ST|LETTO

PRAISE FOR *STILETTO*

"Big Pharma and Big Tech in the glamorous and rainy landscape of Seattle make a fertile backdrop for crime and for the promising young detective Anna Crane's first case tracking her elusive prime suspect, Eleanor Kieran. In this very fine, enthralling novel, Peterson is expert with details of murder and with the intricate human relationships that make her characters triumphantly alive."
—DIANE JOHNSON, author *Le Mariage* and *Le Divorce*

PRAISE FOR *DUCK AND COVER*

"A bittersweet and utterly beguiling novel."
—*PUBLISHERS WEEKLY*

"Peterson would seem to hold out just about as much hope for the family as she does the planet."
—*NEW YORK TIMES* "Notable Book of the Year"

PRAISE FOR *ANIMAL HEART*

"Brenda Peterson weaves a haunting love story into a fast-moving plot. Animal Heart is based on facts that are terrifyingly true, and it captures the exquisite beauty of a world that we are devastating and destroying, piece by piece. Please read it."
—JANE GOODALL, author of *Reason for Hope*

ST|LETTO

A NOVEL

BRENDA PETERSON

By the author of *Duck and Cover*, a *New York Times*
"Notable Book of the Year"

SHE WRITES PRESS

Published 2023
Printed in the United States of America
Print ISBN: 978-1-64742-430-5
E-ISBN: 978-1-64742-431-2
Library of Congress Control Number: 2022919516

For information, address:
She Writes Press
1569 Solano Ave #546
Berkeley, CA 94707

Interior Design by Tabitha Lahr

She Writes Press is a division of SparkPoint Studio, LLC.

"What is addiction, really? It is a sign, a signal, a symptom of distress. It is a language that tells us about a plight that must be understood."

—Alice Miller

*For my beloved siblings who
helped shape this book—
Tracey Conway, Paula Peterson,
and Dana Mark Peterson*

PART ONE

I

ELEANOR KIERNAN

April 29, 2019

She'd made a mistake escaping by boat, miscalculating tides, and foolishly braving the high wind small craft advisory. Whitecaps slammed the hull, each wave a cold, spinning caldron of sea foam. Eleanor Kiernan gripped the outboard's tiller, sails strapped tight, navigating riptides of Dungeness Spit into the Straits. Low-slung mists obscured a waterlogged dawn's weak sunlight and the eerie seep of fog. She'd never sailed alone, in such a tempest of sea, without Leo at the helm.

"Steady, Brodie boy." Eleanor Kiernan had clipped her Scottie dog's life jacket to the sailboat's railing with a carabiner. "We've survived worse storms."

But she didn't know how she would ever endure this—the sight of Leonard Cushman's body splayed out on a Persian carpet, his throat gashed, his blood bright, not yet congealed, and familiar green eyes holding her in his startled, accusing gaze.

There was no escaping *him*—even if she did elude the police. She just needed time to think, to plan her upended life. Leo's death changed everything, like a hurricane shredding a once sturdy house, detouring the future.

Wind slashed her, salt spray prickling her numb cheeks. "It's spring, for God's sake!" Eleanor shouted at the whistling squall, pulling her knit cap down over her spiky, red curls. Her voice was swept away by a gust shoving the mast sideways. "In Boston, it's sunny and seventy degrees!"

As water sloshed over the deck, Eleanor tightened her slicker. She should have packed a balaclava in her tidy duffel bag, along with provisions for her plan to hide out on one of the remote San Juan Islands. If she found safe harbor, she would have to pick up more gear and supplies while she moored briefly at her San Juan Island beach cottage.

Her sailboat sank into a loud wave gully, then rose menacingly. "Time to stow you below, Brodie!"

Eleanor let go of the tiller long enough to unhook her dog and prod him into the small cabin. Brodie curled up on the bed. It always amazed Eleanor that her Scottie could nap on such turbulent waves. She'd had no sleep. The storm had forced her to take refuge overnight in a ramshackle motel in Port Townsend, not her usual Victorian bed-and-breakfast. No one would've expected to find her in such unlikely lodgings. If she were not running away, she'd have chosen an elegant resort.

A rogue wave almost capsized her boat. The clank of riggings and ropes woke Brodie, who barked and growled, running around below deck. Her dog, like her, preferred the East Coast weather where spring was balmy and dependable, not the Pacific Northwest, where people wore parkas even in summer. Eleanor had lived in Seattle for seven years and loved its evergreen luxury, its laidback but sophisticated style, its iconic coffee houses, and its crowded bookshops. She'd not yet acclimated to the unpredictable seasons, perpetual charcoal skies, and rain. Every day she checked the Boston weather.

Some weekends the rumor of Seattle sun would finally prove true. Last month, Leo had called Eleanor for a Sunday sail on this same boat that was now her only hope of a getaway. He was always the most at home on water.

"Think I'll stay in," Eleanor had demurred.

"Nonsense," Leo said.

Leonard Cushman, her boss and mentor, was a man used to getting his way, especially with Eleanor, whom he considered his protégé, perhaps even his heir, at the pharmaceutical company Fortura.

"I'm swamped," she'd stalled. "My brother's not doing well."

"Frankie's *never* doing well," Leo snapped.

Eleanor hesitated. Maybe she should go, especially if Leo suspected her betrayal. For the first time in their years of working together, Eleanor was afraid of Leo. She worried he'd somehow found out she was covertly cooperating with the Justice Department's FBI investigation to expose Fortura's culpability in creating the opioid crisis. If Leo knew of her mutiny, he would not only have fired her but he might have also hired someone to silence her. Leo was brutal in his business dealings. There was even a rumor another whistleblower at Fortura had suffered a suspicious death on Leo's boat.

She had refused the invitation, so was grateful when just several weeks later, Leo showed up, uninvited, at her twin brother's funeral. Frankie's death was not a surprise—Eleanor had long dreaded it, but his loss threatened to unhinge her. Frankie had died after an overdose of Neocodone—an opiate Eleanor and Leo had created.

Leo arrived late to the gravesite carrying a bouquet of white roses, Eleanor's favorite. Tentatively, he touched her shoulder as they stood together in the mournful accompaniment of Seattle drizzle, its soft, mournful patter a fugue.

"Don't know what to say, Eleanor." The raindrops from his stylish hat dripped onto her raincoat. "I'm so very sorry."

"Please take your hat off, Leo," she said under her breath. What she wanted to scream was, *This is your fault. This is our fault!*

"Your brother was in so much pain," Leo's voice was uncharacteristically gentle. He reserved his authoritative baritone for other employees.

"Frankie's pain was bearable," Eleanor murmured. "His addiction was not."

Leo visibly flinched. "I know how dearly you'll miss your brother, Ellie."

He always deferred to Eleanor, as if sensing both her sensitivity and rebelliousness. Eleanor's startling eyes, the color of dark lilacs, were too penetrating to be traditionally pretty, her body almost boyish, and her mind quick and intriguing. At work and in her personal life, she was discerning, aloof. Her twin brother's addiction and her demanding job had taken up most of her time.

With his self-assured, trim physique and thick, salt-and-pepper curls, Leo often charmed women. But not Eleanor. In their early days, Leo had informed her, "I respect you, not just for those swank Harvard credentials you don't flaunt at cocktail parties but also"—he'd added with a smile—"for your passion about everything—except me. It's a relief, really. No fawning. You're my favorite nemesis."

At the graveside, Leo took off his hat and lowered his head. He reached out to take Eleanor's arm, but Eleanor stepped back. She shook her flame-red hair, flattened and frizzy from the rain. Her high cheekbones seemed more sculpted, suggesting she'd lost weight. Her brow was etched with grief, her usually expressive eyes a bloodshot smear. For the first time, Eleanor mirrored her twin's gaunt desperation.

"You can't hold yourself responsible, Eleanor," Leo said. "Or me. There are so many psychological triggers for addiction besides drugs."

She held her tongue. Leo had a point. Her brother had been depressed much of his adult life. Eleanor feared if it hadn't been their Neocodone, it might have been meth or alcohol or some other drug that destroyed Frankie. The twins' father had died young from a climbing accident on Mt. Rainier, attempting the same treacherous ice crevasses, into which Frankie later fell and broke his leg. The injury left Frankie in chronic pain. Their mother, an American history professor at Boston University, had named them after the two people she most admired: Eleanor and Franklin Roosevelt. Their mother often reminded Frankie of Eleanor's impressive career. As if to emphasize her disappointment in her son, she didn't attend Frankie's funeral.

The last time Eleanor saw Frankie, she'd angrily warned him, "Be sure to write your social security number on your arm in Magic Marker so they'll know who you are when they find your body." Instead, her twin had tattooed Eleanor's phone number on his ankle.

Eleanor bowed her head. Several mourners fidgeted, shifted, and anxiously lit up cigarettes at the gravesite. Eleanor recognized Toni Fleishman, Frankie's lover from rehab—a platinum blonde in a flattened beret, chain-smoking. Toni despised Eleanor and blamed her for Frankie's overdose. Frankie's pallbearers, friends from various rehab stints, slowly lowered the blue silk shroud into the grave on a simple, wooden plank. Frankie's will had insisted on a green burial, popular in selected areas of Seattle cemeteries for its environmental benefits.

One of Frankie's friends began her brother's favorite song: "Bring Him Home," from *Les Miserables*. As the tenor sang, "Let him rest, heaven blessed," his tone was so like Frankie's pure falsetto that Eleanor gasped.

"Bring him joy," the soloist sang on, "he is young . . ."

They were young, barely forty. Too young to die. Eleanor would never bring her brother home. Steadying herself, she tossed the bouquet of pale roses onto her brother's shroud and then threw in a handful of muddy, black soil.

As the dirt slid over her brother's shroud, Eleanor's fury at Leo finally subsided. For a moment, she thought she might faint. Eleanor lightly touched the sleeve of Leo's raincoat. "Thank you for being here . . ."

She'd given Leo the London Fog a year ago for his European trip. It was the only gift she'd ever offered her boss because she was tired of seeing Leo ruin his expensive tailored suits in Seattle cloudbursts. The only gift Leo had ever given Eleanor was after a string of break-ins at their office. It had surprised Eleanor when she opened the gaily wrapped present to find a slim six-inch knife with a blunt-cut carbon-blued steel blade. The expensive leather sheath was inscribed with her initials: E.K.

"It's an F-S British commando dagger," Leo had explained. "You hold the stiletto like this . . . between the thumb and the forefinger. You always go for the throat, the jugular," he added with a swift and practiced flourish.

Eleanor was stunned by the stiletto and his graphic demonstration. "Uh, no, Leo."

"Believe me, Eleanor, a fighting knife like this might save your life. These death threats against us at Fortura are real."

Eleanor thought the stiletto was a strange way to show his affection. She'd reluctantly taken Leo's disquieting gift and hidden it at work in her lab desk.

At the grave, she leaned against Leo, at last allowing the tears.

He startled under her tender weight, as if unsettled, shifting his feet in the soggy grass. Leo drew a long breath and said, "I can stay on with you awhile, Eleanor."

"No," she said quickly. "I need to be alone now." When she uttered the word, "alone," pain pierced her heart.

As a twin, she'd never really endured the haunting isolation other people talked about. "I'm all alone," they'd confess. Eleanor had pitied them and had deftly avoided three marriage proposals, preferring serial monogamy with a few unavailable men, most of whom Frankie didn't like. Whenever she'd had to decide between her twin and a partner, she'd always chosen Frankie.

As the mourners respectfully left Eleanor to her solitude, a sharp and unfamiliar pain throbbed throughout her body. She might do anything to stop this bone-marrow ache. Loneliness. She'd lost the great love of her life. Frankie was her fix.

THERE WAS NO LAND IN SIGHT AS Eleanor tried to right the sailboat. She pointed the bow at a 45-degree angle into each wild wave. How would she navigate now without her twin and Leo, the two most important men in her life? To calm herself, Eleanor tried to summon one happy memory of her twin. Staring into the waves, she remembered her brother in the Blue Ridge Mountains. It was before his fall and before Frankie's stamina failed him from too many drugs. He had always been the better athlete.

"Up here," her brother had told Eleanor, his tanned face turned toward the sun, "mountain folks are so used to the wind, they learn to walk with it pushing them forward. They even lean back into it to right themselves. If the wind stops, you fall flat—no wind to balance you. It's like a *chinook*, a warm wind at your back."

How dearly Eleanor wished her brother was with her, always at her back. How she longed to explain to Leo her desertion and despair. She longed now for a warmer wind than the battering blows and howls of the thunderstorm threatening her boat's flight.

She gunned the outboard through a turbulent Haro Strait, hoping to see on any horizon the humpbacked silhouette of San Juan Island. The wind was so fierce that her boat listed precariously, almost parallel with the water. The waves' fists and splatter against her waterproof pants made a plastic patter.

Ropes fluttered, snarling around her boots like leg cuffs. Reaching into her backpack, Eleanor grasped for the knife to cut them. The nylon was tough as sinew—and her stiletto was still streaked with blood.

II

ANNA CRANE

April 29, 2019

Seattle wasn't always adrift in the blue-gray marine wash of a wavering watercolor or a drowned city. Sometimes a storm's bluster stripped and suddenly cleared skyscrapers of their foggy cloaks. Then, it was so startlingly sunny, everyone complained and shaded their eyes from a sky determined to expose everything.

Anna Crane was comfortable in the blare of sunlight from a childhood spent in the sun-drenched, subversive Florida Keys. But she was anxious this morning because her recurring nightmare lingered like a hangover. All her life, Anna's dreams had been accented by visceral, haunting images, which often, and terribly, came true. This familiar nightmare was the worst—mud splattered over her sister's bright, yellow slicker. Muck and murder.

"Rise and shine, Detective." Captain Dimitri's call woke her at 7:30 a.m. Dimitri's voice was as agitated as she felt after her restless night. "Your first *live* murder case."

Anna would never correct the captain— "live murder" was an oxymoron. Like so many things about her past, Anna kept her private life as a wordsmith, a struggling songwriter and singer, a closely held secret. She preferred to let her criminal justice degree from the University of Washington do the heavy lifting when Captain Dimitri first interviewed her.

"Sir . . . text address?"

"No," Dimitri said. "I want you here at the station first. I'll brief you and Rafe myself. Forensics is already working the scene."

It worried Anna she was so tired for her first day as the youngest detective in homicide. She was thirty-five and measured her five years working on cold cases by how many she had solved. She'd never told anybody at work, except Rafe, how her intuitive gifts had helped her close many unsolved cases. All her superiors knew was that her work was impressive and surprisingly successful. Now Detective Anna Crane would at last get to interview suspects at an active crime scene. In this homicide squad dominated by veteran, by-the-book men, it was Anna's chance to prove herself.

When Anna arrived at the station, Captain Dimitri growled and shook his head. "Here you go, Detective." He dropped a coffee-stained folder on her desk. "I'd never let you cut your teeth on such a high-profile murder, but we're short-handed with so many guys tracking the damn fentanyl case."

For months, the more seasoned detectives had been trying to figure out how street drugs like cocaine and even some prescription opiates were being laced with fentanyl, a synthetic painkiller 50–100 times more powerful than morphine. Anna had closely followed the case. There was some new and disturbing evidence that the pills weren't from the usual suspects, like China or Mexico, but were possibly manufactured here in some Northwest pharmaceutical lab. The lethal pills were stamped with brand names like Xanax or Percocet, so they appeared harmless. But several high school students were near death on ventilators in nearby Harborview hospital after trying to give mouth-to-mouth resuscitation to friends who'd overdosed.

"Any new leads?" Anna asked.

"*Nada*," Captain Dimitri shook his head sadly. "Except another kid died today."

Another death in the fentanyl case would ratchet up pressure and public attention on her department. Anna hoped she and Rafe could quickly close the homicide that Captain Dimitri was reluctantly entrusting to them. However, she had an uneasy feeling this murder might be as complicated as the unsolved fentanyl case.

"Vic's a Big Pharma bigwig," Captain Dimitri said. "Beat cops on the scene have already notified next of kin for you. Of course, they all alibi each other. Families always do." Captain Dimitri gave Anna a weary salute. "Make me proud, Crane."

His thick Russian accent didn't disguise his anxiety. Captain Dimitri had come to Seattle as a teenager when his parents had whisked him away from Russia to escape his fate of being drafted into the Red Army. He prided himself on his excellent English, especially when teasing his officers. In his texts, Dimitri used exclamation points like emojis. Dimitri believed the ability to chide or tease an underling was a sign of leadership. Anna expertly weathered her goading and irascible boss. The captain reminded Anna of her aerospace engineer-father who had no patience for anything but facts on file, who always regarded his oldest daughter askance and strangely. At best, he was bewildered by Anna; at worst, he believed, even with her straight As, that Anna was incompetent in the "real world."

After Anna had chosen a career in criminal justice, her father protested, "You're too sensitive to live. Maybe you're on the spectrum? How're you ever going to survive as a cop?" He'd been shocked when Anna made it through a criminal justice degree, Phi Beta Kappa, and the rigors of police training. He'd predicted she'd never last at the job.

"On it, sir." Anna opened the file, her pulse rising as if she were about to run a marathon.

Captain Dimitri gave her a pointed look. "Will we see you tonight, Crane? Counting on you to win for us."

Anna tried to keep her expression bland, but she was not looking forward to being Dimitri's "ringer" on his karaoke team competition. Their captain had learned English when his family immigrated to the United States by singing in the many karaoke bars in the city. His birthday party tonight at Hula Hula on Capitol Hill was mandatory. She'd have to miss her cherished chorale rehearsal to join in the rowdy competition.

"I'll do my best, Captain," Anna said dutifully. Apparently, she hadn't kept her singer-songwriter chops secret enough. Word was out she had a voice.

She glanced over at her partner, Rafael Bartelli, who signaled a thumbs-up as the captain marched into his office whose glass walls were so smudged it was hard to see him.

Anna and Rafe had been paired as one of the few woman detectives and an openly gay male detective. Depending upon his mood or their successfully solved cold cases, Captain Dimitri called them either "The Girls" or "Deadheads." Though Seattle was an ultra-liberal city, Captain Dimitri often played catch-up with the twenty-first century.

Anna read the brief file carefully, noting their murder victim was an organ donor. Of course, a body kept in the icy morgue for days could not fulfill a donor legacy. But this posthumous concern for others was noteworthy. So was the vic's vast fortune and philanthropic generosity to every Seattle art gallery or hospital wing.

Rafe circled her desk and slipped a cinnamon roll next to her teacup, a sample of his husband's culinary talents.

"Morning, *Detective.*" He flashed her an affectionate wink. Rafe was the only one to directly congratulate her on the promotion. He always explained Anna's dedication to her work as "elevation of duty." Now Rafe leaned down and whispered to Anna, "Any hunches?" Rafe had always appreciated her intuitive abilities had accounted for some of their success in the most baffling crimes. But sometimes he teased her. "What's a pre-cog doing working cold cases?" he'd ask.

Anna had never been able to explain to Rafe, or to herself, how she simply knew things, how she accessed information, or how she deduced something beyond any logic.

Working in the basement's dingy office, away from the white heat of active investigations, Anna was free to allow the insistent but often inexplicable insights that helped her understand motive or the execution of a crime. She struggled with this skill as both blessing and curse. Anna would never call herself "psychic." She wasn't that good, and she wasn't sure or comfortable with this other way of knowing. Often Anna wished someone besides Mr. Cooley, her beloved, middle-grade science teacher, had trained her as a child when the premonitions and nightmares first began. She'd dreamed of her sister's death long before it finally happened.

One night in high school, Anna had awoken from a nightmare of discovering her sister, Lizzie, face-down in red mud, dead, tire tracks crisscrossing her slicker and a squeal of brakes as a car raced away.

Terrified, she'd run to Lizzie's bedroom and found her sister retching in their shared bathroom, Lizzie's black hair pulled back in the tight bun their ballet mistress demanded, her thin body trembling as she bent over the toilet. Lizzie sobbed between bouts of vomit. She was sixteen and in rigorous training for a position in the *corps de ballet* of their local Key West dance company. It was all Lizzie had dreamed of during their childhoods of exacting ballet classes. Anna enjoyed ballet, but it wasn't her only passion.

"You can't keep doing this, Lizzie." Anna held her sister's head, gently pressing a cold washcloth to the nape of her neck. "It's not healthy."

"Just a stomach bug." Lizzie stood, her long, muscular legs wobbly.

"No, you're doing this to yourself." Anna sat on the edge of the bathtub, studying her sister intently. The once lithe, waif-like body was now shapely with breasts almost as generous as Anna's.

Lizzie had always struggled with her weight. Daily, she stripped naked and took a deep breath before stepping onto the scales as if it were a gang plank. The number would flash her weight as if condemning her to execution. Every time her ballet teacher cocked an eyebrow at Lizzie's lovely but developing torso, the young girl collapsed in shame and self-doubt. Curves that made boys now flock to Lizzie and Anna in the high school hallways had recently cost Lizzie the soloist roles she'd always been awarded.

"Look at this!" Lizzie traced her thighs in disgust. "My quads are bulging. I've got Grandma's hips. They're why I just lost the Rosaline role in *Romeo and Juliet*. I couldn't fit into the costumes anymore."

Anna held her sister as she wept, shushing her softly. She didn't know what to say. Anna had inherited those same hips, the shapeliness in her Cuban grandmother's generation suggested strength, balance, and easy childbearing. But for a ballerina, the round slope of hips was a liability. It ruined the visual line of a woman posed forever on point, her lean, graceful arms lifted high as if she were simply alighting from flight, touching down from some ethereal realm of swans and fairies.

While it was heartbreaking to see her beautiful sister so willing to destroy her health, Anna understood the drive. She, too, had been devoted to dance since she was six. But when Anna's own body no longer fit in the strict tutus, she'd switched to martial arts where strong core muscles, nimble reflexes, and flexibility from their ballet years was an asset—a building, not a stumbling, block.

Anna read Lizzie's weight like a warning light on their scales: 127 pounds, perfect for Lizzie's 5'9" height, just an inch taller than Anna and ten pounds less. Anna also weighed herself every day, the curse of any young girl who was just beginning to take dating seriously. Anna herself was on a pre-graduation diet, having ordered a size smaller than her usual 12 for her high school graduation party dress.

"What if we end up triple-D like mom?" Lizzie wailed as if breast size were a fatal diagnosis.

"Boys will love it," Anna said. "Girls too."

"But not ballet directors." Lizzie leaned away from Anna's arms to hang over the toilet bowl, shoulders heaving.

Anna lightly touched her sister's head, the bun now unraveling, curls wet and sticky. "You'll get the next part," she whispered, hoping it wasn't a lie.

And Lizzie did. In her sophomore year, she lost so much weight she was invited to join the prestigious Key West Ballet Company. But her blood labs were bad. All during her dance career she suffered an auto-immune disease, anxiety, and fibromyalgia. Still, Lizzie danced, stepping on those dreaded dictatorial scales every day, until at thirty, she finally moved up to Atlanta and made principal soloist in a small local ballet company. She was thriving, finally happy. But then, Lizzie was killed by a hit-and-run homicide, yet unsolved by Atlanta police. Every time Anna's nightmare recurred, she tried to see more details: a license plate, a face of the driver. But the vision yielded nothing more.

Anna had been on track in Seattle's police force to make detective, but after Lizzie's death, she'd applied for a job in cold cases. Everyone in the station knew that Anna, like many of them, had survived an early brush with violence or an unsolved crime, which had also launched them into detective work, as if every criminal they caught could compensate for those they had lost.

Rafe perched now on Anna's desk. "Tonight, you can't lie and say you lost your voice. It's sing or die."

Rafe riffled through the open file folder on their victim. Unlike Anna, who camouflaged her curves in black slacks, standard cream blouse, and flowing dark-gray silk jacket, Rafe allowed his flamboyance full display. Today, in honor of their karaoke night, he was outfitted in a purple Hawaiian shirt and tight, black jeans.

"I really don't like to miss my chorale rehearsal," Anna said.

"Where's *your* Hula Hula swag?" Rafe teased. "You can't beat my karaoke team with just a good voice. Here . . ." He rummaged in his briefcase and brought out a fluorescent-pink tank top with a dancing girl and tiki statue. "It's vintage . . . on sale."

She took the skimpy tank top. "Save this for your Ru Paul collection. To wear this, I'd have to be flat-chested and blind drunk."

"Virgin Mai Tai for me." Rafe shrugged good-naturedly, but there was a slight tension in his eyes. Anna knew Rafe was seven years sober after his gay party days. Since he'd married, he rarely went barhopping. The required karaoke party might be difficult for Rafe. Of course, she must be by his side.

"Aloha, partner." She relented and tucked the garish tank top in her small backpack.

Anna's only usual hint of color and subversiveness was her curly black hair disciplined into a ponytail and tinged with blue highlights—this week—and her fire opal earrings, which she never took off. Even though Anna knew they were considered bad luck by some gemstone collectors, she wanted to test superstition.

"Nervous?" Rafe asked under his breath as he studied the file. "Lots of eyes on us with this case." He knew her too well and could read every worried tell of brow or lips. There was no hiding from him.

She was glad her partner was gay; he was so determinedly buff and handsome she might have been tempted to flirt or even surrender to his considerable charms. Now, they could be close without the troublesome complications of sex. Instead, they enjoyed the physical shorthand of trust—a much better bond when one's life was at risk.

Rafe studied the developing murder report. "Wow, knife wound to the throat." He let out a whistle under his breath. His eyes, the caramel color of moist earth, widened.

A sudden shiver went through Anna's body, like the quick-silver rise of mercury in a thermometer. Her second sight was trying to get her attention. Anna intuited, without knowing how, that the murderer was someone the victim trusted, not an anti-drug crusader attacking Big Pharma.

"Maybe family or friend," she mused aloud and stood up.

"Yup," Rafe nodded. "Always the closest. Someone you know."

"With me, Rafe?" She tried to make the request more an invitation than a command, even though she was his senior in the strict hierarchy of the station.

Rafe never minded her taking the lead; he joined her, stride for stride. In their mud-splashed squad car, it was Rafe's turn to choose a radio station.

"Rap or opera?" Rafe asked, fiddling with the dial.

"Both hurt my ears," Anna said.

"*The Magic Flute* it is, then." Rafe plugged in his iPhone's Spotify playlist of Mozart's playful opera and hummed along to Tamino's duet with Princess Pamina. Anna had patiently endured hearing the whole plot of this Masonic fairy tale, though she did enjoy the young couple's underworld descent and admired the malignant Queen of the Night.

Anna would have preferred Coldplay, Celia Cruz, or the educated drone of NPR. As Sarastro's baritone rumbled, Anna pleaded. "Let's compromise . . . an opera star singing something I can understand. How about Renee Fleming's *Haunted Heart*?"

"Is *your* heart still haunted?" Rafe teased.

Rafe had been a good listener when she broke up with the talented tenor in her chorale. They'd sung a "West Side Story" duet, which still tenderly echoed in her head. The affair had been a disaster, and Anna almost left the chorale after their last concert. But the other altos and a protective Rafe had convinced her the chorale needed her voice more than she needed the unfaithful tenor.

"Your love affairs are better than any rom-com," Rafe often said. "I'm happy to just be a voyeur." He glanced at her now with a grin. "But Anna, online dating really *does* work."

Anna shook her head. "I know. I know. You met the love of your life. 'So happy together!'" She sang the pop tune.

"Let me do your dating profile," Rafe persisted. "I'll post a sexy photo of you singing karaoke with your gorgeous curls untethered from that boring ponytail. How about, 'Single, shy martial artist seeking harmony in an erotic duet.' Maybe a black-and-white profile pic to show off those haunting Sophia Loren eyes of yours?"

Anna cringed and took a curve too fast. She'd never hear the end of it if Rafe got more intimately involved in her romances. It was enough that he delightedly listened to her disastrous love affairs. The only thing that appealed to her about his potential dating ad was her pride in having just received a brown belt in aikido, the Japanese martial art that gracefully reverses an attacker's energy against themselves.

"Oh, God, no, Rafe, no online profile for me," she said. "Romance should be a mystery, not an advertisement."

In answer, he couldn't help but sing sultry lines from Cole Porter's "Love for Sale."

Despite herself, Anna sang along with her best Lady Gaga harmony. When they arrived at a gated community in Golden Gardens near the Salish Sea, a security officer, probably a retired cop, checked them at the front gate. The guard was so burly, he barely fit into his little office, which was the size of an old-fashioned telephone booth.

"The place is already crawling with you guys," he muttered, as he greeted the detectives. "And the kid on duty last night forgot to turn on the security cameras. He did write down a few license plates in the visitors' log, but who can read his graffiti?"

"We'd like to see those logs," Anna asked. She gave the security guard her most gracious smile. Her respect signaled to him she understood, that like many ex-cops, this older man had to work after retirement. "Might need to ask your help again, sir," she said, as if to salute him.

"How come you're only charming, Anna, when you want info?" Rafe asked, as they drove through the wide curves and mini mansions. The well-manicured neighborhood was abloom with pink magnolia trees, tulips standing at attention, fragrant lilac bushes, hot-red azaleas, and a blizzard of cherry blossoms like brilliant hallucinations. God on acid.

Yellow crime scene "Caution" tape draped around the driveway of a three-story white house with columns as pretentious as an antebellum plantation. Several squad cars, red lights blazing, were at the scene.

"Detective, you just missed forensics." A female cop at the door nodded to Anna. There was a barely perceptible criticism, not just that Anna was late to the scene but that she was perhaps too inexperienced for such an important case. "No signs of a break-in. No money stolen." The cop rattled off her notes, then nodded toward the grand staircase. "Some staff here awaiting interview. Body in the study."

As they strode into the large office, Anna's pulse quickened. She'd seen many bodies in various stages of dissection at the police morgue. But Dimitri was right. This was her first live murder. Unlike in cold cases with their tidy files, dated crime-scene photographs, and witness statements, Anna sensed the palpable presence of death here. It was ominous, an oppressive atmosphere, like a thunderstorm hung heavy, brooding. As they entered the study, Anna sensed the emotional current running through the room. Despair? Disappointment? Surprise?

On a brilliantly patterned, blood-spattered, blue Oriental rug, Leonard Cushman lay face up in his spacious office, powerless and naked.

III

ANNA

April 29 2019

Snapping on latex gloves, Anna kneeled and studied Leonard Cushman's half-naked body. Perhaps the perp stripped Cushman to get rid of any DNA? Or was this a lover's vengeance? Anna fought an instinct to smooth the victim's tousled hair so that he would be less unkempt, less unloved. Scanning this crime scene, Anna sensed something was deliberately misplaced in this well-appointed study. A misdirection.

Unlike some other intuitive people, Anna didn't most often read people's colorful, shimmering auras like clairvoyants. Anna's clairsentience was more subtle; she only sensed things like a psychic peripheral vision. Clues, insights, and inexplicable knowledge would just come to her, especially when she was not searching for them. Her most acute sense was hearing.

"So, you just know things without knowing exactly how or why." Rafe had shrugged and grinned when she'd first confided in her partner about her intuitions. "I don't care how you get your info, just don't keep it to yourself. I can always check out what you intuit to see if we can match it with evidence."

Carefully, Anna inspected the thin knife wound, blood already congealed in Cushman's throat. Like many Seattleites,

Cushman appeared to be addicted to gyms. Any attacker strong enough to kill face-to-face with one stab must have been equally athletic, relying on the element of surprise. Because of the precision of the stabbing, it implied someone with maybe surgical training.

Anna studied the man's face. A murder victim's last expression could hold a good amount of information. His slight uplift of the dark eyebrows, the wide-open green eyes indicated shock or dismay. Leonard Cushman was not traditionally handsome, especially frozen in this fatal gaze. But the set of his jaw, his distinctive brow, and his arrogance were apparent in the curve of his thin lips, even with their dark ooze of blood. This was a man born and bred to expect dominion. Yet here he was, a victim, death the victor.

She was surprised at her physical reaction to this first hands-on encounter with a murder victim. Kneeling here beside a man who was so recently alive filled her with awe, even reverence. She'd long ago left her mother's Catholic influence, but there was a spirit lingering here. Anna bowed her head a moment. No prayers came to mind, only a deep quiet. Anna sang softly, "See what you lost when you left this world . . ."

Rafe entered the room and pulled on his crime-scene cap and gloves. "'Sweet Old World' from *Wrecking Ball*," he said.

"Surprised you know it."

Respectfully, Rafe gazed down at the body and was quiet for a few moments. "Everyone should have a voice like Emmy Lou's at the end," he said. "Purest melancholy."

He scrutinized an evidence bag with a coil of paisley fabric. "Forensics found this sash. Looks like it's from Cushman's robe, but no sign of the robe."

"So, he might have been expecting a lover," Anna said. "Even in his office."

Rafe held up another evidence bag with a cell phone. "Apparently the vic was clutching his cell when he died." Rafe deftly lifted Cushman's cell phone from the plastic evidence bag. Rafe was a whiz at passwords and soon had unlocked the victim's phone.

"How did you figure out Cushman's passcode, when forensics couldn't?" Anna asked.

"It was the date his company went public," Rafe answered, scrutinizing Cushman's texts, recent calls, apps, and emails. "Look at this," he said. "Cushman's Find Friends app has only one person he's shared his location with. Cushman must be very lonely—or just paranoid."

"A woman?" Anna asked. "Name?"

Rafe shook his head. "No name. He only calls the person, 'Great Blue.'"

"Like the bird." Great blue herons were Anna's favorite, with their spacious wingspans and hoarse, dinosaur caws. Northwest Native tribes believed them to be divine messengers.

Rafe frowned. "Hasn't Cushman's pharmaceutical firm been in the news recently? His lab was burned down. Eco-terrorists rescued all the lab animals."

"Oh, yeah." Anna nodded. It was a big case, though no homicides were involved. She hadn't followed it, except to feel the rescuers deserved kudos, not punishment. Anna loved all animals. She'd been glad to hear chimps were no longer being used in medical research.

"Our vic is a Big Pharma CEO at Fortura. Maybe it's the same anti-drug protesters who broke into his lab who did this? This guy probably had lots of enemies."

"We'll have to follow all leads," Anna said. "Cushman is worth billions. Not exactly an oligarch or Bezos, but rich enough to have family who might like him dead."

"Safe's wide open." Rafe crossed the room and whistled when he saw several tall stacks of cash undisturbed inside the safe. "Not a robbery." There were papers scattered around on the floor as if someone were desperately searching for something. "Forensics says this note was left on the desk." Rafe showed Anna the scrawled note in the plastic evidence bag.

"Please believe me—" The note ended abruptly with an inky gash from a fountain pen.

"Cushman's last words?" Rafe asked. "Who was he writing to?"

The note drew Anna's attention more than the ransacked safe. "And who uses fountain pens these days?" she said. "We'll check to see if it is Cushman's handwriting."

Anna stood up and stepped slightly away from the corpse as Rafe respectfully again covered the victim, except his face, with the blue paper cover.

"Did Cushman live alone?" Anna asked.

"Think so. He's divorced, stepson grown, twenty-something. Ex-wife also lives in Magnolia and is in Paris half the year. There are some full-time staff here. Maid discovered the body. Gardener and cook are downstairs waiting for our interview."

"You go talk with them," Anna said. "I want a little more time with Cushman."

As Rafe left, Anna drew a steady breath and focused on the outflung arm from under the blue cover. There was the pale shadow of a wedding ring etched around Cushman's ring finger like a scar, betraying the recent divorce. The man's complex Swiss Chopard watch, with spinning moon phases, exact sunrise-sunset times, and perpetual calendar, adorned his wrist. Like the timepiece, Leonard Cushman was now a limited edition.

There was a spilled bottle of Bordeaux staining the rug. The carpet was also blotched with blood. Forensics would have to help her understand the bloodstain pattern analysis. She refocused her full attention on Leonard Cushman. *What is here that cannot be seen but can be sensed or overheard?* Anna knew especially troubled spirits often lingered with the dead. Sometimes she heard them.

As a child, Anna had mystified the doctor when she complained of noises and voices in her head. The world sounded too loud, and young Anna often wailed in pain. The doctor concluded her ears tested fine but sent Anna to an audiologist. He conducted a more sophisticated hearing test, making Anna sit with her back to him in a glass booth while he reached to press buttons for tones—from ultra to subsonic. Anna would raise her hand to signal she'd heard the notes—the moment *before* he hit the button. At first, the audiologist wrote off her quick, audio responses as a child's eagerness to please. But once he noticed how consistently Anna knew when he was just about to trigger the frequencies, he realized Anna had some special sense.

"Anna seems to be able to . . . well, to hear the *suggestion* of sound," the audiologist marveled to her mother. He struggled to explain. "Her ears are like our ultrasound, like hearing . . . what is *not* spoken. Super sensitivity. I'd invest in some good headphones for her so she can get some quiet."

Of course, the headphones never helped since what Anna heard was also in her mind. She knew it would be no good to tell the audiologist she had the ears of a dolphin or elephant. Over the years, she'd tried to train herself to block out some noise, especially any ethereal haunting voices. But a skill she'd honed was intuitively eavesdropping on conversations echoing in the air *after* they'd been spoken. She'd developed audio-sentient memory, the way some people used photographic memory, to recall recent conversations. It was like listening to voices lingering after the dialogues.

Now studying her first active crime scene, Anna attuned intently and heard the faint tones of an argument. *Man or woman's voice?* She couldn't make out gender or words, just the emotion of it. Conviction and rising righteousness in their tones. But the debate was oddly impersonal, even philosophical. This office setting for this conflict was not about any seduction; it was maybe a long-simmering struggle, which turned suddenly violent. *Motive?* Anna tuned in, closing her eyes more tightly. She expected outrage like a vengeful hum and furious static lingering after a murder. But what she heard touched her. A high note of hope. Even expectations. The warm timbre of devotion. On both sides.

The coroner strode into the bedroom, with a grimace both wry and efficient. Horace Exum was a large but agile man, even paler than most Seattleites because of his long hours in the morgue.

Horace gave Anna a quick and critical once-over glance. "I see you're not in cold cases anymore, Detective," he declared, as if this were a disturbing diagnosis.

"Good morning, Horace." Anna nodded to the rotund coroner as he knelt beside her to examine the body.

"Not for this guy."

A field job like this was usually reserved for crime scene pathologists. Maybe Horace was here because he didn't trust a novice on the murder of such a high-profile victim.

"Can you give me any idea on time of death?" Anna asked.

Horace slipped on his gloves and checked the body for temperature and lividity. "Just a ballpark . . . killed between 11:00 p.m. and 4:00 a.m. I'll know more when I get him on my table." The coroner scrutinized the bloodied carpet and its dark splotch dried at the edges to tell him how old the blood was. Horace took some time analyzing the viscous slash of the wound before he checked the corpse's knuckles and fingernails. "No obvious signs of a defensive struggle. Probably knew his murderer. Someone had to come close to deliver such a lethal cut."

This jibed with her intuition. After all, Leonard Cushman was stripped half-naked.

Horace pulled an evidence bag out of his pocket. Inside was a slim black leather knife sheath. "Left behind under the desk."

"Why would the killer leave the knife's sheath?" Anna wondered aloud. "Fingerprints?" she asked Horace.

"Forensics already checked," Horace said. "None. Wiped clean." The coroner studied the expensive sheath. "It has a British Army insignia." He let out a low whistle of admiration. "Looks like the knife was a stiletto . . . an F-S commando dagger. Sheffield. Not some Chinese knock-off." Horace sat back on his knees. "Got one of these myself. A real collector's item. Made famous when it was used in WWII on D-Day."

An ex-military man, Horace still had the instincts, if not the physique, of a soldier. "The fixed-blade stiletto is the fighting knife of choice." He jabbed the air to demonstrate a stab. "It's so slender with its diamond double-edged blade. You slip it right through the rib cage and muscles . . . pierces the heart." Horace stood, his knees cracking audibly. "Murderer might have surgical or military training. Or has good taste in knives."

"Maybe this murder was a message and had something to do with Cushman's drug business?" Anna suggested what she knew would be the most held theory, though she suspected this was not a common murder. It was too intimate, more passionate than political. "Or someone the victim knew well."

"The murderer had to get close enough for just one fatal slash to the throat. Slip the stiletto in and then twist up to attack the brain stem. Lights out." Horace shook his head.

Anna studied the sheath inside the crinkling plastic. There were gold-embossed initials, E.K., carved into the soft, supple leather. The sheath was more like a feminine glove than a stiletto sheath.

"Do you think a woman could have killed him?" Anna asked.

"Sure, could be a woman, if she knew what she was doing," Horace said, but his expression was doubtful. He stood up and stripped off his gloves. "Can't say more until my PM is finished. Later."

Horace often helped detectives most by not getting in their way. Now he was out the door. His forensics minions would come back to complete the job with their dutiful dusting for more prints and fine-tuning of the scene.

Alone with the murder victim, Anna stepped away from the body. *What else is here?* A scent. Bitter. Not perfume. It was astringent, as if someone had tried to clean up something. Not spilled wine. *What is it?* Opening her eyes, Anna followed the scent to the nearby table. Forensics had already removed the two wine glasses for prints. But there was a stain on the table as if something spilled had been hastily wiped off. Anna bent down and sniffed, surprised at the sour but familiar smell. Kombucha. Whoever had killed Cushman was not a connoisseur of fine wine but someone who swilled the fermented tea that was popular all over the city.

Anna smiled at the image of a billionaire with his Bordeaux, toasting a visitor who drank this beverage once the passion of old hippies. Vinegary but also fruity and fizzy, kombucha was an acquired taste.

She studied the murder victim one last time. Sprawled, legs akimbo on the elegant rug, Cushman was so alone. Anna knew most people were victims of intimates—a harrowing fact that made her keep her distance from almost everybody. Maybe it was why she'd been so comfortable working with the dead. The departed were more often past hurting others. Not always. Cushman's will might reveal those he'd disinherited or those who might be determined to kill him. If money were the motive, she'd also have to interview those people at Fortura who stood to take over after Cushman's demise.

Anna sighed and stared again into Cushman's fixed eyes. In a flash, she knew: He truly cared for whoever had killed him. She questioned whether it was romantic or paternal. Was the murderer perhaps family? A competitor? Protégé? Prostitute? Did a man like Leo Cushman really need to hire a lover? Was he so lonely?

A pang of sympathy for the victim struck Anna. Except for the probable use of a fighting knife, this murder didn't feel premeditated. There was something more doomed and emotional about it, like the last resisted act of a tragedy. Then Anna intuited something she'd have much trouble logically explaining to anybody else.

Was the stiletto the victim's gift to his murderer?

IV

ANNA

April 29, 2019

"Let's get to know Leo Cushman better," Anna told her partner, as they drove toward the gleaming new Fortura skyscraper, Cushman's headquarters. Seattle had been seized by another dot.com "cloudburst" of construction in this once sleepy South Lake Union area, thanks in part to Amazon's relentless expansion. Pedestrians, mostly young and tech-looking, thronged at stoplights, jittery in their headphones and bulging backpacks, awaiting green walk signals with the impatience of schoolchildren.

"DINKs." Rafe dismissed them as parts of double-income childless couples with a grimace.

"More like SINKs—single income, never kids," said Anna, coolly assessing the masses of people glued to their phones, then realizing she might also fit the acronym.

Her partner was one of the happiest spouses she'd ever known. Rafe often told stories about his doting husband and their adopted five-year-old son, Nate. His long-awaited and sunny marriage was the antidote to all the sorrow, blame, and bloodshed they witnessed in their detective work. Anna envied

Rafe this domestic solace, but she often curtailed her own dating during a difficult case so she could keep her focus on work.

Since Rafe was navigating the steep hills and irritating one-way downtown streets, Anna was free go over notes on Cushman's domestic staff, whom her partner had interviewed at the crime scene.

"So, the maid says she let in an unexpected guest about ten last night." Rafe recited all the details. "Visitor was tall, platinum blond, maybe in her late twenties, early thirties. Maid said she'd never seen her before." Rafe smiled faintly. "Apparently, the woman was not a natural blonde, maybe wore a wig. Visitor was somewhat down on her luck . . . '*Rubia . . . solia ser bonita . . .*'"

"Pretty, but she's seen better days," Anna translated. Where she grew up in the Keys, most locals spoke Spanish along with the Cuban exiles.

"And she was polite as if maybe this was her first time at Cushman's home."

"Polite?"

"Even murderers can have good manners." Rafe grinned, let the brake go, as the car backslid into first gear as they lurched up a hill.

"Get anything important from the gardener or the cook?" Anna asked.

Rafe's witnesses at the crime scene had added a few more interesting details. "The gardener said Leo Cushman was frequently visited by one of his employees, a young woman who loved his shade garden, especially the tango hummingbird mint and enduring summer crepe. The gardener said it was difficult to grow well in a rain-soaked city. This visitor took some clippings for her own garden up in the San Juan Islands. She was an amateur pilot and had flown Cushman as a passenger. In fact, Cushman was the one who'd taught her to fly."

"Great Blue?" Anna asked.

"Nobody seems to know this Great Blue person's name."

"Can you check Cushman's phone to find Great Blue's location?"

"Nope, already tried. The person must have disabled the phone."

"Let's check Cushman's business finances and see if there's any record of a plane and airplane log with anyone else's name piloting it," Anna said. "Cushman's copilot must also have a license."

"Will do." Rafe pulled into the crowded parking garage of Fortura Pharmaceuticals. "Oh, and the cook, Mrs. Salvatore, said Cushman usually ate alone, too busy to entertain properly. With his wife and stepson out of the house, the only person he ever had for dinner was a coworker . . . his protégé, Eleanor Kiernan."

"Ah," Anna nodded. "EK—the same initials on the stiletto sheath."

"Right."

"Is she blonde?"

"No, red-haired, thin, athletic," Rafe said. "Mrs. Salvatore said she's smart as a whip but not stuck up." Rafe pulled into the Fortura parking garage and jumped out of the car, waiting for Anna to join him. "The cook said this Kiernan and Cushman argued all the time."

"Did she say what exactly Mr. Cushman and this woman argued about?" Anna asked.

"Everything . . . business, politics . . ." Rafe punched the button and within seconds an elevator arrived with a bright *ding-ding*.

"Kiernan might be a possible person of interest."

The elevator doors opened onto a spacious lobby. Anna noticed the artwork of local painters she admired with their delicate watercolors. But there were a few chaotic abstracts that struck Anna as a nervous breakdown on canvas. Or hallucinations. She preferred impressionistic art with some relationship to nature, like Monet's waterlilies or Turner's seascapes or Pacific Northwest Native art. Anna admired a stylized painting of salmon spawning by a local Haida artist.

"Detectives Crane and Bartelli," Anna told the receptionist. "We're here to see Leonard Cushman's executive assistant."

"Yes, of course." The receptionist did not make eye contact. Her identifying lanyard with company photo read Jasmine Wolf.

"And we'd also like to ask you a few questions about Mr. Cushman," Anna said.

There was a faint blush to Jasmine Wolf's high cheekbones. The woman was stunning, perhaps Native American. She was either shy or perhaps hiding something.

"Ms. Wolf, do you know if Mr. Cushman had any enemies? There were many threats and protests about his company, even a boycott."

The receptionist hesitated, frowning, with no eye contact. She took a quick breath and rearranged a fountain pen on her desk, spinning it around. She did not answer.

"Did Mr. Cushman give you the beautiful Mont Blanc?" Anna asked, remembering the scrawled note in Cushman's bedroom. *Did Jasmine Wolf write it? Or did Cushman write the note for this woman, his lover?*

Startled, the receptionist nodded. "He's very . . . he *was* . . . very generous." Tears streamed from Jasmine's downcast eyes.

Those eyes held so much devotion and pain. *What happened between her and Cushman? Is she truly in love with him? Did she have the typical affair with a corporate boss?*

"Yes, generous . . ." Anna encouraged softly. Anna reached into her pocket and handed the receptionist the clean handkerchief she always carried. It came in handy; and people responded as much to the soft cotton as to her solacing gesture. "Can you tell me something about Mr. Cushman that might help us understand him better?" Anna asked. "We are trying to get a sense of him in life—as well as death."

The receptionist made eye contact for the first time. There was a brightness in her expression now, eagerness to talk about this man she had so obviously adored.

"Leo, I mean Mr. Cushman, was a sailor." Jasmine smiled at some memory and continued. "My father always led our tribe's canoe races. When we needed a new canoe, Mr. Cushman gave our tribe a grant, even helped choose the cedar tree from British Columbia. Our canoe is the best on the Salish Sea."

"Quileute?" Rafe spoke up for the first time. "Your tribe? I've heard about your canoes." Rafe's husband, Terrance, was a distant descendent of Chief Sealth, the revered Native statesman after whom Seattle was named.

Pleased, Jasmine said proudly, "Yes. Quileute."

"What was your relationship with Mr. Cushman?" Anna asked. "You were . . . close?"

Immediately, the receptionist's face closed. Jasmine glanced around quickly, as if afraid someone else might be listening. She picked up the sleek, black fountain pen and hid it in her top drawer. Jasmine Wolf nodded them toward the hallway. "Mr. Cushman's executive assistant, Jackson Poole, is waiting now for you in his office. Second door, left."

It was clear there was nothing more the woman would give them. Instinctively, Anna doubted Jasmine was their murderer. Her grief was too real. But, of course, it could be remorse.

When they entered Poole's plush office suite, the man greeted them with a slick smile and a clipped accent, which screamed Ivy League. He was thin, anemic-looking, and preppy for Seattle. He wore an expensive dark-blue linen suit suggesting he had a tailor. Anna instantly disliked Jackson Poole and suspected lying came easily to him.

"How can I help you, detectives?" Poole asked and offered them two chairs. He kept his place behind the polished mahogany desk.

Just like a Big Pharma exec, Anna thought, noting the endangered hardwood that too often was the badge of the powerful.

"We're trying to establish Leonard Cushman's last twelve hours," Rafe said. "You must keep track of his schedule, calls, meetings?"

"Of course," Poole said too quickly, as if he'd already eliminated everything to really help their investigation.

Poole handed over a leather-bound Day-Timer. Anna noted Cushman had not scheduled any guests for the prior night on his work calendar. She also noticed Cushman used a fountain pen and a few of the entries were smeared and unreadable. At first glance, Cushman's handwriting was like the note scrawled on his office table. Cushman's last week was full of meetings with staff and a rare office visit from his ex-wife, Eloise, and stepson, Hugh. They would have to double-check Cushman's family, even if they had already provided convenient alibis for each other.

"We're looking for a young woman, perhaps a blonde," Anna said. "Or a redhead. She and several other people might have visited Cushman's home late last night."

Poole hesitated long enough to suggest to Anna he knew something he was not about to tell her. "No idea. We have a lot of blond and red-haired women working here."

Rafe pressed him. "And just to rule you out, Mr. Poole, where were you last night at 11:00 p.m. or later?"

Jackson Poole leaned back in his chair and folded his arms across his chest. "I was here in the office working late . . . the janitor can vouch for me. I was preparing for a big meeting this morning with the board of directors."

"Did any of Mr. Cushman's employees visit him at home?" Anna asked. "Perhaps an employee with whom Mr. Cushman had running disagreements?"

Flicking off a piece of lint from his suit, Poole nodded. "I suspect you're asking about Eleanor Kiernan. She is brilliant, but Eleanor is Mr. Cushman's biggest critic." Poole warmed to his own critique of Kiernan. "You didn't hear this from me," the man said, "but Eleanor is mourning her twin brother . . . he overdosed just last month."

Anna kept her back straight and her expression bland, scribbling in her notepad. But her breathing quickened. Kiernan might have a personal motive for killing Cushman.

"I can give you Eleanor Kiernan's contact info for now," Poole offered, a faint, obsequious smile on his narrow face. He obviously took pleasure in throwing suspicion on his coworker. A rival? "Eleanor didn't show up for work today. No one's been able to get ahold of her. Rumor has it she's left town."

Now they were getting somewhere. If they couldn't locate Kiernan—and especially if she'd skipped town—they'd also have to get a search warrant for her home.

Jackson Poole tapped his cell phone and rattled off the address, phone, and email for Eleanor Kiernan. Then he placed his manicured hands back on the desk, as if to say he was done answering any more questions.

Rafe leaned over and whispered to Anna, "Eleanor Kiernan has no social media presence. Can't even find a photo of her online. And no pic of her on Fortura's website. Only her credentials. Lead researcher, biochemist."

Anna nodded and fixed on Cushman's executive assistant. "Please tell us more about Mr. Cushman and Eleanor Kiernan . . . romantically involved?"

Poole burst out laughing. It surprised Anna he had such a hearty, full-bodied laugh. Despite herself, she liked Poole a little better. He might be a liar, but Anna instinctively admired anyone who laughed so amiably.

Poole glanced out the skyscraper's window at the ferry boat gliding across the sound like a floating birthday cake.

"Well, some might say Eleanor and Mr. Cushman were stuck in some . . . well, some endless struggle. You know, karmic."

The executive assistant now seemed to be telling the truth. "What kind of struggle?" Anna asked.

"Well, they disagreed violently about our new fentanyl-like drug that Fortura is marketing." Poole began to explain as if he were suddenly a science teacher. "You know, detectives, fentanyl is even more successful at reducing chronic pain than Neocodone. At first, we thought its only use was for anesthesia. But our formulation is awesome for—"

Anna held up a hand to interrupt what sounded more like an ad than an explanation. She'd once had a fentanyl lollipop for a biopsy and knew its giddy, carefree effects, where the world was perfectly right and she was almost invincible, even as a huge needle penetrated her spine.

"Illegal fentanyl laced pills are killing kids," Rafe said flatly. "A girl in my son's middle school took what she thought was Advil from her mother's purse and died."

Poole held up his hands. "Not our problem, officer," he said. "We rigorously test our drugs for—"

Anna had had enough of the man's denials. "Please don't leave town," she said to Poole. "We will need a follow-up interview."

"Of course," Poole answered crisply. "You'll find Kiernan's lab on the fifth floor."

Anna and Rafe took another elevator to the lower floor, where they hoped to interview Eleanor Kiernan's lab mates.

"Kiernan seems like our first real person of interest," Rafe said. "You already noted her initials on the stiletto sheath."

"If only it were that easy," Anna said. "We'll track her down. But let's keep an eye on Poole. I don't trust his patter. Check his alibi." Because they were the only passengers on the long elevator ride, Anna said in a soft voice, "You know, Rafe, I really think this murder was intimate . . . family or friend . . . someone Cushman really trusted." Anna hesitated to confide in her partner her strong intuition at the crime scene about the murder weapon. "And . . . well, I think the stiletto was a gift Cushman gave to someone he cared about."

"Okay," Rafe sighed. "I'm not going to make you tell me exactly how you got this ESP info. I'll just see if I can figure out the same thing with actual *evidence*."

Anna frowned. He was right, of course. The challenge for her was always proving her intuitions in some logical way that made sense to others. Her sometimes unreliable intuitions haunted Anna. On the one cold case she cared most about solving, Anna's sixth sense was always silent, as if she were not allowed to know. Sometimes Anna wished she could issue a gag order against her sister's last cries, always echoing in her nightmares.

The only person Anna had ever confided in about her frightening premonitions and nightmares was her middle-grade science teacher, Mr. Cooley.

"Mr. Cooley, what's wrong with me?" Anna had tearfully demanded of the only adult she trusted.

"Not a thing!" he'd pronounced firmly, then pushed a junior microscope toward her like a shield.

She squinted to scrutinize the squiggly samba-like dance of cells on glass. Unlike the other eighth-grade students, Anna didn't just want to study a strand of her own dark, curly hair or a pink snapdragon petal or black mold. Anna had insisted on pricking her own forefinger for one bright drop of her frothy, velvet blood.

"Maybe you'll be a scientist someday." Mr. Cooley smiled at Anna's bowed head.

All year, her teacher had carefully observed this highly sensitive, popular girl. But recently, she'd grown more introverted, strangely quiet. Mr. Cooley would often find her sitting alone at lunch when she was usually surrounded by girlfriends. "Are you . . . having some trouble at home, Anna?" he asked softly.

"No, it's just me. I'm . . . different."

"How . . . *different?*"

"I'm a weirdo." Anna shrugged. "Sometimes I . . . well, I get pictures in my mind or know things I shouldn't. I hear colors . . . sometimes see . . . well, weird waves of light . . . dream about people dying. It scares people. I've got to keep my mouth shut more."

"Ah," Mr. Cooley said and nodded. "Information can come to us in many ways if we're open. Sometimes that happens to me. I've done a lot of research and can teach you how to keep your own counsel, Anna. Don't be afraid or deny your gift. It's called synesthesia and 'clairsentience'—or *clear seeing*. Sighting like yours is the rarest. It's another way of being smart."

He explained hers was a skill she could develop, but she must also learn to discreetly share her premonitions or knowing with others—*only* after she'd matched her second sight with quantifiable facts. Mr. Cooley continued. "It's sad because most people just tune out their intuitions. This kind of dumbing down doesn't help us advance as a species."

"Are animals clair-sen-tient?" Anna struggled to pronounce the word correctly. "Do they see all the colors and hear sounds before they happen?"

"Animals have extraordinary sensory skills . . . what to humans might seem *extra*sensory. You know, bats and dolphins navigate by seeing with sound. A snake sees the heat of a mouse prey. An elephant calls to her mate in a language of infrasound, much lower than human hearing. Animals need their keenest senses just to survive." Mr. Cooley smiled. "They can't *not* know things. Or pretend they don't know. There are predators who would take advantage. An animal who denies *all* senses just doesn't survive."

Anna studied Mr. Cooley with real interest. "Should I pretend I'm an animal when I know things other people don't?"

"Yes, we *are* animals! And sometimes you can really help others. You can develop these intuitive skills so they don't overwhelm you. But you just can't tell a lot of people about this, Anna. Remember, you can always be wrong. You must be more scientific and back up your senses with something others can also see and hear. Be careful who you trust and tell what you know. Choose friends who won't insist you be any *less* than who you are."

As the elevator door clanged open, Rafe nudged Anna. "Anything more I should know? Any ESP from the ether?"

Anna shook her head. "Nothing yet. But I think we should track down Kiernan."

Anna kept returning to Eleanor Kiernan as a possible suspect, not only because Kiernan was missing but also because Anna's sixth sense now told her this woman was important for some reason. It was an intriguing lead to investigate—a critic and Cushman's only friend, but perhaps also a guilty and despairing protégé. Kiernan's brother had overdosed on the very drug she and Cushman had created. These were the first viable motives for this murder—vengeance, justice, and penance.

V

ELEANOR

May 1, 2019

This was not the time—hiding out on an isolated island
beach—for Eleanor to remember her therapist once
telling her, "You'll never come into your own until Leo
Cushman dies."

Camped in this moss-hung Douglas fir forest, Eleanor
certainly did not feel she'd come into her own. But she was
relieved to see splashes of morning sunlight through the
ancient forest. The most savage storms often ushered in this
rare but glorious Northwest sunshine. For all her grief and
terror, she'd slept through the fierce gale in her sturdy tent
and down sleeping bag. By now, the police would have discovered Leo's body and might have landed on her as a possible
suspect because she had suddenly left town. Eleanor needed a
refuge and solitude to plan her next move. She had retreated
to the misty contemplation of these timeless, thousand-year-
old trees.

Eleanor whistled to her dog, who was running anxious
circles around their campsite. "Breakfast soon, boy," she promised Brodie, who snapped at her heels.

The Scottie lifted his shaggy, wheaten snout to happily inhale the aromatic scent of her freshly caught salmon, seasoned with black pepper and Irish butter, sizzling in her tiny skillet over the hungry fire. Eleanor refused to eat the freeze-dried backpacking fare—berry granola, mac and cheese, or chicken coconut curry Leo always stored in his boat cabin's cabinets—unless she had to camp here a long time.

She had everything she needed now, having picked up provisions from her Friday Harbor beach house—a cell phone charger, fishing pole, camp stove, water, trail mix, dog food, and leftovers from her well-stocked fridge. A tiny hatchet for chopping wood rested on her little woodpile. Her iPad and cell phone were silenced so no one could easily track her. They were useless anyway, with no signal on this practically uninhabited island of Sucia, just north of Orcas in Boundary Pass. Everything else she needed, including her wetsuit, was stowed on Leo's sailboat. His boat was always ready to go. Leo's tidy *San Juan*, usually docked on Elliot Bay Marina, was where he really lived. Now that Leo was dead, the boat would be hers.

"You know I'm leaving you this sailboat in my will," Leo had told her just last weekend on what was their last sail together.

"By the time you're gone, Leo, I'll be too decrepit to sail." she'd laughed.

Eleanor shivered and buried her face in Brodie's thick fur. "Now Leo *is* gone."

She bent over to embrace her Scottie, who leaned against her knees. There was a rustling in the underbrush when a coyote casually strolled by their campsite. Brodie barked and bounced around on short legs like pogo sticks, as if the intruder were trying to attack their hideaway. Brodie's ruckus set seagulls squawking on shore like sentries.

"Shhhhh, Brodie, it's okay."

But nothing was okay. It might never be okay again. Eleanor stood up, shaking, and zipped Leo's heavy windbreaker over her layers of fleece under wear, vest, and down jacket. The scent of Leo's sage and sandalwood aftershave lingered in the slicker's Gore-Tex folds. She could smell him days after his death; she fought off more tears—and more guilt.

Brodie yipped and jumped up, begging to share her breakfast. She had remembered to bring his folding food bowl and shared half of her fried salmon with him. Though she wasn't hungry, Eleanor forced herself to eat the salmon feast. She had to admit the flaking flesh was always more flavorful when stoked by fire. Even so, Eleanor only ate half her salmon. She'd stow the leftovers in her large cooler in the boat's cabin.

She debated whether to keep the campfire stoked for warmth from the cold morning sun and insistent marine mists. The plume of smoke might attract company and signal her presence if anybody had discovered Leo's sailboat was missing from the marina. The twenty-one-foot *San Juan* was outdated but because of Leo's passion for shining teak and Tilex scrubbing compound, his boat barely had seen barnacle or brine. It was the only modest thing about Leo. His private plane was top-of-the-line, and his several houses were like overgrown invasive species in a city whose dot-com millionaires disdained displaying wealth, except online.

"I'd be embarrassed to live in your mini-mansions," Eleanor had always teased Leo. "But I'd happily live on your boat."

Now, she was doing just that. How long could she last here on Sucia? Should she set sail today for the border? Eleanor had a friend from her Fortura lab who now lived on a sailboat off Galiano Island in Canada. Would he take her in and shelter her in his community of rogue sailors and runaways from city life?

When she'd asked her friend why he was leaving such a lucrative corporate job, he'd said, "Can't work anymore for a company so compromised by profit over health." He grinned. "Fortura is caught up in criminal crosswinds. We born sailors always watch to see which way the wind blows. We're devoted to something as invisible and almighty as air."

Leonard Cushman was also such a wind-struck sailor. His maritime devotion was what Eleanor enjoyed most about her mentor. On the water, Leo surrendered to the wind. On the water, Leo was almost humble.

He was also a patient teacher. Just last weekend he'd teased Eleanor as she took the tiller. "You're luffing, Ellie . . . again."

In the fickle spring wind, Eleanor had valiantly struggled to adjust the slack sail. It flopped loudly, catawampus to the crazy wind.

"Luffing is a big-time sailing sin," Leo had teased her.

She allowed Leo to climb over her on the slim sailboat to protectively cup her head and call, "Ready about?"

"Yes, Captain my Captain." Eleanor smiled. Poised for his tack, she braced herself.

Eleanor also steadied herself for what she was about to tell her boss. She was on the verge of quitting his company. It was news best delivered when Leo was most receptive to another force besides his own. Like wind. Or his favorite protégé. Eleanor dearly hoped when she threatened to leave Fortura, Leo might reconsider his rejection of her pleas to help the families of those who had lost someone they loved to their painkiller. She would, of course, not tell him about working undercover for the FBI.

Several years before, when Eleanor's research had proved their painkiller was terribly addictive used long-term, not just for end-of-life or cancer patients, Leo had kept her report like an admission of their guilt. But he hid the only copy from the feds and his Fortura sales force, who were making huge bonuses.

"Hard alee!" Leo shouted.

Like a shot, he let out the sheets, line flashing through his gloved fingers like heat lightning. The mainsail swung over them with a creak of teak, and the white jib thwacked toward the wind as he bent low in the boat, then sprang to the other side to pull it in.

"Now, Ellie, you haul her in!" Leo shouted, handing her the jib sheet.

With all her might, Eleanor heaved. She braced one foot against the rail, arms aching as she heard the *chink-chink-chink* of the winch catch and the sail skirt tuck in tight.

"Better," Leo said. "But we lost wind."

Losing wind, running before the wind, close-winded, windward—the secret of sailing was wind. But who knew where it was coming from or where it would carry them?

"Pretend you're a baby bird in flying school," Leo said. "You don't have wings, you have sails." Leo opened a bottle of beer. It was the only time he indulged in such working-class drink. Even so, his IPA of foamy gold was from a local micro-brewery, already famous internationally. "Now, where is the wind?" he asked her.

Eleanor gazed up at the telltales, two strings of red yarn streaming from the shrouds. The wind was fragrant with the clean tang of fresh water. "From the south."

"Find your point of sail."

Eleanor fixed on Mt. Rainier's white dome. The volcanic mountain was so benevolent, but it was volatile . . . alive. Rainier was where Frankie had once fallen into that icy crevasse and broken his leg, and the doctor prescribed endless opiates for his pain.

"See ripples in the sail?" Leo demanded. "Means you're wasting wind. Turn into it . . . right, good!"

Eleanor pulled tight. "Wind off the starboard side," she said as the pale sheet fluttered. There was a slight whisper of wind, then a darkening in the water.

Leo pointed to a distant spot on the lake. "Tack!" he cried.

Quickly she performed a series of short, staccato tacks.

"Close your eyes," Leo said softly. "Feel the wind?"

She did. The wind was moist and brisk, a breeze as generous as it was fickle.

"Now, follow it."

She had followed this man for almost a decade, apprenticing herself to someone she respected as a true believer and healer. But like any disappointed convert, she wondered if she'd mistaken Leo's success for greatness, his passion for principle, and his drive for devotion.

Eleanor opened her eyes to realize her hands had made subtle adjustments on the tiller. They were flying—running with the wind. It was a moment of astonishing clarity, like the first time she and her brother had balanced on their two-seater bicycle.

Wind is like water, Eleanor thought. If she could feel it, she could flow with it. Sailing had more to do with sensing than seeing. And trusting. For too long, she'd trusted Leo.

"My turn," Leo called and clambered over Eleanor to take the tiller.

The mainsail swelled as if blown by the faintest breath of some holy being.

"Jibe ho!" Leo called, and they both ducked as the boom slid across the boat. A robust gust filled the jib. At the helm, Leo lay way back, exuberant, skipper's cap almost skimming the lake.

Eleanor lay back, too, as waves splashed her sweaty skin. Above them, the windsock flew full force.

"We're off!" Leo cried joyfully as they both leaned backward into the wind, their bodies stretched out over the rails. A wild wave drenched them, but Leo just laughed. "Funny thing about getting high on the water," he roared. "We're heeled."

Exuberantly, they sailed all day until it was almost dusk, with late, spring light and a sliver of new moon rising. Leo was buzzed from his multiple micro-brews. It was time for Eleanor to tell Leo of her desertion, if not her betrayal. The wind was also abandoning him.

"Leo," Eleanor began thoughtfully. "I've been thinking . . ."

"Always a good sign for us." Leo grinned, distracted, cocking his tousled head to listen for the lost wind.

Us, Eleanor knew, meant the company. She forced herself to continue. "I'm talking with some other biochemists in global health . . ."

"Great," Leo nodded. He fiddled with the flapping sail. Luffing. "What do they say?"

Eleanor took a deep breath, "They say I should come work . . . with *them*."

Startled, Leo swung toward her, letting go of the main. The boom swung uncontrollably, almost striking her. "What the hell, Ellie?"

Eleanor ducked just in time to avoid the boom. "Listen, Leo, there are some wonderful NGO researchers working on international programs needing my skills—it's so innovative and inspiring."

"I never pegged you for a nonprofit bleeding heart."

"And I never believed you were *just* about making money, Leo," Eleanor said. "What about making meaningful contributions?" When Leo simply shrugged and busied himself with a resistant knot, Eleanor pursued, her anger rising. "When you first brought me on at Fortura, you were all about finding a cure for chronic pain, for helping people heal. You promised we'd do something remarkable together."

At last Leo faced her, his eyes darkening and pained. "We *are* doing remarkable things—" He stopped, seeing her frown.

"You've changed, Leo." Eleanor took a deep breath. "All the money has changed you. You're not the same man I worked with side-by-side in the lab. Where's the empathy, the imagination? It's what first drew me to you and your work."

"Easy for you to condemn me for making money, Ellie," Leo said. "You come from money. Always had it. You've never had to work for it from the bottom up . . . like me."

She shook her head, gazing across the glassy bay at Mt. Rainier—a pale goddess in skirts of mist, like another world shimmering on the horizon. Maybe Leo was right. Maybe if she'd suddenly made her first fortune after an immigrant background of poverty, she'd also be changed. She'd had the ease of a family trust fund, of always knowing there would be enough to support her dreams and help others less fortunate.

"In South Africa . . ." Eleanor continued, "maternal-infant health fatalities are three times the world rate. Global Health scientists there have invited me to join—"

"For Christ's sake, Ellie, if you care so much about maternal health, why don't you just have a kid?" Leo snapped. "Frankie's dead. Find somebody else to try and save."

Eleanor eyes blurred with spray. "I didn't save Frankie, did I?" she shouted, so furious she considered throwing her heavy thermos at him. Leo looked so arrogant and condescending in his sailor's cap and ridiculously expensive sunglasses.

Why did she ever think of this man as her captain? Eleanor wanted to bring Leo Cushman and his company down. Yes, she'd agreed to become a whistleblower against Fortura's crime; but was still uneasy about harming her mentor. She'd stayed on at the company, hoping she could convince Leo to do the right thing and settle lawsuits from those families who'd lost those they loved to overdose. After she'd made sure Leo was not liable and did the right thing, she had planned to leave Fortura to do penance for all the pain and heartbreak they'd caused. Fortura had made her Leo's accomplice, complicit in all the drug deaths. The thought sickened her. She was furious at herself . . . and him.

The *San Juan* sailed on in silence, with only the flap of the sail as the wind abruptly deserted them. Luffing again.

"You'll really give up on us?" Leo finally asked, his voice surprisingly subdued and sober. If there had been any wind, she would not have heard what he whispered. "Don't, Ellie . . . don't leave me."

Eleanor did hear him. But she was too angry and troubled to answer. The lake was still and forlorn. A few motorboats cruised by, headed for shore, passing them like a ghost ship. Flatly they floated. Becalmed. Dead in the water.

BRODIE BARKED AT A PASSING KAYAK as it glided gracefully by their remote island beach. A kayaker waved cheerily and called out. Eleanor scowled and retreated into her tent. She did not need the company of other chatty campers who might be able to identify her if the police had put out an APB for her or alerted the media with her photo. She glanced at her watch, wondering how long it would take detectives to realize she'd stolen Leo's sailboat—now technically hers—and run. Most boats in Seattle marinas simply docked and set sail at will. No one paid attention. Perhaps no one would report Leo's boat missing. Her most fervent, but probably futile, hope was that no one would suspect and follow her.

VI

ANNA

May 1, 2019

Turbulence from a swiftly moving thunderstorm shunted their float plane sideways as they flew over emerald-green islands, shrouded with purple mists. In this sheltering Olympic rain shadow, the San Juan Islands were usually sunnier than Seattle. But the late-afternoon rain chased away the spring sunshine.

Even in her noise-canceling headphones, Anna winced at the roaring noise. She didn't mind the queasy lift and drop of the small plane. Anna loved flight—unless it was her runaway suspect's.

"We've lost a lot of time," Rafe grumbled as the float plane lurched sideways. Unlike Anna, Rafe preferred to stay on the ground. He was also out of sorts because he might have to spend a night away from his family.

"At least we have a good excuse to miss more of the captain's karaoke parties." Anna grinned.

It had taken time to plod through interviews with Eleanor Kiernan's codirector of Fortura's research lab, who'd revealed the most possibly incriminating evidence—Kiernan kept a stiletto fighting knife in her lab drawer, but she mostly used it on camping trips or at work as a letter opener. Once, to the dismay of Fortura coworkers, she wore it on her belt at an office Halloween party when she dressed as a pirate. The stiletto was a gift from Leonard Cushman. It was also missing. Only the custom-made sheath, with EK initials was left behind. *Why?*

Such a strong lead for the possible murder weapon. When the detectives searched Kiernan's house, they'd found signs of a hasty departure, which necessitated this float plane to the San Juan Islands. Both Cushman and Kiernan kept beach cottages up in Friday Harbor. When Anna and Rafe had searched Eleanor Kiernan's home, they'd also discovered a note for neighbors.

Brodie and I are gone for awhile.
Please water the bonsai every 2–3 days.
Thanks, EK

The note was already with forensics to check the handwriting against the unfinished note on Leonard Cushman's office table. There was an APB out at local airports and ferries for Eleanor Kiernan in case Anna's suspicion that she was escaping to Canada was incorrect. Certainly, a woman who was desperate and had deep financial means might run anywhere in the world—but not without her dog. When Leonard Cushman's boat was also found to be missing at Elliot Bay Marina, the detectives hoped their now-prime suspect would seek a familiar place to hide.

"We need photo ID of Kiernan from forensics," Rafe said.

There had been many photos of her Scottie in Kiernan's home but none of her. Why did someone as accomplished as Kiernan keep such a low profile? A ding on Anna's phone and then the blurry driver's license photo of Eleanor Kiernan appeared. Thirty-nine, organ donor, short-cropped red hair fashionably cut. Anna thought Kiernan was a little like Annie Lennox, except the rock star would never costume herself in an unironic corporate suit. Unlike most driver's license photos, which are much like mug shots, Kiernan's photo showed off her best feature—the attractive slant of her high cheekbones and piercing eyes. But her eyes, even in the bad photo, were anxious, brow furrowed. No smile. Anna wished she were more visually intuitive to read this face clearly. She'd glean much more about the woman if she could hear her voice.

When Anna showed Rafe the photo of their suspect, he nodded.

"Red hair," he said with satisfaction. "Bet she's the shade-garden lady the gardener told us often visited Cushman." He fiddled with his iPad. "Hey, look at this. Her twin, Frankie, was the extrovert of the pair, super active on Facebook. Posted this family photo."

Anna squinted, studying the photo of two frowning tod-dlers, an almost identical boy and girl, with red curls and startled, bright blue-violet eyes; they were bookended between imposing parents. The father's face was angular as a hatchet. The elegant mother wore a museum-quality emerald necklace.

"With such Boston Brahmin parents," Rafe said, "I might also turn to drugs."

Their float plane banked over a lush lavender farm and Lime Kiln Point. Then, it skimmed over the crowded marina, pastel Victorian-style homes, art galleries, and tourist shops on the main streets. On the landing strip, they were greeted by the Friday Harbor sheriff, a no-nonsense woman who probably kept her island well-patrolled and mostly crime-free.

"Hop in." Sheriff Conway nodded toward her red Jeep, which was clean and waxed to a high hand-polish. A criminal could see his unlucky face mirrored in the Jeep's shine.

Taking the passenger seat, Anna explained, "Kiernan's on the run. You know her?"

"Six-degrees of separation." Sheriff Conway laughed. Her ruddy, open face contrasted with the sharpness in her dark eyes. She seemed like a woman who missed nothing, while appearing amiable and even a little remote. "But Kiernan keeps mostly to herself when she's here. Doesn't mix much with the locals. I always got the feeling she came to Friday Harbor to get away by herself, unless her brother was with her. Then, I'd sometimes see them riding motorbikes or horses at the local stable. Or sailing in Leonard Cushman's sailboat."

"Did you know Cushman?" Rafe asked, leaning up from the back seat.

"Who doesn't?" Sheriff Conway replied and expertly took a long curve with one hand on the wheel.

"Cushman and Kiernan . . ." Rafe asked. "Lovers?"

"Cushman squired lots of women around the island. Roche Harbor, fancy places. Not Kiernan. She and her boss weren't tourists. Acted more like homebodies, locals."

"Does it surprise you Eleanor Kiernan is a possible suspect?" Anna asked.

Sheriff Conway hesitated, glancing over at Anna, her keen eyes assessing whether she should really offer her professional opinion. "Who else do you place in the frame for this murder?" she asked.

The question impressed Anna. It was not only direct but also suggested the sheriff obviously had another idea. "You think it's someone else?"

"Well," Sheriff Conway said with a frown. "I never saw Cushman up here with his son or his wife. Not exactly a tight family. You talked with them yet?"

"They alibi each other." Rafe shrugged. "Soon as we find Kiernan, we'll get back to Cushman's family."

Sheriff Conway nodded. "Well, I'd keep an open mind about anyone's who's going to inherit so much money." She frowned, then added, "And there were death threats against Leonard Cushman, even here. I had to follow up on several of them. Two antidrug activists, Yamasaki and Fleishman. I had to arrest them after they attacked Cushman's plane. Sprayed red paint and graffiti all over his shiny little jet."

Anna liked this sheriff. She was anything but small-town. "What did the graffiti say?" Anna asked.

"Drug lord and kid killer!" Sheriff Conway said, shaking her head. "I'm just glad this murder wasn't on *my* watch." Sheriff Conway grinned. "I don't envy you this case—"

The sheriff quickly answered a ding on her cell phone. Anna noticed the phone was in a tidy holster on her belt, where a gun might be. *Did the officer even carry a gun?*

"Right," said the sheriff and hung up. "Cushman's sailboat was spotted at our marina late last night. Someone at the marina saw Kiernan and her dog at the dock. She's gone again now."

"Where do you think she'd sail?" Anna asked.

"Maybe she'll try to hide out in the one of the less inhabited Gulf Islands just over the border. Know them?"

Anna knew them well. Ancient rainforests and old-growth trees made these wild and isolated islands one of Canada's best-kept secrets.

"Yes, you can get lost and never found if that's where she's headed," Anna said. She faced Rafe. "Can you radio Canadian Coast Guard and let them know we're on the way?" Turning back to the sheriff, Anna asked, "Got a motorboat?"

"Does any island sheriff *not* own a motorboat?" Conway smiled. "I was just waiting for you to ask. I'll text my deputy to get everything ready."

So far north at that time of year, there would be some sun until almost nine o'clock—time and just enough light to search for the murder victim's stolen sailboat.

"DAMN!" SHERIFF CONWAY SAID, AS she revved the engine on her police boat. "Thunderstorms worse up north. Best put on your life preservers."

Anna and Rafe obliged. Anna was relieved it was late May and they'd only have to contend with rain. Last winter, when she'd sailed the tumultuous waters of the Strait of Juan de Fuca, she'd had to wear so many base layers and a bright orange dry suit so thick she felt like the Pillsbury Dough Boy. But it had warded off the waves and wind chill. Now, the simple waterproof slicker and red knit hat she always carried in her backpack was enough to protect her from the spitting rain. Rafe wasn't as well prepared. He hunkered down in the cabin, his thin fleece jacket buttoned up tight.

They made good time cruising through Boundary Pass toward the border when Sheriff Conway got a tip from the Coast Guard that a sailboat matching Cushman's was spotted farther north near Mattia and Sucia Islands. If they could catch up with Kiernan before she crossed the border, they'd have a better chance of intercepting her. If they missed her tonight in this well-known fog zone, she might disappear into the Gulf Islands.

Anna assumed Kiernan would be well-prepared to camp out on some remote island. If Kiernan were the meticulous researcher her job demanded, she'd have a plan, either way.

"I'd like your opinion," Anna shouted over the wind to the Sheriff. "Why would Kiernan run if she wasn't guilty? I've been working mostly cold cases, and this is my first active murder investigation," she admitted. "My captain probably regrets giving it to me."

"Well, I met Eleanor Kiernan once after she called island's emergency medics. They called me to the scene because her brother was strung out on drugs, unresponsive. There's a lot of cross-border, illegal trafficking in opiates." Sheriff Conway shook her head. "Never seen anybody so calm in a crisis. I guess that'd make Kiernan capable of . . . well, of planning to off her boss. We haven't had many murders in Friday Harbor," Sheriff Conway concluded, "but those I've investigated have been pretty high-profile."

Anna recalled a movie star—she couldn't remember his name—who, like many wealthy Hollywood types, had moved to Friday Harbor. They were charmed by its pristine beauty and their sophisticated techy neighbors. But many of the Californians left because they couldn't endure the brooding rain. And wireless reception was always spotty at best.

"We've lost any signal," Rafe complained, as if it were the end of the world.

Anna smiled at her partner. Rafe was no nature boy. Bicycling Seattle's increasingly congested city streets was his only nod to adventure. Anna knew Rafe would much rather be at home with his husband and their young son, Nate. Anna was Nate's godmother—an honor she took very seriously. Sometimes she worried if she and Rafe were killed in the line of duty, Nate would never get over losing both father and surrogate mother. Anna swore she would never let it happen, but here they were chasing a possible murderer, exposed out on the water with no backup yet.

In times like these, Anna tuned into her intuitive skills. It was always harder to summon them up than to simply receive them whenever her sixth sense caught her by surprise. As the motorboat lurched over turbulent waves, Anna closed her eyes.

Again, she saw Cushman's body, the red, expert slash at his throat from the probable stiletto. She scanned his office, searching in her memory for what she initially sensed might be amiss . . . misplaced. Certainly, the spilled kombucha had surprised her. But there was something else nagging at her. Anna frowned, focusing. *Why was he naked if the murderer was not his lover? Who was the late-night blonde visitor?* Cushman didn't seem like the type to call upon prostitutes. The coroner had said he probably knew his killer and was intimate with her—or him. In her memory, Anna again scanned the scrawled note on Cushman's bed stand. *"Please believe me."*

Then Anna knew, without knowing how or how to prove

it. These last words were Cushman's, meant only for Kiernan. *What was he pleading with her to believe? Why?*

The motorboat leapt up over a ferry boat's wake, and Rafe gave out a startled yelp.

"Yikes!" he shouted, but the wind drowned out any other words.

Anna kept her eyes closed, visualizing the crime scene. She breathed evenly, relaxing. When she summoned up a meditative calm, she could see most clearly. Another detail had been troubling her. *If Kiernan's stiletto was the murder weapon, why did she leave its sheath with her incriminating initials at the scene?*

Just then the sheriff's radio let out a burst of static. "Suspect spotted," crackled a deep male voice. "Sucia Island beach."

Sheriff Conway nodded in satisfaction and said something in a language Anna did not understand. She supposed it was the language of the Coast Salish tribal people who'd lived and sailed here for thousands of years. Anna wondered if Kiernan were desperate, violent, or frightened enough to resist arrest.

Sheriff Conway continued her rapid-fire conversation with the tribal police. It didn't surprise Anna that the sheriff spoke this Native language. She also appeared to enjoy a cordial relationship with the Native officer. This was not always the case with tribal police.

The sheriff explained, "My cousin's the tribe's police chief. He's given me the exact location of the sighting and will meet us there soon to assist."

Anna nodded, her heart pounding. Instinctively, she reached for her holster. She had never carried her gun until now. This would be their first arrest in a current murder case. She caught Rafe's eye. He, too, was anxious. It showed in the way he squared his shoulders, pulling his jacket even tighter. It was much cooler with the sun setting.

As their motorboat skipped over strong waves, Anna almost lost her balance on the deck. Sheriff Conway reached out a firm hand to steady her. Sometimes when Anna had physical touch with a person, her intuitions were the most accurate. Faint images now flickered in her mind. *A Native man, eyes haunted, as he shoved a needle into the beautiful, stylized red-and-black wolf tattoo on his thin forearm.*

"Call your son!" Anna blurted out to the sheriff before she could think better of it. "He's in trouble."

Sheriff Conway let go of Anna. She nodded sadly, not asking Anna how she knew about her only son's heroin addiction.

"He's always in trouble," the sheriff said, and then added, "But thank you for seeing. I will call him."

Anna was relieved the sheriff did not question her second sight but simply accepted and was even grateful for it. How different Anna's life would have been if her visions would have been heard, even welcomed.

Sheriff Conway abruptly cut the motor as they cruised into a calm inlet. Even in the dark fog, they could see the twenty-one-foot sailboat tucked in and anchored. A slender woman in a black slicker was hoisting supplies from the sailboat to a rubber zodiac. A white, shaggy dog balanced in the sailboat's small zodiac awaiting her. Barking furiously, the dog was menacing.

As they eased near Kiernan's sailboat, the suspect surprised them all by firing up her engine and heading her zodiac straight toward them. Again, Anna fingered her pistol and planted her feet on the motorboat's floorboards to steady herself.

Rafe shouted out, "Eleanor Kiernan, we're arresting you on suspicion of the murder of Leonard Cushman."

With the dog growling fiercely, Kiernan steadily navigated toward their motorboat. If she was going to ram them, she'd only succeed in harming herself in her smaller boat. Death by cop. Anna braced for a possible collision.

Kiernan was now close enough for Anna to read her expression more clearly. Anna had expected perhaps despair and the recklessness that precedes violence or self-destruction. But instead, Kiernan's face was calm and competent as she cut her engine and deftly came alongside the motorboat. She held up both hands in surrender as Sheriff Conway tossed down a rope to tow her Zodiac closer. The Scottie seized the knotted rope, teeth chomping and fraying it back and forth as if its thick length were a burrowing animal.

"Brodie, leave it!" Kiernan commanded. Her dog reluctantly complied but not without a mighty tug that pulled the sheriff's motorboat close enough for Sheriff Conway to reach down and lend Kiernan a hand.

There was no need to handcuff her. The dog scrambled aboard and instantly adored Rafe, leaning against him and wagging his tail. Rafe read Kiernan her rights, and she settled on the boat's splintered wooden seat. Her expression was melancholy, surprisingly open.

"I want to help you find whoever killed Leo," she said, her high cheekbones raw from the wind, her eyes lucid even in the dark.

It was what many murderers told arresting officers when they were finally caught. A ruse, a distraction. But Anna wondered if this might be true for Eleanor Kiernan.

"Then why did you run?" Anna asked.

"I knew you would suspect me," Kiernan answered simply. "I needed time to figure things out."

"You could have done that in custody," Rafe commented drily. "Or in Seattle."

He nodded to Anna and jerked his head to point out a stiletto knife in its large sheath on Kiernan's belt. It was obviously not the knife's proper sheath but was made from thick canvas. Anna suspected it would perfectly fit the sheath they'd discovered in Cushman's office.

Anna realized her partner was convinced they'd caught the killer. It was in the triumphant tilt of Rafe's head. She wasn't so sure. Kiernan's expression was firm, her curly red hair matted from wind and rain. She did look like a woman on a mission.

"And have you?" Anna asked Kiernan. "Have you figured things out?"

"No," Kiernan admitted with a frustrated scowl. "But I will." She studied Anna carefully as if she were researching a subject in her lab. "*We* will."

VII

ANNA

May 2, 2019

Anna studied her suspect intently. Kiernan was self-possessed, reserved, and attractive, even in her splattered black slicker and gray beret. Anna imagined if Eleanor Kiernan had been arrested in her corporate headquarters instead of a stolen sailboat, she'd be wearing the camouflage of success—maybe a linen jacket draped with a fashionable silk scarf—her style more the rich, flowing fabrics of Eileen Fisher than the tidy fit of Ann Taylor.

"I know it sounds like a bad film noir," Kiernan said to the detectives in the dim Seattle interview room the next day, "but I'm being framed."

Listening to her soft-spoken, surprisingly husky voice, Anna could tune into Eleanor Kiernan more accurately. The woman's voice had the rich, alto undertones of a blues singer. Her tone was mesmerizing, like the intimate confidences of a late-night radio host. But in her throaty voice Anna heard Kiernan's grief. Or was it guilt?

Anna straightened in her chair, not wanting to give any sign she sensed this woman's sorrow. She was careful in her questioning, worried she might make a mistake or miss something important. Her boss was intently watching this interview through the one-way mirror.

"Framed?" Anna asked in her most neutral tone. "By whom?"

Kiernan exhibited a faint suggestion of surprise, as if she was startled a detective could use the proper, but old-fashioned pronoun. The woman's sudden superciliousness, her obvious sense of privilege, put Anna off. She was glad to detach from any sympathy she might have for this potential murderer.

"I'm not sure . . . yet . . ." Kiernan mused. "But I have some ideas."

"*You* have prime suspects?" Rafe asked drily. When he was overly tired, her partner sometimes resorted to sarcasm, not his usual interview style. "Do tell."

"No need to be snarky, Detective." Kiernan then said quietly, "I'm here to help you find Leo's killer."

"Maybe we should deputize you," Rafe said. "It's what we do for all suspects who try to flee the country and have no alibis except 'home alone.'"

Kiernan folded her arms over her chest and sighed. "I've got nothing more to say until my attorney arrives."

It was the wrong strategy. Anna regretted her partner's remarks, but she forgave Rafe his fatigue. They'd all had a sleepless night, catching the early flight back from Friday Harbor to Seattle with Kiernan and her Scottie in tow. Now, the dog was with Kiernan's neighbors.

"Would you talk with us a little more while we wait for your lawyer?" Anna asked.

"Yes." Eleanor Kiernan nodded. "I told you I want to help you find Leo's killer."

Anna let the silence deepen, hoping it might evoke more from Kiernan—make her anxious enough to blurt out something they could use against her. But their suspect kept her own counsel, her hands folded tightly together on the interview table. They were working hands, not well-manicured as Anna might have expected: hands that were adept at tying complicated sailor's knots as she had made her escape; hands skilled in gutting fish, which is why, Kiernan said, there was blood on her stiletto. They were waiting for forensics to reveal if there was any human blood or DNA besides Kiernan's staining the knife handle. Rafe suspected it was not just fish guts. If the blood matched Cushman, they'd have their murder weapon.

Anna decided to try a different strategy to startle their suspect into talking. "Did Leonard Cushman give you the stiletto we found on you?" she asked.

Their suspect was taken aback. At last, she nodded, took a breath. "Yes, Leo gave it to me after all the death threats toward Fortura. I keep it in my desk at the lab. Everybody knows it's there. Sometimes I bring it home or pack it when I camp."

"You took it with you when you made a run for it," Rafe said. "Surprised you didn't ditch it after you murdered Cushman."

"No! I would never hurt—" Kiernan jerked back in her chair, wood scraping loudly on the concrete floor.

Anna winced at the sound—both the harsh screech of the chair legs and the hoarse, almost guttural, sorrow in Eleanor's voice. Anna was unwillingly drawn to this woman's grief over losing her twin. If Anna had ever found out who had killed her sister, wouldn't she want to take vengeance, as Kiernan might have, against the murderer? Anna straightened in her stiff chair, struggling to keep her detachment. Captain Dimitri was judging Anna's performance. She mustn't appear in any way sympathetic to the plight of this suspect.

Kiernan dropped her gaze. Before Rafe's accusation, she had made steady eye contact, especially with Anna. Her violet eyes were unsettling, but it was more difficult to read Kiernan now she fixed her eyes only on the interview table with its permanent rings of old coffee cups and scratches.

"I really hoped you might understand." Kiernan shook her head.

"We do understand," Anna said softly.

Anna recalled their quick search of Eleanor Kiernan's home office with its meticulously researched wall of articles on the opiate crisis. The yellow highlighted headlines had caught Anna's eye.

FORTURA DEVELOPS NEW PAINKILLER, LIKE FENTANYL, 1,000 TIMES MORE POWERFUL THAN MORPHINE

MORE AMERICANS DIED FROM OPIOID ADDICTION IN 2018 THAN IN THE ENTIRE VIETNAM WAR

115 PEOPLE DIE EVERY DAY FROM OPIOID OVERDOSE IN THE US

MORE THAN 900,000 PEOPLE HAVE DIED IN THE US OF OVERDOSES SINCE 1999

Kiernan had tacked on her bulletin board many more exposés of Big Pharma crimes. For years, Fortura, Purdue, and other opioid companies had lobbied Congress to change the label of their painkillers from short-term to long-term daily use. The misbranding created a marketing "tsunami" for opiates, enabled by FDA officials on the take, who later claimed they were tricked by the drug giants. Some of the same FDA officials who approved opiates for long-term pain management—with no scientific evidence that the powerful opiates were not addictive—went on to accept lucrative jobs at the same Big Pharma companies they had federally reviewed.

Rafe clicked on his iPad to pass it across the interview table to Eleanor Kiernan. It was her twin's obituary. *Franklin Kiernan. Dead at 39 . . . an opiate overdose.*

"Revenge for your brother's death," Anna suggested quietly, "it's a very strong motive for murder."

Kiernan gazed at the obituary; her head bowed. She was quiet for a long time and then in her melodic, choked voice, read the poem from her brother's obit.

"We must laugh, and we must sing.
We are blest by everything.
Everything we look upon is blest."

This grieving sister's fractured tones and the obvious devotion for a lost brother moved Anna. Despite herself, tears edged Anna's eyes. She herself found solace in Yeats's poetry. Often, when crafting her own song lyrics, Anna sought the calm of cadence and images to discipline her pain into words. This morning, she'd written in her journal the shards of her recurring nightmare about her sister's hit-and-run death.

"Car tracks tattoo her arms.
Brambles and thorns strangle dancer's legs.
Still on point."

Anna couldn't help keenly feeling Eleanor Kiernan's anguish. Loss and resolution were what usually drove Anna's investigations. This case was already shadowed and complicated because Anna didn't much like the victim. Cushman's drugs destroyed so many lives. In cold cases, Anna had never sympathized with the murderer. Now, Anna was uneasy to find herself wondering if she might regret delivering Eleanor Kiernan to a lifetime of prison. If Kiernan had killed Cushman, perhaps she was justified. Murder might be the only way to find justice for Big Pharma's greed.

Sensing Anna's distraction, Rafe took over the interview. "In the space of one month, you lost your brother and now

Leonard Cushman, the two most significant men in your life. Maybe grief drove you to do it. Maybe you're just in denial. Sometimes murderers tell stories of their innocence—with so many vivid details—that they believe their own lies."

Anna leaned in closer and encouraged in almost a whisper, "Yes, we saw your study with the wall of opioid articles. It was like your own murder board."

Eleanor hunched over the interview table as if Anna had dealt her a blow.

Anna pressed on. "I can understand your motive for killing your boss, trying to hold him accountable not only for your brother but also for all the others. And . . . perhaps some guilt on your part?"

"I've been trying to stop Leo for years!"

"Well, he's stopped now," Anna said simply.

Eleanor Kiernan sat back with a hopeless expression. She fell silent.

They had only a few more minutes before Kiernan's lawyer would arrive. Anna tried a different tactic. "You're actually *not* our only suspect," Anna explained almost amiably. "We're pursuing other lines of inquiry . . . and if you really are serious about helping us, I'd very much like to hear your ideas . . ."

"Finally." Kiernan sat forward and intently met Anna's eyes. Her voice was clipped and professional. "Ask yourself these questions. Who had the most to gain from Leo's death? If I'm out of the way, who will run Fortura? Who might want to keep me quiet by discrediting all I'm doing to end my company's part in the opioid crisis? Who knew I had a key to Leo's home and that I kept a stiletto in my lab desk so they could frame me?"

Instantly alert, Anna nudged Rafe under the interview table. *Kiernan had her own key to Cushman's home!*

Rafe's eyes widened with this new, incriminating evidence. Kiernan could enter the victim's house any time. That was opportunity.

Kiernan rushed on, as if believing she had seized the upper hand. "Leo left me controlling shares in Fortuna in his revised will. He promised me. But I can't run a company—or change it—from prison, can I?"

"*What* new will? Anna asked quietly.

Kiernan frowned. "Leo was very secretive. "I wanted to vet the new will for myself."

"So, you went to Leo Cushman's house the night of his murder?" Anna steadily asked. "To see his new will?"

This question startled Kiernan. She refocused her scrutiny of Anna with more regard and some alarm. "I never said I was there *that* night."

"You had a key to Cushman's house. You could have let yourself in. No one can substantiate your alibi." Anna leaned forward. "We have Mr. Cushman's phone records," she said softly. "He called you quite late the night he was murdered. Did you go there? Did you argue, as people say you and Mr. Cushman often did?"

Shaken, Kiernan folded her arms and sat back, gathering herself, as if realizing she'd foolishly given away too much and was carefully considering how much damage she'd done to herself.

Anna pursued her. "No signs of a break-in. Or robbery. Forensics will probably find your fingerprints all over the safe. Was Leonard Cushman lying about any new will putting you in charge of his company? You lost control and stabbed him, grabbing the one thing he *did* leave you?"

Kiernan shook her head back and forth so vehemently; it reminded Anna of the woman's Scottie dog seizing the sheriff's motorboat ropes when they arrested Kiernan.

Rafe pushed on. "It wasn't really premeditated, was it, Eleanor? Just necessary. Or will you try to tell us it was self-defense?"

Eleanor Kiernan's face drained of color. She was about to say something, perhaps even confess. Suddenly, an unctuous attorney entered the small interview room with the usual requests for a private conference with his client. With him was a tall, authoritative Black man with a bulging briefcase.

"FBI," the second man said and flashed his badge. "The Justice Department is overseeing this case as part of an ongoing investigation."

The agent was determined, as if this dramatic entrance was always his favorite part of the job—stealing suspects away for his more important investigation. There would be a territorial battle, Anna knew. Her boss didn't take well to being usurped by other agencies. At least she could count on Captain Dimitri's resistance. It might buy her a little more time with Eleanor Kiernan, even with her attorney present.

"My client has nothing more to say." Her lawyer sat down, possessively taking Eleanor by her arm. "If you're not going to charge her, Detective, you'll have to let her go."

Anna noted Eleanor Kiernan instinctively slipped out of her attorney's grip but nodded gratefully at the FBI agent. *Was Eleanor Kiernan a whistleblower turned vigilante?*

As they left, Eleanor faced Anna and took a quick breath.

"Do *you* believe me?" Kiernan asked, keeping her eyes riveted on Anna.

It unsettled Anna. This impressive woman was reaching out to the very person who could imprison her.

"Do you?" Eleanor asked again, her expression fierce and yet somehow vulnerable.

Anna heard the plaintive note in her voice. She struggled not to let Kiernan's pleas or her melancholy soften Anna's resolve to confirm her guilt. Anna gathered files together on her desk. At last, she focused on Kiernan.

"No . . ." she began. But seeing Kiernan's stricken face, Anna added, "Not yet. I'll believe you when you tell us the whole truth."

Captain Dimitri stepped into the interview room, slamming the door behind him. "We now have motive, opportunity, and means enough to charge your client," he declared to Eleanor Kiernan's lawyer. "Her stiletto is our murder weapon. Blood on the knife *is* fish guts, just like your client says." He glared at Eleanor, a scowl of satisfaction on his craggy face. "But there's a tiny speck of blood on the knife handle you didn't wipe clean . . . It's Leonard Cushman's."

VIII

ELEANOR

May 1, 2019

"Don't *ever* meet with the police again without me present," her lawyer, Bart Adams, sternly advised Eleanor as he sat with her alone in the dingy interview room. "Why didn't you wait for me to advise you?"

"I thought I could handle them," Eleanor confessed. She spoke in a whisper.

"They're not rats in your lab, Eleanor," Adams snapped.

"I'm afraid I said too much."

"I'm sure you did." The lawyer shook his head. "And what the hell is the FBI doing mixed up in your case?"

Eleanor was mute. She had sworn under oath not to tell anyone about her whistleblower status with the Justice Department's investigation of Fortura. As Adams laid out the rules for any future interviews with the police, Eleanor realized she must trust no one, not even Leo's lawyer. She'd called Bart Adams in desperation because her own lawyer was not a criminal defense lawyer and was out of town anyway. But she knew this man represented the company and Cushman's family.

"Isn't representing me a conflict of interest?" she asked.

"I'm a corporate lawyer, not a criminal defense attorney," Adams said. "But you're in a bind, and I'll help as much as I can. Now, tell me everything you told the cops."

Eleanor only confided in Bart Adams what she had unwisely admitted to the detectives—she possessed a key to Cushman's home. She did not mention she believed she was the major beneficiary in Leo's missing, revised will. *Does Adams even knew about it?*

As the lawyer droned on, Eleanor was distracted. She wondered why she had a strange kinship with the female detective. It wasn't just because she was also a woman in a traditionally male role. Anna Crane had most probably experienced the same sexism plaguing Eleanor as she rose through the ranks of Big Pharma to become Leo Cushman's most valued scientist. But there was something else about this detective undermining Eleanor's defenses. She had an unexpectedly keen intelligence and yet a hidden sympathy. Eleanor could sense it in the other woman's expressive eyes. Detective Crane was perhaps misplaced as a detective; Eleanor would have taken her for a therapist or teacher. But perhaps this sincerity was just a strategy belying the detective's offense. Eleanor resolved to do some research on Crane, as she always had anyone who threatened her brother's and her own survival.

"Remember as a suspect you are out of your element here," Adams advised. "Homicide detectives will take advantage of every slip of your tongue. They are not interested in the truth, only a quick conviction."

A part of her, the straight-A student, was paying close attention, even taking notes with the Mont Blanc fountain pen she'd bought for herself when Leo promoted her to lead research scientist. But her deepest thoughts were focused on the terrible moment when she'd discovered Leo's body. His nakedness, the way he clutched his ever-present cell phone, his familiar green eyes, fixed, all the light gone.

Perhaps Leo had some premonition Eleanor was also in danger. That was why he'd called her to come over so late, even by Leo's insomniac standards.

"Can't it wait?" Eleanor had mumbled drowsily, glancing at the clock. Almost midnight. She had just settled in for the night with a new Tana French mystery.

"No," Leo said firmly. "There are some things you need to do."

"Do what?" Eleanor asked.

It would just be like Leo—ever the calculating deal-maker—to offer Eleanor more control in his company in return for some acquiescence to compromise her ethics. He'd bribed lobbyists and congressional reps to overlook the growing opioid problem and influence the FDA. She'd have nothing to do with any more of his deals, even if it gave her more power at Fortura. Maybe he would ask her to resign in return for some share of his company shares.

"Eleanor," Leo had continued in a suddenly weary voice, "I'm so tired of fighting with you. Can't we finally reach some compromise?"

The irritating word "compromise" always triggered her. From the root word, *compromissus*, it meant to make a mutual promise—to agree again to do something together, instead of this endless struggle to persuade each other.

Raising herself up on her elbow in bed, Eleanor had sighed. But she couldn't stop herself from one more attempt to reach him. "Leo," she began, "In your heart, you're the scientist who longs to heal people. You truly want to help those in pain."

"Like your brother," Leo said quietly.

Eleanor hesitated and conceded. "Like Frankie." She knew she'd been hard on Leo at her brother's recent funeral. She both longed for and dreaded the day when her whistleblowing was revealed to Leo. She wouldn't mind losing Fortura; but it would be hard to leave Leo.

"That's why I'm changing my will," Leo said. "To leave Fortura in your capable hands. I don't want to lose you. *You're* my legacy, Ellie. My real heir. The better part of me. I've already left enough money to my family . . . and I've told a few others who really deserve it. I've provided for them, too, in my new will."

"Is this for real?"

"Believe me," Leo said. "I want to settle some of these lawsuits and establish a fund in your brother's name to help other addicts. But I need to make sure you'll have the power to do this." His voice was strained. "There are many in the company who would fight you or even fire you. Or worse. They want to keep stonewalling. There are even people in my family who might wish you ill—when they don't inherit my controlling shares."

As Leo anxiously rushed on to confide disturbing details of his new will, Eleanor allowed herself to feel a tentative triumph. Maybe she'd convinced Leo to hold the company somewhat accountable. But she wasn't sure if the new will was simply a ruse to keep her from leaving him.

She sat up in bed and slipped into her sandals, hoodie, and jeans. "Okay, Leo, I'll be right there," she said. "I can let myself in."

When she had entered the back door, Eleanor was careful not to wake up any of his live-in staff. She tiptoed up the grand staircase and into his office. There was the man she'd thought was invincible, fallen, face-up on the floor, his throat gashed, blood bright, not yet congealed. Horrified, she listened for Leo's pulse, but his wrist was cold, rigid, his vacant eyes staring up at her. Eleanor gasped, her heart thudding. She was dizzy, faint.

Kneeling beside Leo, her heart throbbing furiously, Eleanor did not scream or weep. Instead, she gave this man, who had inspired both her love and despair, a long, last look.

"Who would do this to you, Leo?" she asked, as if he could answer. Leo always had all the answers.

Tenderly, she touched his forehead feeling the delicate chill on her fingertips. She would always remember the dark quiet in the room and how empty her whole life suddenly was without him.

"I'm so sorry, dear Leo." She took a deep breath. "I'll . . . I'll find out who did this."

She stood, unsteady on her feet, and shivered. *Was she also a target? Death threats? Was the murderer still in Leo's house?* A bolt of fear surged up her backbone as Eleanor listened intently for any sound of footsteps or movement. None.

Glancing around the room, Eleanor noted Leo's safe was open, papers obviously rifled through and falling out onto the floor. In one quick stride, Eleanor crossed the large room. She searched for the new will Leo had called her about. Her heart fluttered. No will.

There was, however, what she had so long suspected but never found: Leo's secret red file folder, but it was empty. It had included names and contact information for FDA insiders on the take, lobbyists, and congressional representatives, along with financial records of generous contributions to their campaigns. Eleanor had already given a stolen copy of this file to the Justice Department. She wondered who had taken it and why. Was it someone inside Fortura or an opiate activist who'd finally hit the motherlode of Cushman's crime? There was no sign of the original documents of her own research detailing the addictive effects of Neocodone. Leo had probably long ago destroyed them.

Eleanor stashed the empty red folder in her backpack and glanced down at the nearby bedside table with its spilled wine glass and a note in Leo's quick, almost inscrutable cursive. "Please believe me . . ." it began before the ink blotched. It poignantly echoed what Leo had asked of her on the phone. *Was his last note meant for me?*

Trembling, Eleanor reached into her pocket for her cell phone to call 911. But suddenly, she stopped. On the floor beneath the safe was a stiletto. *Her* stiletto. She recognized it from the tiny nick on its blade she'd made on a camping trip. It was streaked and smeared with Leo's blood.

Where's the sheath? Who stole the stiletto from my desk?

Eleanor's chest constricted, her body trembling. She must flee. *Now!*

She grabbed the stiletto, sticky in her hand. Stowing the slim knife in her backpack, Eleanor ran stealthily down the back stairs to make her escape. She needed time to think. Most of all, she needed a sensible plan.

IN THE DIM, WAVERING LIGHT OF THE interview room, her lawyer said, "We need a strategy for your defense if they decide to charge you. You say you discovered Mr. Cushman's body? Walk me through exactly what happened that night."

"Yes . . . yes, of course." Eleanor shook away the horrible memories. She tried to settle her emotions and her thoughts so she could decide how much to confide in Leo's lawyer before getting her own criminal defense lawyer. To determine if she should trust Bart Adams with the truth before she got her own counsel, she tested his loyalties. "Mr. Adams, are you the lawyer who recently drew up Leo's *new* will?"

The attorney gave her a startled, quizzical look, as if he were rarely caught unprepared. "What new will? Leo would have told me if there were changes to his estate. You'll hear all those details when we officially read the will next week. For now, let's focus on just you."

She felt a flush of alarm, her throat tightening. *Did Leo lie about a new will? Did his murderer steal it from the safe along with the incriminating info in the red folder?*

The attorney took Eleanor's arm. "It's obvious you're not telling me everything, Eleanor. Fine with me if you prefer your own lawyer. Let's get through arraignment and make bail."

She wouldn't solve Leo's murder or find out who framed her if she were in prison. "Yes, bail," she nodded. "Then, I have to get home to do some research."

Bart Adams smiled. "Of course, you do." He nodded in his irritatingly paternal way.

"You haven't even asked me if I'm guilty." Eleanor frowned.

"Defense attorneys don't make a habit of asking," Bart Adams replied drily. When he saw her surprise, he quickly added, "We always assume clients are *not* guilty." He avoided her scrutiny. "That's how we'll plead."

At the arraignment, Eleanor's mother was the only one who had believed in her innocence. She proved it by sending a bank wire to post bail from the family trust fund when Eleanor called her. Eleanor had always been too proud and independent to accept any money from her mother's wealthy Boston family, especially since she could have covered the cost herself. But without her brother, she had no one else to confide in about her arrest. Her mother had texted Eleanor.

> Bail in a murder case is exorbitant, dear.
> You've already proven yourself a flight risk.

Eleanor's first move after making bail—besides finding herself a new criminal defense lawyer—was to rush home and restore her kitchen to the spotless splendor of her work lab. Cleaning was a way of preoccupying her body when her mind was focused on solving a problem. Her twin had not inherited Eleanor's orderly Virgo habits. When Frankie was overwhelmed with his troubled thoughts, he'd turn to drugs.

Eleanor deep cleaned her granite kitchen sink with baking soda and vinegar, restoring its gleaming black composite with vegetable oil. As she used a rag to buff her sink into a submissive shine, Eleanor tried to remember all the times she'd confided in her brother about crimes she believed Leo and his company was committing. She berated herself for being indiscreet in telling Frankie about Fortura's opioid cover-up. Of course, Frankie wouldn't keep her confidence. He never really had.

"Was it one of your friends from rehab, Frankie?" Eleanor mentally addressed her brother as she emptied sour kombucha bottles, placing them in her tidy recycling bin designated for tin cans and glass.

"Did you finally go postal on Cushman?" She imagined Frankie's grin. *"Well, some other people I know might also want him gone."*

Perhaps the person who murdered Leo was one of Frankie's unsavory pals or dealers. Maybe Frankie had even told one of his rehab friends about the stiletto hidden in her lab drawer. There was the weird girlfriend. Frankie seduced one in every rehab stint. Possessive. Furious.

"Don't worry, sis, anything we say in rehab is confidential," Frankie had always assured her.

But she didn't trust him. Weeks before his death, Frankie had surprised his sister by inviting her to visit his rehab center to meet a few of his new friends. For her first and only visit with Frankie's rehab pals, Eleanor didn't bring food; she knew most of the addicts had little hunger for home-baked sweets, no matter how tempting. Their hunger was bone-deep, unsated. Instead, she brought flowers from her garden, including the late-blooming white winter roses Frankie loved.

Even though the rehab walls were adorned with gorgeous original paintings by local artists—misty seascapes, old forests, swaying wheat fields, and a radiant Van Gogh-esque night sky—the in-patients walked by them, immune to their vivid colors. Eleanor had seen more life on cancer wards when visiting friends in the hospital. In rehab, people passed her by, deeply preoccupied, their faces flat and fixed on some inner demon. Without their beloved drugs, life was dulled and diluted.

In the Schick Shadel visitors' room, Eleanor had taken her seat next to Frankie, determined to say nothing and just listen. Frankie was surrounded by his usual rehab groupies—a bedraggled dirty blonde with fingernails bitten down to the nubs and a nervous adolescent boy who obviously believed her brother was a role model.

As they chatted about the unusual heat wave, their call-and-response was like a melancholy Greek chorus. In a synchronized choreography, all of them lit up cigarettes. The boy nodded, his face shrouded in smoke; the woman sipped coffee, her blood-shot gray eyes riveted on Frankie. She leaned forward hungrily at his every word. She even cast a suspicious glance at Eleanor, as if jealous of their life-long twin bond. Eleanor assumed this ravaged woman and her brother were already breaking rehab rules forbidding romantic relationships.

As if sensing the woman's jealousy, Frankie soothed her with a radiant smile. "Toni," he said soothingly. They held eyes intimately as if they were the only two in the visitors' room. "Don't worry. She won't come between us. Ellie never does."

Frankie's friends laughed, and Toni Fleishman sat back, lighting another cigarette. Eleanor couldn't prevent a little gasp escaping her. It was the terrible truth—her twin never let Eleanor interfere with his romances, where Eleanor had always put Frankie first before her boyfriends. None of them preoccupied her as much as her brother.

Toni had kept her eyes focused on Frankie. She tracked his every move like a heat-seeking missile. Eleanor admitted a pang of pity for the disheveled young addict. Her platinum hair hung in dirty pigtails, her too-bright lipstick was smeared from cigarettes, and her hands were jittery. Eleanor assumed her twin would abandon Toni as soon as his time was served.

Perhaps Toni suspected he'd give her up before he would ever let go of opiates. It might explain why Toni was so proprietary.

Eleanor had to admit she understood Toni's desperation. She'd known it all the way through university and on holidays when Frankie skipped any semblance of family gatherings to devote himself to some new fling or addiction. The irony was whether it was his twin, his friends, or his lover, Frankie had found his one, true passion in drugs. Opiates were a cruel mistress—an unrequited love.

Toni glared at Eleanor. "You've made a fortune off of people like us . . . you and your damn drug company."

"Uh, Toni," Frankie said, "Eleanor is not here to argue. She's here for me."

Toni pushed on, her face seized with a fury, which made her once lovely face blotched and ugly. She pointed an accusing finger at Eleanor. "You have no idea what it's like to ache for something so much your body breaks down without it." Toni shifted away from Frankie's outstretched arm. "Fevers, the shakes, rotten teeth. I used to be beautiful . . . a model. Now, look at me!"

Eleanor stared at her hands, wishing Frankie would reach out to her instead of this pathetic addict.

"I said, *look* at me!"

Reluctantly, Eleanor met Toni's defiant gaze. Without a word, she took in the young woman's split lip, the meth-yellowed teeth, and naked, thin forearms scarred by infected track marks and tattoos. It was difficult to believe Toni had ever sashayed down a runway with the arrogant nonchalance of a top model.

Frankie pulled Toni closer to him. There was nothing left to embrace but her bones. "You still are . . . beautiful."

Next to this broken addict, Frankie appeared vibrant, his cropped red hair curled tightly like Eleanor's, his eyes keen, if not so clear.

Eleanor excused herself, claiming she was late for a meeting. Frankie shrugged and flashed her his dazzling, crooked smile. She couldn't bear seeing one of his front teeth broken. This was only Frankie's third rehab. Given time and his addiction, Frankie might end up as broken as the woman he was trying to comfort. Eleanor shuddered to imagine her twin as the ghost he would likely become.

IX

ANNA

May 3, 2019

At their messy murder board, Anna and Rafe sipped morning tea and coffee in rare disagreement. She'd treated him to Starbuck's mocha latte, but he preferred pricey Elm Coffee Roasters. Too much caffeine gave Anna jitters. Earl Grey clouded with half-and-half was her favorite. No sugar.

"Quite a cast of characters," Rafe muttered, studying all the photos of possible suspects amidst the clutter of crime scene photos.

Her partner's moodiness increased with each new murder suspect Anna added. Captain Dimitri had given them only a few more days to come up with a credible alternative to Eleanor Kiernan, whom Dimitri had already advised they charge with the murder of Leonard Cushman. Kiernan had easily made bail and her trial date was set. Rafe insisted they focus on gathering their evidence for her trial.

Anna studied the board, calling out each name in a meditative chant.

"Jasmine Wolf, Jackson Poole, Eleanor Kiernan, Cushman's ex-wife, Eloise, his stepson, Hugh . . . and maybe some antidrug activists."

"Look, Anna," Rafe insisted. "Captain Dimitri's right. Kiernan fled, she had motive: revenge for Cushman's part in the opioid crisis and grief over her brother's death. She had means. Her stiletto *is* the murder weapon. Finally, she had opportunity. By her own admission, she had a key to the victim's home. Her fingerprints are all over the safe, and Cushman's blood is on her stiletto." Rafe sat back at his desk, "Case closed."

"I know, Rafe, I know."

Rafe pressed his point. "You also know the stats. If we can't figure out the perp within the first forty-eight hours, our case—like most other murders—will end up filed under 'Unsolved.' Do we want our first live case to go cold?"

Rafe was probably correct about Eleanor Kiernan's guilt, but Anna wanted her intuition to jibe with their overwhelming evidence. It didn't—not quite yet. She was missing something. The familiar foreboding—a sense of physical dread, like an unsettled stomach, a pitch off-key, slight lightheadedness—made her hesitate and hold back. She knew something was terribly wrong about this case. Anna had to wonder if her uneasiness was just because she also understood the anguish of losing a sibling. *Is empathy blinding me to Kiernan's guilt?*

On the cork board, Anna pinned up two more photos with red thumbtacks.

Rafe groaned when Anna scrawled their names on Post-it notes. "Yamasaki?" Rafe asked. "Fleishman?"

"Didn't you see the file Sheriff Conway sent down from Friday Harbor on the Obliterate Opioids activists who spray-painted Leo Cushman's plane? Roger Yamasaki and a junkie, Toni Fleishman." Anna put up the crime scene photo of the luxurious Phenom 100 light jet scrawled in black-and-red slashes with the accusation, "*Drug Lord! Kid Killer!*"

"Oh, yeah." Rafe nodded with a sigh. "Those two seem more like bad graffiti artists than killers. Alibis?"

Anna didn't tell her partner that Yamasaki's alibi was as

blurry as his driver's license photo. Or that Toni Fleishman claimed to have been in rehab the night of Cushman's murder. They'd have to confirm. Anna was determined also to keep her focus on the people they had yet to interview.

"Forensics is doing more testing. We must do a follow-up interview of Cushman's ex-wife and son," Anna argued. "I'm just not convinced by their mutual alibis."

"Jackson Poole's alibi was confirmed by the janitor," Rafe snapped, then reminded her, "Kiernan's the only one *without* an alibi."

When Anna said nothing, only stared at the murder board, Rafe sighed. "Really, Anna, what more do we need? Why keep on interviewing other possible suspects?"

"I wish you would've backed me up more with the captain," Anna said. "Especially about the stiletto sheath left at the murder scene, like it was conveniently placed there for us to discover. Maybe Kiernan really is being framed. There's a lot about this case that's just not making sense to me."

Rafe threw up his hands. "You've got better evidence from the great beyond?"

"I've been right before," Anna said, stung by his disbelief.

"You've also been dead wrong," Rafe concluded.

Rafe's increasing doubt in her was a mirror—and a mutiny. It haunted Anna when her intuitions were sometimes off, especially when they mattered the most. Anna cursed herself now for ever having confided in Rafe about her unpredictable sixth sense or having told her partner too much about her sister's unsolved murder. Her intuitive flashes often were a flaw, not a skill. She should have just pretended to play by all the well-worn rules, the factual chain of evidence and nothing else—nothing so unreliable as her own psyche's perceptions.

Anna had never told Rafe about the time her premonition was dead on. It was a winter night in 2015, when Seattle was overwhelmed with a rare blizzard. Few people in the city, except transplants, knew how to drive well in snow, so traffic was a nightmare with multiple accidents clogging every highway. In stop-dead traffic, Anna sat stalled on I-5, watching emergency vehicles struggle to get past cars idling because of a fatal accident. Anna had heard about the fatality on her radio, always tuned to the frequency of police chatter. She was about to listen to her audiobook when suddenly she was seized with the sensation of pure alarm. Dark foreboding shadowed her.

Panic crept up her spine like a jittery shiver. *Someone is in danger! Who?*

Anxiously scanning her mind for the faces of those she loved Anna's attention at last settled on her sister, Lizzie. But why? Her little sister had just joyously moved from the Keys to an Atlanta up-and-coming ballet company.

Trapped in freeway traffic and swirling snow, Anna immediately speed-dialed her sister's cell. No answer. Anna dialed the ballet company office. Her sister hadn't shown up for rehearsal for two days, which truly alarmed Anna. Her sister never missed rehearsals, especially when she was the new principal soloist.

It was then Anna realized she didn't have phone numbers for any of her sister's friends in Atlanta. Anna called Lizzie's best friend in Key West. No answer.

Fear tightened her chest so terribly, Anna could hardly breathe. She must reach Lizzie before . . . *Before what?*

Traffic was at a standstill, so Anna closed her eyes to intently concentrate. Lizzie wasn't answering her cell or her texts. Slowly, a number appeared to float in Anna's mind. *Why not dial it? If it is a wrong number, nothing is lost.*

Anna was profoundly relieved when a woman answered. The voice was so choked, Anna almost didn't recognize it was her sister's.

"Lizzie," she asked. "You, okay?"

"Anna? How did you . . ." Lizzie began, then sighed. "Of course, *you*'d know."

"All I knew was I had to call you. Whose number is this? Where are you now?"

Sobbing, Lizzie managed to explain she was in a neighbor's apartment. She'd ravaged the man's medicine cabinet and was just about to take an overdose of strong painkillers she'd discovered. "I told God, if you aren't ready for me, make somebody stop me." Lizzie's voice was strangled. "*You* heard me, Anna."

Anna wanted to scream at her sister. *One of these days, I won't be able to stop you!* But instead, Anna kept her voice steady, low, and calm. "I'm catching the next flight out to be with you. Lizzie, what's going on?"

"I lost the role," Lizzie whispered. "After my move, after all my work!" Lizzie choked back sobs. "The director insists on a Balanchine body, and I've gained five pounds! I tried Gyrotonic training for strength. My hamstrings are practically bulging. I'm a horror in a tutu. I hate myself."

"Is your neighbor there with you? Let me talk to him."

Silence. Then Lizzie confessed quietly. "I broke in here . . . my neighbor has lots of painkillers . . . and I . . ."

"Broke in, Lizzie? It's illegal."

"Says the cop." Lizzie huffed.

Anna could feel her sister was about to hang up. Anna didn't question why the neighbor's phone number had appeared in her mind just when Lizzie was about to commit suicide. What she always did question was how to take care of such a fragile little sister. Lizzie had always been unstable. In high school, Lizzie had attempted suicide by crashing her car after a boyfriend betrayed her. Ballet was what had always saved Lizzie. The discipline, the rigorous routine, had grounded Lizzie. Now, dance had also betrayed her.

"Is there anyone who can stay with you now?" Anna asked. "Until I get there?"

Silence. Then a sigh, "My neighbor . . . home soon. Obviously, you have his number."

"I'll take the red-eye and be right there in the morning. Please, *please*, Lizzie, promise me you won't do anything to harm yourself." Anna surprised herself, by almost adding, *Or anyone else.* Why had she even thought of blurting it out? Lizzie had never been violent. All her harm was against herself.

"I . . . I promise."

Anna waited, listening with all her senses attuned to what Lizzie was not saying. All Anna heard was the screeching pitch of despair, like keening so high, it hurt Anna's ears.

"Call me every hour until your neighbor comes home, okay?"

"Okay." Lizzie exhaled and her sobbing eased, but then she succumbed to hiccups. "You saved me, Anna."

"I'll always try . . . try to save you, Lizzie," Anna promised, feeling inept and helpless, overwhelmed with the burden, which had always been her beloved little sister.

She hadn't been able to keep her promise. Only a few months later, her little sister was killed. No sixth sense or nightmare had warned Anna the night a hit-and-run driver stole Lizzie's life. Nothing. When it really mattered—*nothing.*

Just like she had nothing now to make Rafe believe in her premonitions and concerns about their case. Her partner waited impatiently for Anna to answer his doubts. He drummed his fingers on her desk, the dark pinewood scarred with scratches and nicks from all the competent detectives before her time. Anna glanced up at the disapproving clock. Its face was cracked, and it hung cockeyed.

"You're right, Rafe," Anna admitted darkly. "Sometimes, I *am* terribly wrong."

X

ELEANOR

May 4, 2019

As she waited for her FBI handler, Thomas Filson, to arrive, Eleanor paced anxiously before her office's own makeshift murder board, studying the suspects she believed might have killed Leo Cushman. They were a diverse lot: Jasmine Wolf, Cushman's devoted but often denied lover; Jackson Poole, Leo's envious executive assistant; Toni Fleishman, her brother's vindictive lover from rehab who had been jilted by Frankie's death; Leo's ex-wife, Eloise, and stepson, Hugh. Then there were the death threat notices against Fortura.

Eleanor's board was a single, elegant pane of glass balanced on her cherrywood desk. She didn't post photos on the glass, only yellow and green sticky notes, each scrawled with a name and Eleanor's data. Green was for "Probable Suspect" and yellow was a "Possible Suspect." Eleanor had given up using her fountain pen because the black ink smeared so easily when she tried to add information on the sticky notes. Instead, she had to settle for a bold, red Faber-Castell artist pen.

Though she was serious about conducting her own private investigation of Cushman's murder, Eleanor realized her research was amateurish and scanty, compared with what the detectives could access. She also realized there was enough evidence already against her to convict. Eleanor didn't have much more time to figure things out. Reluctantly, she added a green sticky note to the glass board. On it was penned her own name in the perfect penmanship the nun sisters at St. Pious school had praised.

"Good penmanship is a product of a disciplined mind," Sister Ruth Ignatius had sternly taught.

Eleanor wondered what Sister Ruth, the only nun she had ever admired—who had taught her biology and earth science with the brilliance of a true believer—would think of her as a murder suspect. If all Catholics had been as inspiring and rigorous in their study as Sister Ruth, Eleanor might have stayed in the church of her Irish ancestors. But Eleanor discovered early on the blinders of dogma and its dismissal of science as if it were simply a rival belief system.

Yet, Eleanor had to admit, the facts in Leo's murder cast suspicion squarely on her. She'd need professional help if she were to escape a prison sentence. That's why she'd asked her old college friend and now FBI contact, Thomas Filson, to dinner. Remembering his penchant for fine foreign foods, she'd bribed him with a promise of homemade prawn pad thai and red curry. For dessert, there would be mango with sticky, black rice. Years ago, when they'd dated at university for a few months, Thomas had treated her to every four-star restaurant in Boston. Later, she'd learned he wasn't a trust-fund baby, like many other Harvard students, but on scholarship. After their break-up, a mutual friend told Eleanor that Thomas had gone into credit card debt to date her.

Eleanor couldn't remember why she'd broken up with Thomas years ago, but she was sure he recalled it clearly and carried a grudge. Perhaps that's why he was wary about getting together with her again, off-duty.

Of course, Thomas was on time. He'd always been on time,

even early for their college dates. But now, instead of a nervous, lanky, young man with dreadlocks and an air of radical wit, he stood as a solid and impeccably dressed early-forties government agent whose self-confidence was not as endearing as had been his youthful rebellion.

"Thank you so much for coming, Thomas." Eleanor said. "I didn't know for sure if you'd really accept my offer."

"If I'd known you were such an accomplished chef, Ellie, I'd never have taken you to all those expensive restaurants." Thomas Filson bent down to pat her Scottie and scratch his shaggy neck. Brodie growled, but then happily padded after the man. "Ferocious guard dog you got here." Thomas laughed. Even off-duty he wore his Oxford cloth shirt, a stylish, blue-striped tie, and a sports coat.

Eleanor considered taking him directly to her office to show him what little progress she'd made on her own investigation. But she knew he would be more likely to really help her after enjoying her cooking.

"Whiskey?" She offered a cocktail as he took his seat in the rocking chair across from her on the sofa.

"No, better not," Thomas said with obvious regret. "I've got to keep my wits about me with you . . ." He hesitated an instant. "No whiskey. How about wine?"

Eleanor again glimpsed the young Black man from years ago at an elite East Coast college, trying to fathom white folks and their inbred, exclusive ways. She tried to remember what his Harvard scholarship was for—psychology, criminology. She dared not ask him what future FBI agents studied. Her ignorance would tell Thomas just how little she remembered about their brief but passionate romance. What she remembered most was his deft touch, those surprisingly supple fingers patiently investigating her body, not the usual hurried blur and push of most young men. Thomas was a gifted lover, but outside of the bed, he'd never been a good listener.

Like now. He was rattling on about his success at the FBI; he hadn't asked her a single question about her own investigation or her life since they'd been together in university. She could understand why he was not yet married. Women were not always looking to be in the supporting role for a self-proclaimed hero, not unless they were desperate for a boyfriend or broke. Eleanor was neither.

Her brother had been a devoted listener. It's why every phone call when they were living at home and dating usually was for Frankie. Perhaps having a twin sister to practice an intimate and conspiratorial confidence had trained him well for relationships. Or perhaps his characteristic curiosity and easy-going nature made Frankie a perfect partner. He was truly fascinated by people—from the homeless man chanting nonsense on the corner to the smarmy politician soliciting his vote at a fundraiser.

Eleanor reserved her attention for people who had something important to teach her, like Sister Ruth or her favorite bio-chemistry professor or Leo. Most people she found boring, even immature, their lives consumed with chit-chat and mundanities, their self-interest condemning them to small-minded goals. Eleanor wanted to cure and save people, if only from themselves.

"I'm always surprised at how brazenly people lie in any investigation." Thomas shook his head, as he reached for the Bordeaux on the coffee table to pour a second glass for them.

"No, not for me." She covered her crystal wine glass. *Is he trying to get me drunk?*

Eleanor wondered if Thomas assumed her invitation meant there was any possibility of ending up in bed again together after all these years. Had he bothered to diligently research her as she had him? She hoped he'd found the information she'd requested about Toni Fleishman's possible criminal history.

"Hungry?" Eleanor asked and invited him into her dining room.

He was droning on as she served up their dinner. Eleanor forced herself to be as patient with his endless soliloquy as he'd once been with her young and inexperienced body. She focused on his strong but sensitive hands, the expert way he wielded the porcelain chopsticks, plucking her pad thai noodles even in single strands. She wondered where he had learned such a nimble touch. Certainly not in his crime work. But then again, maybe his investigations were exactly where he'd picked up such careful dexterity. Eleanor imagined what Thomas would have done had he been the one to discover Leo's dead body. A crime scene demanded scrupulous attention to detail, picking up the tiniest piece of wine glass or a single hair, securing it as a vital clue, without contamination.

Eleanor had done nothing right at the crime scene. She had clumsily rushed around the office, dashing from the open safe while clutching her own stiletto someone had deliberately placed so the police would surely discover it and accuse her. She hadn't even wondered who had been in Leo's bedroom drinking the fermented brew Leo truly despised.

They were almost ready for dessert before Thomas finally turned his attention to her request for information on Fleishman.

"Got more on the woman you asked me to check out from your brother's rehab. Burned-out top model, addict, activist. She got arrested with some guy named Roger Yamasaki."

Suddenly alert, Eleanor asked, "Arrested? What for?"

"Spray painting a private plane up in Friday Harbor." Thomas delicately gave her a rather triumphant smile. "It was Leo Cushman's plane."

A chilling wave of alarm and energy washed over her. Leo had never told her about the incident. "You think Toni and Yamasaki could have gone from protest to murder?"

Thomas was sober, his tone serious, almost paternal. "You're smart enough to realize, Eleanor, that *you* may also be a target of whoever killed Cushman, right? If, as you say, you're being framed for his murder, the real killer might want you out of the way, too, or plan to get rid of you so the case will remain unsolved. Closed prematurely, with you taking the blame—posthumously."

"All the more reason for you to help me find Toni Fleishman," Eleanor said. "I do think Toni might mean me harm. She was so menacing when I met her in Frankie's rehab. And Toni was there at Frankie's funeral. Do you think Frankie ever told her where I live?"

"I can try to track her down . . . *unofficially*," Thomas said. "But the agency can't work with you anymore on the Fortura investigation, or at least not until you're cleared of all charges."

"Are you saying I'm no use to you now as a whistleblower?"

Thomas smiled regretfully. "You must be very careful about what you do, Ellie. You're out on bail, which can be revoked. From the agency's point of view, you don't make such a credible witness anymore against Fortura—not with a murder charge hanging over your head." Thomas shrugged. "We can't really take over the investigation because pushy Captain Dimitri has pulled rank on us. But he's right. It is their murder case."

"It's *my* life!" Eleanor tried to keep her voice from rising.

"You're their prime suspect," Thomas said. "They think this case is locked up."

On an instinct, Eleanor asked, "Can you do me one more favor? Look up more details on an Elizabeth Crane hit-and-run case in Atlanta, Georgia, in 2015. She's Detective Crane's little sister. I found her obit, but not much more. Is the case unsolved?"

Thomas sat back in his chair, frowning. "Anything else can I do for you? I guess I'm your personal PI now."

"I really do need your help," Eleanor implored him.

"And I need you to tell me the truth." He fixed her with

his dark, penetrating eyes. "Why am I here? We could have done all this information exchange by phone."

Taken aback, Eleanor realized he was right. *Why did I ask him in person?* It was only then Eleanor remembered why she had broken off their affair. He'd come too close to her. Though Thomas never seemed to listen, he somehow, from the beginning, had seen her willful solitude and her loneliness, how abandoned Eleanor was in university and living for the first time far away from her twin.

When Frankie had come to Boston to visit his sister, he'd barely had time for her, preferring to hook up with her roommate who offered him pure psilocybin, an illegal hallucinogenic drug for visionaries. In university, Thomas had easily detected Frankie was sublimely high. It didn't take a major in criminal justice to figure out her twin's rapturous details of a parallel universe with ten-part, ultrasonic harmonies were the product of those magical mushrooms.

"I have to change my life," Frankie had giddily announced to Eleanor and Thomas in her dorm room. "Drop out of college. Many other worlds need me."

"No arguing with an addict." Thomas had dismissed Frankie's fungi flights.

"He's not an addict!" Eleanor had protested. "He's just *exploring*. Psilocybin is not heroin. It's not addictive. Some cutting-edge scientists are even using it to treat anxiety and for end-of-life assistance. My brother has always been a seeker, open to spiritual—"

"He's a druggie," Thomas had declared. "He needs your help, not your consent. I won't report your brother, not if you get him some drug counseling."

She didn't know what would have happened if she had taken Thomas's advice in those early days of Frankie's addictions. Instead, she'd abruptly broken up with Thomas—now she remembered it clearly—by email.

Ashamed, Eleanor gazed at this man whose advice she had summarily ignored years ago. She realized just how much she now needed his alliance and clear vision. Like Frankie, Leo had for too many years blinded Eleanor to painful realities about those she loved.

"I don't know who else to turn to, Thomas," Eleanor honestly admitted. "I . . . I'm lost without Frankie." She leaned forward, her elbows on the dinner table—a gesture her Brahmin mother couldn't break in her.

Thomas nodded. "Ah, there's the Eleanor Kiernan I knew"—his expression shifted from skeptical to fond—"and once loved."

Startled, Eleanor also leaned back. "Loved?" she asked softly. "Oh, Thomas, I was terrible to you in college. You saw the truth about Frankie. I should've listened to you."

Instead of gloating, as he had every right to do, Thomas reached out and took her hand. His touch was unnervingly familiar, calm. Again, he showed the same physical patience as he waited for what Eleanor could not yet give him, or anybody else—her trust.

Sensing her retreat, Thomas sighed, allowing her the distance she had always required. "Well, listen now, Ellie," he said. "Toni Fleishman may be a danger to you." He consulted a small notepad from his pocket. "Apparently, she veers between addiction and activism. Rehab and jail. Now she's involved in the Obliterate Opioids movement. You know, those staged die-ins at all the museums and hospital wings to whom Fortura donates blood money." Thomas frowned. "She's angry and unpredictable. Fleishman and Yamasaki sent death threats to specific Fortura employees . . . including *you*."

Thomas sat back, studying her reaction. He had obviously retreated into his FBI agent personae, a professional and detached advisor, perhaps a protector. Or maybe he believed his job was done. He'd given her all she'd wanted—and it wasn't him.

This time it was Eleanor who took Thomas's hand. It was warm and as familiar."Thank you," she said warmly. "This may help keep me out of prison."

"And, I hope, keep you alive." Thomas stood up and glanced at his watch. It wasn't expensive like Leo's. It was a working man's watch with wheels within wheels of time and dates and a silver chip to mark north, south, east, and west, perhaps like his own firm moral compass. "Thanks for the fine dining," he smiled faintly.

There was resignation in his lips, those full—and now she realized it—lovely lips she had once so enjoyed and yet abandoned for Frankie. *Everything was always for Frankie.* Eleanor would have given up her own life for her brother. Maybe that was how the hapless, hopeless crusader, Toni Fleishman, felt. She'd sacrifice Leo Cushman's life, and her own, for Frankie, whose first and truest love was not a person but a painkiller.

As she said goodbye to Thomas at her turquoise door, he paused. "Oh, and the other thing you asked me to look into . . ." he said. "I'm already on it . . . checked out Detective Crane the minute I first met her in the police station. There's a buzz about her in the force. She once even applied as a trainee to the agency. But she was rejected. Not really our type. The Lizzie Crane hit-and-run case is unsolved. Georgia sheriffs aren't really up to snuff. But I did find a restraining order in 2015."

"Against Lizzie Crane's lover?" Eleanor asked intently.

Thomas glanced at Eleanor with a good-natured grin. "Nope, the restraining order was issued against Detective Crane's sister." He lightly kissed Eleanor on the cheek and scolded her. "First rule of any investigation . . . don't assume the obvious is correct."

Eleanor didn't know exactly what to do with this privileged information. She only knew it was important to perceive something about the detective who might prove her guilty of a murder she didn't commit, someone who might even believe her innocence.

As she closed her front door, Eleanor reflexively checked her text messages. There was one from her mother, her lawyer, and from Jackson Poole, Leo's executive assistant.

> Sorry to tell you, the board
> has placed you on administrative leave.
> Mandatory!

Poole punctuated his text with a yellow emoji of a sad face.

Eleanor sighed and wished she hadn't dismissed Thomas so early. He was good company. If Thomas had lingered longer into the evening, if she had invited him to stay for more than just a meal and information, Eleanor might have locked both her deadbolt and her doorknob. Instead, she was so anxious to get back to her murder board and add to her green sticky notes—she wanted to tack up Roger Yamasaki's name to her gallery of possible killers—she forgot to set the deadbolt.

NOR DID SHE PAY ATTENTION WHEN Brodie started barking wildly, running in circles around her desk. That was how someone broke in through the kitchen door after midnight. The next day, the house cleaner would find Eleanor Kiernan unconscious on the floor of her study, her body rather comically covered in crumpled yellow and green stickies.

XI

ANNA

May 6, 2019

"How's your head?" Anna asked the woman who had been their prime suspect. Kiernan lay in the hospital bed with a wide swath of her skull shaved and bandaged. Anna noted with some concern that Kiernan's eyes were bloodshot, pupils wildly dilated—wide open but not alert. Her pale face bore the flat affect and detached expression of closed head trauma. Expressionless. One finger was pinched with an oximeter, her hand bruised from the IV.

"I'm fine," Kiernan said dully. "How's my dog?"

Her voice was somewhat slurred as she sucked on the brief relief of a fentanyl lollipop. She refused to press the Dilaudid pain button, which would release a stronger opiate dose into her IV. Eleanor preferred discomfort to disorientation.

"Brodie is fine—getting fattened up at your neighbor's," Rafe said.

Anna felt some guilty confirmation that the attack on Eleanor Kiernan had forced Rafe to admit they must reconsider her guilt.

"Your Scottie probably saved your life." Anna smiled. "Forensics are checking for fingerprints and any DNA on his collar. He put up quite a ferocious fight for you."

"Good boy." Kiernan attempted a smile, though her lip was swollen, split, and stitched.

"Now that you're conscious," Anna leaned forward, careful not to jar the hospital bed, "we do need to ask you a few questions. Are you up to it?"

Eleanor punched the controls of her bed to raise herself to a sitting position. "Of course," she murmured, distracted for a moment by a nurse taking vitals.

As the two detectives perched uneasily on the uncomfortable chairs next to Eleanor's bed, Anna was aware of the doctor's orders not to question the patient too long. Her head injury was mild but had left her in obvious pain, and she was easily fatigued.

"Up for it, yes," Eleanor murmured, one hand gingerly touching the back of her skull.

"Any idea who might have attacked you?" Rafe asked.

"That's *your* job, Detective," Eleanor said. "Who do you think did this to me?"

Anna hesitated to answer. It was the victim's right to know who might have wielded the blunt instrument, which had left Kiernan with a slightly fractured occipital. But Eleanor Kiernan was still a murder suspect, awaiting her trial, and perhaps still couldn't be trusted. Sensing Anna's dilemma, her partner spoke up again.

"The neighbors only got a glimpse of your assailant," Rafe began. "Medium build, wearing a black hoodie—"

"Was it a woman or a man?" Kiernan asked. She winced, as if it hurt to talk.

Anna noticed the woman's usually direct gaze was clouded and distracted, not just from the drugs but also from the injury. Anything she might say would be possibly scrambled but important information if they were to solve both Leo Cushman's murder and who had attacked Kiernan. *Is it the same perpetrator?*

Rafe glanced to Anna for direction. "We don't really know the gender," he lied.

Kiernan's neighbor, Isaac Wright, had clearly seen a man running out her back door into the narrow alleyway. The neighbor had also seen a woman in huge sunglasses, revving a red car in the alley. The man had thrown himself into her sedan, and they sped away. A red car. Isaac didn't get the license plate.

The detectives weren't yet willing to share any of this information with the victim. All Anna added was, "We think your attacker had an accomplice. Do you have any idea of who might want to harm you? Can you remember any detail before you were struck from behind? A sound? A smell?"

Kiernan cocked her head as if listening to something just out of earshot. "All I heard was Brodie barking crazily," she began, then said slowly, "But right before I passed out, I heard a scraping sound maybe . . . subtle, uneven . . . like someone dragging one leg a little behind the other." She paused. "And a weird smell . . . smoky, like tobacco. Then, before I could turn around, nothing."

Rafe jotted down all the details. "Good. Anything else?"

Exhausted, Kiernan fell silent. She lay back in the hospital bed, covering her swollen eyes with one palm. "Turn down the lights," she complained. "Glare."

It wasn't clear if she were stalling or simply in pain from her head injury. Rafe obligingly dimmed the fluorescent lights. They all sat quietly at an impasse.

The hospital was serenely situated on Lake Washington. Kiernan's window opened onto a gray-scape of wind-carved trees and turbulent waters. Whitecaps splashed against the break walls, and a long, steel silhouette of the floating bridge rose above the waves. Seattle weather was the most unsettled and unpredictable in the spring, ranging from early heat to chilly fog. The silence of the room's occupants was soon accompanied by the thrum of raindrops against glass—the floating world.

It was strangely meditative, their standoff, the percussive rain, and the mists filtering into the dim hospital room—even communal. Anna had always loved weather and what one of her favorite local poets, Tess Gallagher, called the "faithful rain." Of course, Anna never confessed to her coworkers that she read poetry, which, like her cursed sixth sense, would separate her even more from the other detectives. Only Rafe, who loved opera, also shared in her passion for poetry. Sometimes, on long stakeouts, they'd even read their favorite poems to each other.

For Anna, this was recent work by Arthur Sze, especially his poem, "Cloud Hands." It would have surprised Anna to learn Kiernan was on the board of Copper Canyon, a Port Townsend publisher of international renown and Sze's publisher. But then she remembered Franklin Kiernan's obituary had quoted William Butler Yeats.

Kiernan was very still, her breathing now steadied. Anna thought she might have drifted off to sleep. But just as she and Rafe were quietly rising to leave, Kiernan spoke, her eyes closed. "I know you're not telling me everything you know, detectives, about who did this to me . . . or who killed Leo." She took a long breath. At last, she opened her eyes, those bright beacons, and fixed on Anna. "I propose a quid pro quo."

"What?" Rafe said.

"Detective Crane well knows her proper pronouns," Kiernan smiled faintly. "So, she probably also knows some Latin."

Annoyed, Rafe snapped, "I know what quid pro quo means . . . or as we uneducated cops say, tit for tat."

Anna asked, "What's your offer, then? Something the FBI told you? We know you've been working undercover with them. What do you know about Leonard Cushman's business that might have gotten you killed too?"

"You first," Kiernan insisted and crossed her arms, waiting.

Her expression was expectant but somehow cagey. With an arch of her brow, her pale face naked without makeup, Kiernan seemed to scrutinize Anna as if the detective were cultured on a glass slide, intimately revealed, all secrets magnified under an all-seeing biochemist's microscope.

While Anna didn't trust Kiernan, she admired her. Strong conviction, like seeking justice, was a firm taskmaster. *Is this why Kiernan kept her Fortura job?* Kiernan didn't need the corporate income. Anna had asked the department's financial forensics expert to research Kiernan's accounts and discovered her family had wealth enough for no need to work a day in her life. *Why doesn't she work for a non-profit to help cure the opiate crisis?*

"All right," Anna said. "We can give you this. Leonard Cushman had another late-night visitor the night he was murdered. Several visitors, in fact. None logged in. If you're telling the truth now—that *you* discovered him already dead—then one of those visitors probably killed him *before* you say you arrived."

"A woman?" Kiernan straightened up so quickly in her hospital bed, it obviously gave her a transient dizziness. Again, she held her head, but this time more in frustration than seeming pain.

Anna nodded. "Yes, there was a woman."

"Blonde, platinum blonde?" Kiernan asked.

Now it was Anna's turn to be alert. She hesitated to answer, but then she nodded.

"I'm sure it was Toni Fleishman!" Kiernan concluded with satisfaction. "She was in rehab with my brother and blames me and Leo for Frankie's death." Kiernan held her head and gripped the hospital bed for balance. Then, as if exhausted from the effort of giving the detectives her best evidence, she fell silent again. "Toni Fleishman made specific death threats . . . against Fortura . . . against me."

Anna and Rafe exchanged a meaningful glance, recognizing Toni Fleishman's name from her Friday Harbor arrest for attacking Cushman's private plane. Anna leaned forward eagerly, Rafe scribbling the information in his notebook. "We already know about Toni Fleishman, but not where she is. Do you know?" he inquired. "Does your FBI handler?"

"Toni may be in rehab again, Schick Shadel," Kiernan answered. "And you might want to also check out this guy. . . oh . . ." Kiernan grimaced in pain. "Can't remember his name right now. Japanese American."

"Yamasaki?" Anna asked. "Roger Yamasaki?"

"You already know about him, too?" Kiernan asked. "Do you think they killed Leo and attacked me in their antidrug crusade?"

"We know they were responsible for vandalism . . . we're checking their alibis for the night you were attacked, and Cushman was killed."

Though Anna no longer believed in Kiernan's guilt, she also sensed there was much more the woman was not telling. Keeping Kiernan somewhat culpable for Cushman's murder offered leverage to find out what she was hiding.

"Do you have any more information from your FBI handler you'd like to share with us now?" Anna asked. "It certainly might help establish your innocence."

"I have more information on Toni . . . it's at home in my office . . . a file from the FBI."

"Do we have permission to search your office?" Anna asked. "Again?"

"Or do we need another search warrant?" Rafe added. "If you really think Fleishman is the one who attacked you and killed your boss, granting us access would be important."

"Uh, no, not yet . . ." Kiernan backpedaled. "When I get home, I will share the file with you, but there are some other things I'm not ready to . . ."

"I thought you said you wanted to help us solve this crime?" Anna said.

"I do!" Kiernan insisted. "But my other files are private."

"We've given you what we know about the woman who visited Cushman," Anna pressed on. "What are you offering us in return that we don't already know?"

Kiernan shook her head, as if in defeat. But Anna suspected it was just a stall for time. In her mind, Anna scanned her list of other suspects. Had Cushman informed his ex-wife and stepson they'd been cut out of this supposed new will? In Cushman's official will that Anna had already obtained by warrant, the Cushman survivors were in direct line to inherit controlling Fortura shares. *What is Kiernan holding back?*

Kiernan sighed and shook her head. Then, she suddenly sat up very straight. For a moment she looked like she might leap out of her bed. "Oh, Leo's attorney *didn't* know about any revised will. He didn't draw it up himself."

"Did Cushman have another private lawyer?" Anna asked, intrigued by this new information.

"Don't know," Kiernan answered. "All I know is his revised will had just been witnessed and finalized. Leo said he wanted me to give me a copy . . . *that* night."

Find the new will, if it really did exist, and you'll find the murderer, the mantra thrummed in Anna's mind like the rain outside.

As she stood to leave, Anna said, "You've been helpful. Try to rest, now."

For just a second an expression of regret, perhaps even panic, flashed across Kiernan's face. Anna sensed it as much as she saw it. She wondered, *Is Kiernan still withholding something frightening or even incriminating? Something just as important to solving this case as a revised will and the stiletto she swears was stolen?*

XII

ANNA

May 7, 2019

Today there was no homemade pastry, no fond banter, just resentment. It showed in Rafe's obvious frustration and moodiness. Anna really didn't want to engage in another of their arguments over the Leonard Cushman case or her now unwelcome intuitions. For five years on cold cases, she and Rafe had investigated in companionable sync, sometimes finishing each other's sentences and cases. But their first active murder investigation was proving to reveal fault lines in what Anna had always assumed was a stable, almost sibling-like relationship. This glacial progress in their unsolved case was straining their bond.

"I'm off for a coffee," Rafe informed her as he headed for the door without offering to bring her anything.

Anna didn't answer or ask. Keeping her head down, she pretended to pore over Cushman's phone logs. She didn't want her partner to see how much the loss of one of their fond daily rituals hurt her.

"Later," Rafe muttered.

Just as he was exiting the office, Rafe all but ran into their curmudgeon of a coroner.

Horace burst into their cubicle, flourishing a brown file folder.

"I always say, if you want something done . . ." Horace intoned.

"What now?" Rafe asked. "I thought we already had all your forensics."

"Always double-check even my best path guys," Horace said. "Turns out, there was another microscopic blood stain and DNA besides Cushman's and Kiernan's on the stiletto handle . . . we're trying to identify. Maybe the perp wore gloves, then snapped them off too quickly and left some evidence."

Anna's heart quickened. "Whose blood?" she demanded. "Any DNA matches?"

"Well, it wasn't Eleanor Kiernan's," Horace said definitively. "Kiernan volunteered to give a DNA swab and blood draw to eliminate herself as a suspect."

"What blood type is the unknown smudge? Is the DNA in the database?" Anna asked, trying to hide a tremor in her voice.

"Type O positive," Horace pronounced. "Unknown DNA. No one you've swabbed so far." He perched on the edge of Anna's desk and flipped open a file folder. "Kiernan also gave us something else from her office files . . . a clinical trial report, not something we can use in court, but very handy at this stage of the investigation."

"What?" Rafe demanded, peering over the coroner's shoulder to glimpse the report.

"Some Fortura employees and their significant others participated in the company's 2014 clinical trials that Kiernan ran. She's got their DNA and blood types. Now, so do we."

"So . . ." Anna demanded, the telltale prickling up her spine signaling her to pay close attention.

With his characteristic conceit, Horace strode to the murder board. He ticked off the blood types of each suspect as Rafe dutifully wrote them down on a sticky pad under the suspects' photos. "Jasmine Wolf, type B; Jackson Poole, type A positive; Eleanor Kiernan, type A negative. Leo Cushman's blood type is the rarest, right? Type AB negative."

A rush of her own blood to Anna's head. "This new Fortura DNA and blood evidence on the stiletto is *not* a match for Kiernan, Jasmine Wolf, or Jackson Poole at Fortura, right?"

"Correct," Horace nodded. "Blood types and DNA don't change. They can incriminate or even prove the innocence of someone, years after the murder."

Anna said thoughtfully, "We don't know the blood types or have any DNA samples from Roger Yamasaki, Toni Fleishman, Cushman's stepson, Hugh, or his ex-wife, Eloise," Anna said. "We'll see if we can get a warrant for more blood samples and DNA, especially from Fleishman and Yamasaki."

"Give it up, Anna." Rafe shook his head. "Wild goose chase. So, Kiernan's blood doesn't match the stiletto's and she was attacked. That could've been a set-up. We've got more than enough right now to convict Kiernan at trial with *admissible* evidence . . . like the house key, the motive, the means, opportunity. Forget this iffy blood type stuff."

Horace scowled at Rafe. "Iffy, huh? So now *you're* the forensics expert?" The coroner stood up, dropping the file folder on Anna's desk. "One does have to wonder why Kiernan didn't simply wipe her stiletto completely clean. She's a scientist. Why leave such incriminating evidence as Cushman's blood or any other DNA on her knife, which we know conclusively is the murder weapon?"

"Yeah, right," Anna jumped in. "Especially if Kiernan believed she was being framed. She probably didn't clean the stiletto, hoping it might reveal evidence to prove her innocence. So, she's volunteering new evidence of DNA and blood types for other possible suspects."

"Kiernan may be a scientist," Rafe argued. "But she's not a professional murderer. Or a detective. Rookie killers make big mistakes. Like not completely wiping clean the murder weapon."

"Your call," Horace said, shrugging. "But I'd take this blood and DNA seriously. And more about the other case—the attack against Kiernan. DNA on the dog's collar was degraded. Inconclusive. So was the DNA from the dog's teeth after he bit the attacker." Horace grinned, "You might be looking for a suspect with a dog bite—and because the Scottie's so short—maybe an ankle injury or a telltale limp."

Anna recalled Kiernan had said she'd heard an uneven gait, one leg slightly dragging behind the other before she lost consciousness. Perhaps that was when Brodie bit and sank his teeth into an intruder, who dragged her dog along.

Horace continued. "What we did get from the dog's collar was more blood analysis—type B negative."

Anna studied the murder board, frowning. "Doesn't match *any* of our suspects . . . not yet." She scribbled "Type B negative" on an index card and tacked in onto her board with a giant red question mark.

Horace nodded and handed the file folder to Anna, making a point of bypassing Rafe's outstretched hand. "Okay, do with it what you will."

"This changes everything," Anna began, then realized her grumpy partner was following the coroner out of the office.

"Lunch?" Anna called after Rafe by way of truce. "C'mon. Your choice. My treat?"

"I suppose you'll insist on another damn suspect interview instead of dessert," he groused but waited for her to grab her backpack.

IN SCHICK SHADEL'S OVERLY CHEERFUL visitor's room, the detectives awaited an interview with Toni Fleishman, now on her tenth rehab stint.

"We really need to close this case," Rafe muttered. He grimaced as Anna shoved a stale doughnut into her mouth from the coffee table. "Let's prove to the captain he didn't make a mistake in assigning it to us."

Anna leaned forward, lightly touched her partner's fine-boned hand, noticing the elegant silver wedding band he and his husband created and kept in a drawer until they could finally get legally married. It was a stylized Haida design of two ravens, Rafe's favorite bird. If Anna had a totem animal, it was a wolf.

"Dimitri didn't make a mistake, Rafe," Anna said firmly. "*We're* not a mistake."

She saw by the slight arch of his lips that her words had at least reached Rafe. It was Rafe's "tell," the purse of his lips, which suggested amusement—and a good hand at bridge. When they had played bridge the few times they got together socially, Rafe always won. Anna knew the instant he got the most cards in one suit. She could read her partner's face. Anna was terrible at bridge. Card games bored her.

Now she leaned over and tried to get Rafe to smile, but he busied himself with another packet of sugar in his to-go cup of coffee. She knew his next words would be to grumble about whatever terrible brand of coffee they used in rehab.

"You'd think a high-end place like this, where the only drug allowed is caffeine, would invest in better beans—"

Rafe was cut off by the entrance of an anorexic-looking woman wearing a turtleneck, even though Seattle was experiencing a spring heat wave day of 80 degrees.

"Rehab should open up Starbuck's kiosks for us prisoners," Toni Fleishman finished his sentence.

The woman's hands were splotched with raw track marks, even between the fingers. Anna noted Toni's right eye socket was swollen. She remembered some of the most desperate addicts directly shot up into their eyes. Even with the bruising, Toni's narrow face was rouged expertly, reminding Anna this woman had once been a high-end fashion model. Heavy eyebrow pencil made Toni Fleishman look more like she was off to a retro Goth concert than a fancy runway. Yet there remained some semblance of style and elegant ennui about Toni Fleishman. It was in the way she tossed her thin, bleached hair. Platinum blonde. Anna recalled Cushman's maid describing his late-night visitor as *rubio bonita*, a blonde who used to be pretty.

If this were the woman who also visited Leonard Cushman the night of his stabbing, then they might be staring at their murderer. Perhaps Toni had also attacked Eleanor Kiernan in her antidrug vendetta. Fleishman reeked of tobacco. But there was no obvious limp, just the halting gait of a woman whose bones were seized with severe osteoporosis from years of drug abuse.

Anna sat back and crossed her arms, hoping Rafe would notice she was letting him begin the interview. He nodded slightly, with his suggestion of a smile.

"Miss Fleishman—"

"You're here because you believe I killed Leonard Cushman, right?" Her voice was hoarse, her attitude smug. "Well, I didn't."

"We know you were arrested for malicious mischief attacking his plane up in Friday Harbor." Rafe pursued her.

"What of it?" Toni snorted. "Now they send big detectives like you to follow up on misdemeanors? Roger and I already did our time in jail."

"And did your protests include murder?" Anna asked, almost casually, keeping her tone bland.

Anna's accusation didn't faze Toni Fleishman. She hunched her bony shoulders and snorted again.

"You really think an addict like me and a true believer like Roger could get it together to plan and murder a Big Pharma billionaire like Cushman?" Toni leaned so far back in her spindly chair it almost folded with her in it. "Think again!"

"Yet you found a way to visit him the night he was murdered," Anna said calmly.

She wondered how many wretched people had sat here spilling out their harrowing life stories to a group of fellow addicts. Even the furniture wafted cigarette smoke and confessions. Anna could almost hear the echo of them. She certainly smelled the lingering, ghostly scent of old smoke.

As if on cue, Toni Fleishman reached into her jeans pocket and dragged out a battered pack of cigarettes. She took her time lighting the unfiltered Lucky Strike. It was then Anna noticed her teeth, white and almost unbearably bright. Must be false . . . as false as Toni's denials. This woman knew much more than she would say.

"Franklin Kiernan—" Anna began.

At the sound of his name, Toni almost gasped in obvious pain. Her expression shifted so quickly to one of devotion, it was as if she'd taken an overdose of some truth-telling drug.

"Frankie was the best of us all," Toni said. Her bloodshot eyes welled with tears. She repeated, as if they didn't believe her. "The *very* best."

"Tell us about him," Rafe encouraged.

Now, he was the partner Anna again recognized and adored. His dark eyes were sympathetic, his smile genuine. Rafe was one of the best listeners Anna had ever met. This charmed women. They were seen because his interest was not sexual, simply true. His curiosity was the most seductive of all. She felt a pang of longing. She now envied Toni her partner's attention. It had been a long time since Rafe had listened to her so intently.

"Frankie never had a chance." Toni warmed up to her subject. "Not with that mother and sister of his . . . they . . . well, they *diminished* him. Frankie was never good enough for them. His mother never even bothered to come to her son's funeral! Frankie was always the fuck-up . . . and believe me, they let him know . . ."

"Know . . . what?" Rafe asked. He leaned forward and laid a comforting hand on her track-scarred, yellow fingers. Toni could replace yellowed, rotten teeth but not her stained fingers and gaunt wrists.

"Frankie was their biggest disappointment." Toni lowered her head. "Imagine what a toll that can take on you."

Anna wondered what toll had taken Toni's life down the runway of addiction. She would have to do more research on her background. All she knew was that she was a transplant from LA, where she'd failed as an actress and succeeded for a few years as a model. Perhaps in Seattle, Toni had found the fashion scene less glitzy but cosmopolitan. Rafe had discovered that Toni had even done a few stints on local commercials.

"Did you meet Roger Yamasaki in rehab?" Anna asked.

"Yeah," Toni blew out a stream of smoke. "What of it?"

At least Toni was talking to them now, though Anna doubted she would ever admit to killing Leonard Cushman. Or attacking Kiernan. Anna sat back and let Rafe keep their suspect engaged. It was good to be working in sync again with her partner. While he questioned Toni, she could attune to everything the woman *wasn't* saying.

"Was Frankie Kiernan also involved in your Obliterate Opioids protests?" Rafe asked. "So you decided to focus on Fortura?"

"Frankie knew all about their Big Pharma crimes from his sister." Her green eyes blazed. "Uptight bitch!"

"Did Frankie also tell you where Leonard Cushman lived?" Anna asked Toni. "Did you visit him late the night of April 28?" Anna kept her voice very steady.

"You're just dead wrong, lady," Toni burst out, exasperated. Gone now was any more confiding in the detectives.

"If I'm wrong, tell me why you're innocent," Anna said.

Toni shook her head and her voice dropped. "You just see me as a junkie. But, like Frankie, I got into drugs because of physical pain, a doctor who got rich by pushing the Big Pharma lies, and a brain hardwired for addiction. When the feds stepped in and made my docs stop my scrips," she continued, "I had to get them on the street. Heroin. Meth. It's a miracle I didn't get one of those fentanyl-laced pills killing kids now."

As Anna took in this ravaged woman, her own body flinched, heart thudding, mouth dry, a wave of nausea rising like bile as she unsuccessfully struggled *not* to take on any of Toni's memories.

Lying in a twin bed soaked with her own vomit, stained with the rank smell of diarrhea. Sweating, body skeletal, Toni's skin is pocked with scabs, which she scratches with fingernails bitten to the bleeding nub. Every muscle, from hamstrings to biceps to upper back, aches with pain so feverish, she fears she might spontaneously combust. Burning alive, Toni shivers, goosebumps marching up her arms. She whimpers and cries out, cursing this withdrawal only ending in another desperate fix. Blissful. Brief.

Abruptly Anna stood up from her chair, almost knocking it over. She moved away from Toni Fleishman, one hand bracing herself against the cold rehab wall. *Too close!* her inner voice warned.

It was a risk to intuitively tap into someone who was so ruined, where she took on their pain. Light-headed, Anna's brain zinged, seized with the physical alarm of fight-or-flight. She steadied her breathing and called up an imagined cloak of luminous, protective light to shield her from this woman's anguish.

"Do I give you the heebie-jeebies?" Toni demanded. "Welcome to the club."

Rafe instinctively stood up from his chair and moved to Anna's side, letting her slightly lean against him. His solid shield broke Toni's hold on his partner's psyche. As Anna took a full breath, she had to again consider if working live investigation cases was really the right choice for her. Empathy with the living was not always an asset.

One time, Anna had summoned her courage and secretly attended a session with an intuitive healer—an internationally renowned doctor, who along with her several medical degrees, also employed her psychic skills with difficult-to-diagnose patients.

"In any intuitive healing art, there are two paths of empathy," the doctor had explained. "One is to attune to another's illness so profoundly you actually take it on, briefly channeling it through your own healthy system, and this gives the patient some respite, sometimes even healing."

The doctor had glanced around the crowded room filled with medical students and therapists, obviously professional people. Anna had expected the attendees to be weird or "woo-woo," as her engineer uncle might dismiss them. He had ridiculed Anna when, as a child, she had strapped tin foil over her chest to keep her heart from hurting whenever she physically joined with someone's else's pain.

In the packed auditorium of what Anna recognized were other sensitives, the audience listened to the famed medical intuitive. They were attentive, taking notes, and nodding. Anna relaxed, tapping into the focused energy of the crowd. *This is where you belong*, an inner voice assured her.

"Be cautious," the doctor's mellifluous voice slightly rose as she continued her TEDMED Talk. "Untrained empathy can kill you. You can't *become* someone else's pain without a terrible toll on your own body. You won't last; it's a misuse of your intuitive healing gifts. Instead . . ." The doctor pointed to a large chart of Leonardo da Vinci's famous Vitruvian drawing—a scientific sketch of a man, four arms and legs outstretched to show sixteen perfect, proportionate poses. ". . . imagine you are standing at a certain distance. You decide how far . . . and study the patient with *all* your skills . . . all your training. Practice compassionate *detachment*. Only then will you see clearly."

The doctor gazed out at her riveted crowd, and it seemed to Anna the silver-haired woman's eyes settled directly on her. "*That's* true clairsentience," she'd concluded. "It's how you can help others heal themselves. You are *not* the healer."

Now as Anna faced Toni Fleishman in the dingy rehab visitors room, the detective took a big step back to better observe this wasted woman. The swollen lips split at each side, the eyes rimmed in red veins, the fingernails ridged and dented, and wrists braceleted with savage white scars. How many times had Toni Fleishman attempted suicide? And yet, there was such a fierce life force, like a steady wind. Maybe this woman was weary of trying to kill herself so had focused her rage on Leonard Cushman, her drug lord.

It struck Anna now Toni's eyes were eerily like Leonard Cushman's dead stare.

Anna remembered reading Toni was raised in a series of foster homes. She wondered what had happened to Toni's parents. Anna made a note to find a photograph of Toni from her modeling days to show Cushman's maid.

Rafe gave her a quizzical glance, as if to say, *What's up?*

"We'd like to get some DNA and a blood sample from you, Ms. Fleishman," Anna said mildly. "To exclude you from our inquiry."

Toni snuffed out yet another cigarette in the full ashtray. It was a shaped like a ceramic heart. "Dear, dim detectives, how long will it take you to figure out I'm not Leo Cushman's killer?" Toni snorted. As if to punctuate her sentence, Toni added with a grim laugh. "I'm just his bastard."

PART TWO

XIII

ELEANOR

May 20, 2019

A man who could cook and who was as competent in the kitchen as the office—and the bedroom. None of Eleanor's lovers had ever rivaled her culinary skills.

"When did you learn to cook?" Eleanor asked Thomas, as he entered her bedroom with a flourish of the silver tray set with one white rose, fresh-brewed Columbian coffee, Beecher's cheddar biscuits, and eggs Florentine.

"After you broke up with me." Thomas shook his head and gave her his trademark bemused grin, leaning down to kiss her quickly. She could taste his generous lips, cloves and cinnamon, probably from something else he was baking for her. "It was my way of staying close to you, if only in my kitchen."

Eleanor couldn't remember what she had done to get over her break-up in college with Thomas. Perhaps she took on some extra course credits to busy herself with study. She hadn't time to grieve or miss Thomas because soon after she ended their affair, her brother had been arrested for possession of meth. It was his first arrest but not his last. Their mother had bailed Frankie out with the command Eleanor keep a closer eye on her twin. It was difficult, since Frankie had dropped out of Amherst and rarely responded to her calls or texts, except when he needed money and had overdrawn the severe and suspicious limit their mother had set on his ATM debit card for their trust fund.

"This is delicious, Thomas, thank you."

Eleanor sat up in her bed and reached out a hand to pet her dog, Brodie, nestled next to her. He'd recovered well from the gash to his leg from her attacker. Brodie had given as good as he'd gotten. The police had not yet tracked down whoever killed Leonard Cushman or attacked Eleanor. Because of Eleanor's injury, the judge had placed an indefinite stay on any trial date, pending further investigation and possible evidence. But Eleanor's own new criminal defense attorney warned this was just a temporary reprieve.

"You're nowhere near out of the woods," she'd cautioned.

Eleanor still had dizzy spells from her head injury. The itchy bandage was at last gone to reveal a bald spot and eight-stitch scar. "Bride of Frankenstein," she'd murmured when the nurse first removed her bandage.

"Think of it as a badge of courage," her nurse had said. "A story to tell."

Eleanor did have a story to tell, but she didn't know who to trust with it. Not Frankie, once her usual confidant. Not Detective Crane, who had requested another visit with her now that she was home from the hospital. Maybe she could tell Thomas, now that he'd proven himself a devoted friend, nursing her these first weeks at home and so gently loving her last night. He had even stopped mid-embrace whenever Eleanor was dizzy, her floral wallpaper spinning in psychedelic lavender and gold.

Thomas perched on the side of her bed. He tenderly petted Brodie, who had accepted Thomas's caretaking as his due course. Brodie was not always so welcoming of the men in Eleanor's life. But Thomas knew exactly how to scratch the special place behind Brodie's perky ears, and he'd bribed the Scottie with bits of beef and chicken. Brodie boasted a new red-plaid collar since the police had confiscated his other one.

Thomas seemed pleased Eleanor's appetite for him and his food was returning. "You need to gain a little weight, Ellie," he suggested, leaning over, and daubing a linen napkin at the crumbs on her lips.

Eleanor shook her head gingerly. The dizziness from her closed head injury was the main symptom troubling her since the actual pain in her skull was subsiding. Her compromised balance was why the doctors would only release her if she had a caretaker 24/7. She'd hired a home nurse, but Thomas had insisted on doing the duty.

"I've racked up so many vacation days," he told her.

Eleanor was uneasy about this rekindled romance with Thomas. *Is my attraction desire or gratitude?* With Thomas around, she was less keenly aware of the loss of her brother and Leo. What she missed most was her work. But the doctors told her it was critical to rest her brain. Fortura had now indefinitely placed her on administrative leave but with full pay.

She and Thomas had binged on reruns of *Law and Order*, BBC mysteries—*Vera* was her favorite and his was *Luther*—and even affectionately settled into late-night reruns of *Perry Mason*. Black-and-white television was easier on Eleanor's aching eyes. Besides, Perry always solved crimes, unlike the maddeningly slow Detective Crane. Eleanor longed to return to her own investigation. But Thomas had refused Eleanor entry into her home office with its makeshift murder board and her obsessive search for Leo's murderer.

"Let me do the hunting while you heal," he'd counseled her. "You've already given the police the Fortura DNA and blood evidence. Let's hope they know what to do with it."

His own agency had only come up with a few leads. Most of them, like Toni Fleishman's vendetta, were already duplicated by Detective Crane. Eleanor knew the biggest break in the case was within her bailiwick. She'd only blurted out the truth about Leo's will to the detectives when they pressed her on their first interview. Not only was she the main beneficiary for his controlling Fortura shares but also her sizeable share of Leo's personal, noncorporate fortune would cut others off. The disinheriting would make them suspects. Leo had confided in Eleanor that he'd cut the family out of his new will when he'd pleaded for her to come to him the night he was murdered.

"You must tell no one," Leo had warned her. "It would put you in real danger."

These secrets Eleanor had dutifully kept to herself. She realized they were crucial now for her own investigation. She certainly didn't trust a rookie homicide detective like Anna Crane to figure things out. Eleanor knew that even after she had been attacked, Detective Crane was probably suspicious of her. If the detectives couldn't find the real murderer, they might simply proceed with the trial and convict an innocent person just to solve their case.

"I've got to tell you something, Thomas." Eleanor sat up straight in her daybed, one hand balanced against the curved redwood headboard.

She pondered whether to tell Thomas everything she knew about the revised will— those disinherited, those left large legacies. *Can I trust him?* She studied his clear brow, the taut and dark skin only slightly creased with a deep line of concentration. Without his black-rimmed glasses, Thomas appeared younger, more like the man she'd known in university—an earnest and assiduous student who spent as much time in the library as she did. They'd both grown up to be researchers, she of biochemistry and Thomas of crime.

At this point, Eleanor realized she had to trust someone besides herself. She had to admit she was out of her depth in this investigation, too close to see the crime and others clearly.

Her mind wasn't working right. The neurologist insisted she make no big changes in her life, sign no contracts, and ask for second opinions.

"Tell me, Eleanor," Thomas said. He lay one hand on hers. She could feel his expertise. He was in his element. It was obvious in the attentive tilt of his head, the steady interest in his eyes.

Thomas was, after all, a trained investigator, who sometimes didn't seem to be taking it all in too seriously to inspire a confidence or a confession and reel her in more tightly. She bet Thomas was also a good fisherman. Patient. Perceptive. Deadly.

Eleanor hesitated. What if Thomas wasn't really off-duty in his so-called staycation with her? Maybe he was engaged in a weird kind of official subterfuge by taking care of her. No, she couldn't yet confide in him. He was also too close to the case. If he really cared about her, he might not act rationally but protect her from some truth she needed to know; if he were here to research her as part of his agency's precedent-setting Fortura case, it might only be to make his reputation at the FBI. Maybe they were both undercover. *Under the covers.* She silently groaned to herself at her pun.

Eleanor stalled, thinking of something not too valuable she could confide in him. "I have a stash of my top-secret recipes I keep in my office. They're yours if you help me get downstairs to my file folders."

Thomas laughed. In his laughter was amusement and disappointment. "That's your big reveal?"

She was already leaning on his arm to hoist herself up from the comforter, which threatened to twist around her legs and keep her imprisoned in the bed. "You won't be so disappointed when you see my personal recipe for Ellie's Famous Sloppy Joe's. Take me up to my office, please, and I'll get you the recipe. I ain't a biochemist for nothing. Here's a clue: a little brown sugar and . . . cinnamon!"

"Maybe you can write a cookbook while you convalesce." Thomas grinned. He placed both hands on her slender waist and helped her down the curved and spacious staircase.

As she entered her office, Eleanor gasped. It was pristine and so well-organized, it reminded her of her compulsively tidy Fortura lab's office. Where once her home office had been cluttered with newspaper clippings on the opioid crisis and her murder board pinned with yellow and green Post-it notes, now the walls were clean, her file folders neatly labeled in several stacks on her desk. Instead of her pane of glass with Eleanor's potential suspects, there was a corkboard tacked with photos of everyone Eleanor believed was the possible murderer of Leonard Cushman. Under each photo was a typed index card listing an alibi for April 28, previous criminal records, social security number, and—thanks to Eleanor's own inadmissible Fortura medical records—blood types on each suspect.

"Seattle detectives don't yet know the blood type of your attacker," Thomas said regretfully. "But their forensics is working on it. I've got an inside connection with their coroner. Funny guy." He reached down and fondly patted Brodie's shaggy head. "Coroner tells me Brodie must've left somebody limping badly. Good boy."

The Scottie barked fiercely to reveal that his one fearsome incisor was broken; the incisor had left a wound in Eleanor's attacker.

"Too bad my neighbors didn't think to get saliva DNA from my dog when they first found me." Eleanor smiled and ruffled Brodie's ears.

"Whoever attacked you tore this place apart," Thomas told her and tenderly wrapped an arm around Eleanor's waist. "Broke your glass board to pieces."

Eleanor swayed, overcome with appreciation . . . or dizziness. "Broke my head too," she said and let him help her to the tidy desk.

Outside an evening rainfall blessed her shade garden and rosy, fragrant peonies posing for late morning sun. Eleanor reminded herself she must remember to water and trim her bonsai. Its miniature juniper branches were growing out of control. She glanced over at Brodie, who had settled cozily in his dog bed near the screen door.

Tenderly, Thomas lay Eleanor back on the office love seat, careful as he kissed her not to touch her bald patch on her head and zigzag stitches, which would soon dissolve on their own.

"Think I should wear a wig?" she murmured, teasing his tongue into her mouth.

"How about a lilac one to match your eyes?" Thomas's lips smiled against hers. "Go steampunk."

"So over," Eleanor laughed. "Like grunge."

"So were we once." His breathing deepened. "Everything good comes round again."

Thomas easily lifted her and led Eleanor back upstairs to the bed. She was still in her nightgown, a rich, silk, kimono-style drape of lavender and black triangles. Thomas wore his ubiquitous starched white shirt and jacket. His one nod to being off duty was no tie.

"Are you FBI or *my* agent?" Eleanor pulled off his sports jacket and unbuttoned his Oxford cloth. His dark chest was smooth, not the hairy, matted mess she'd often had to tolerate from other lovers.

"I'm yours, Ellie," he said simply. "I've always been yours."

Eleanor doubted in the years since they'd been young lovers that this attractive man had not given himself, heart and soul, to another woman. They'd never talked about previous affairs, but Thomas was too supple and knowing a partner not to have had much practice. She didn't care about his other flings. His sober gaze, the way he held her close but not cloying, and the nakedness in his expression assured Eleanor she'd made her mark.

Eleanor chided herself, *I never tried to find out how Thomas was after our breakup. Not once.*

It was a sin of omission, she admitted. She'd forsaken his devotion for brief, strictly erotic flirtations and a demanding, inconstant brother. Eleanor felt a pang of concern for this man—would she again betray Thomas as her twin always had her? Maybe it was in their twin DNA to deny love in some futile search for the perfect fix.

As Thomas kissed her breasts, taking each nipple tenderly between his teeth, Eleanor's hips rose to him as if mesmerized by his scent—again the spicy and sweet aroma from his kitchen duties.

"Oh, a man who can cook," she whispered aloud and pulled him closer.

He entered her effortlessly as if he'd always belonged beside her—in her kitchen, in her bed, in her heart, and in the virgin territory, which was now her life.

XIV

ANNA

May 25, 2019

Because her nights were often interrupted by nightmares, Anna had a routine of banking her sleep—sneaking a nap in the early evening before her routine 10:30 p.m. bedtime. On any evening where she was antsy or overstimulated, her mind racing with the day's detective work or some intuition triggering worry, Anna would sip her Yogi Tea and fix a heavy breakfast for supper.

Tonight, it was waffles with maple syrup, fresh berries, her favorite crème fraiche, and a rare indulgence, applewood smoked bacon. Fortified with too much food and stultifying herbal tea, curled up in her old recliner, Anna could snooze and outsmart the insomnia lying in wait for her, always at 3:00 a.m.—the time many mystics declared the veils between the worlds were the thinnest. Her Siamese cat, Tao, enjoyed these evening naps, attaching himself to her body as if he always belonged there.

But tonight, Anna's sleep-bank tactic didn't work. Instead of a precious and restorative nap cheating her night terrors, Anna was jittery and wide awake. Her mind fired like some super-charged computer program caught in an endless loop of images: Toni Fleishman snuffing out her cigarette in a ceramic heart ashtray; their messy and now inconclusive murder board; Captain Dimitri's obvious disappointment in their lack of progress; Rafe's growing impatience with Anna's refusal to consider Eleanor Kiernan might yet be the murderer. Most of all, the face floating before Anna's tightly shut eyes was Kiernan's.

The woman unsettled Anna. She was strangely drawn to Eleanor's pain, her vulnerability, her competence. Anna had made some friends on the force, but none intrigued her as much as this complicated and intriguing suspect.

Keep your distance! Anna scolded herself. Whatever this attraction was, it was unprofessional.

It didn't help Anna's determined nap that a nearby beach party on Alki was full of noise and drunken singing. She heard her alto part to their raucous version of "Take Me to the River." The song only made Anna focus on how much Eleanor Kiernan reminded her of Lennox—those haunting eyes and stylishly spiked flame-red hair.

"Enough!" Anna snapped and jumped up. Her Siamese howled his protest but landed perfectly on his paws.

She grabbed the remote and scanned for some mindless television series to distract her from her obsessive thoughts and the loud beach party. Usually, she'd plop on her headphones and listen to her favorite playlists. But she knew music would only heighten her concentration. She needed to veg and distract herself.

Clicking through her options, Anna watched a little of *Killing Eve*, but the intimacy building between the MI6 investigator and the female psychopathic assassin was no relief, nor was the usually engrossing Netflix *Bloodlines* series set in her native Key West.

"Forget it," Anna said and punched the remote off.

She would answer a text from an old lover, the unfaithful tenor, who was suddenly stalking her on Facebook. Or maybe she would go to the dojo to work off her restlessness with martial arts practice. Or join her usual dancing partners at Little Red Hen, her go-to for swing and two-step. Just then, her cell burst out with music she'd not programmed, some piercing, high-pitched aria.

"How's my Queen of the Night?" Rafe asked. "I'll make a Mozart fan of you yet."

"You programmed my ring tone again?" Anna tried to sound irate, but she was glad he'd called to save her from her own edginess.

"Thought you might be out dancing with some new fling," Rafe teased.

She couldn't admit to her partner she was napping at 7:00 p.m. instead of enjoying the dates Rafe loved to gossip about. "I was just on my way out for chorale rehearsal."

"Sexy duet again with your sweet tenor?"

"Nope, singing a solo."

"You can practice on me."

She could hear Rafe's smile over the phone and was relieved he was in a more upbeat mood. *Maybe a break in the case?* "What's up, Rafe?"

"Forensics got hold of Toni Fleishman's bank info, and it looks like it was Cushman who paid for Toni's last several stints in rehab. Regular deposits since 2017 from his account under the name, 'Philanthropy.'"

"Well, that means he'd known about Toni for at least the last two years."

"Yeah, it was also Toni who Cushman allowed as his only Find-My-Friends contact in his cell phone, under the moniker Great Blue."

"Because his daughter had discovered him out of the blue?" Anna wondered.

"Toni Fleishman's phone was a burner," Rafe continued. "Most addicts use burners to text for a fix. Good thing we confiscated it. Her phone was also one of the last numbers Cushman dialed."

"So, Toni was *rubia bonita*, his late-night blonde visitor."

Anna imagined the reunion when Toni had first tracked down her father. How predictable or karmic she'd also met up in rehab with Frankie Kiernan, whose sister was Cushman's protégé. That might have given Toni, and her cohort Roger Yamasaki, ample ammunition to plot Cushman's demise. She could at once settle a blood feud with the father who had abandoned her and extract revenge for her lover's overdose. Double motives.

"Also, Fleishman's accomplice, Roger Yamasaki, has a pretty good alibi for Cushman's murder," Rafe continued. "The guy really was in an Ellensburg jail, arrested when his Obliterate Opioids protests got rowdy."

"And have you double-checked Fleishman's alibi?"

"She says she was locked up in rehab again."

"Fleishman could have found her way out of the facility. She's an escape artist by now. I'll interview Yamasaki tomorrow. See if you can track down Fleishman now."

"Okay," Rafe signed off. "*Mañana!*"

Anna was relieved her partner had some new leads to follow. His call did have the effect of calming her down. She could now focus on the case in a more organized rhythm.

"No nap," she told her cat as she combed her closet for her favorite dance outfit—a flowing red tunic over black patterned tights and her custom-made tanned leather dance boots, which fit her feet like a glove and glided along the wooden dance floor with feline grace in the two-step. "Going to dance the night away," she announced.

She left some cat treats and toys for Tao, then checked her reflection in the hallway mirror. Maybe she wouldn't have to worry about insomnia tonight.

"MR. YAMASAKI, I JUST HAVE A FEW questions," Anna began the interview the next morning in his shabby Obliterate Opioids headquarters in downtown White Center, a Seattle suburb known for its world-class Salvadorean bakery and Samoan gangs.

She'd carried her gun for this twenty-minute commute from the city. Rafe had teased her about venturing into the gang-war territory of White Center without him. But she was relieved he wasn't along with her. Anna was too tired—and her mind too deliciously slow—to gossip with Rafe this morning. Her legs ached from dancing until early morning. Her dance partner had charmingly moved from swing into her bed, and he had slipped off at dawn. He barely knew any more about Anna than her name—she never revealed her profession. She wouldn't return to the Red Hen to dance again until the case was closed.

In the shabby Obliterate Opiates office, Anna eyed the agitated, middle-aged Roger Yamasaki. He wore a sweatshirt with "SHAME! PILLS FOR PROFIT!" written on it with an image of a spilled bottle of opioids and a skull. The more anxious he became, the more detached she could be. Anna's sympathy was always blunted by her fatigue.

"Mr. Yamasaki, we know about your group's attacks on Leonard Cushman's plane and your death threats against Fortura."

"Someone has to hold Big Pharma accountable for all these deaths," Roger Yamasaki said, sighing. "Hundreds and thousands of them! What really can we do, except try to tell people about this tragedy? It's like giving opiate makers a license to kill."

His shoulders sagged, and, like Toni Fleishman, he was painfully thin. His well-tended goatee and crisp Ichiro Mariners' baseball cap was all that distinguished the man from one of the many homeless vets now bivouacked in downtown Seattle. Yamasaki was bewildered and defeated, perhaps brokenhearted.

"I understand," Anna said. She wondered if he had lost someone to an overdose. Most antidrug crusaders were either acting on behalf of someone else's overdose or their own near escape. She couldn't get too caught up in his anguish. Anna squared her shoulders and sat back, reminding herself to step back from his pain and focus on the investigation. "What we don't know, Mr. Yamasaki, is whether someone in OO might have carried out this murder."

"I already told your partner." Roger Yamasaki's face closed. "Toni and I have iron-clad alibis . . . both of us were behind bars. Me in jail, Toni in rehab."

"Yes," Anna nodded. "So, you say. But could it be someone else in OO?"

At times like this, Anna often tried to call up her second sense to give her subtext, especially when suspects were unco-operative. But she sensed nothing more than the man's obvious pain and sorrow.

"Can't you read the signs, Detective?" he asked with another sigh.

He waved his hands to include the bold, hand-painted protest banners hung around his office proclaiming "FDA APPROVED DEATHS" and "KILLED BY FDA" with photos of lost loved ones. One sign particularly caught Anna's eye:

Fortura Killed My Family! Hold Them Accountable!

It accompanied a vivid blown-up photo of a man and woman in the front seat of a battered sedan, their heads thrown back, flat eyes open—behind them was a toddler in a car seat gazing at his overdosed parents.

Anna had seen hundreds of crime-scene photos, but this one was a gut punch. Her body flinched as she studied the photo. Tragedy was in the toddler's confused, dazed expression as if the little boy were waiting for his dead parents to wake up.

Yamasaki must have noted Anna's obvious dismay at the photo. "Thousands of opioid murders go unsolved." His bald head flushed with rising fury. "The FDA lets Big Pharma monitor themselves. No oversight! Sure, Big Pharma pays fines or settles lawsuits with millions . . . while *they* make billions—like paying a speeding ticket for vehicular homicide!"

Yamasaki's last accusation struck Anna deeply. Her hard-won physical exhaustion was replaced by a bolt of her own grief. The hit-and-run driver who ran down her little sister had probably never even paid a speeding ticket, which left no police record or any way to ever find them.

Leaning over the rickety table, Anna lightly touched Roger Yamasaki's hand.

Instantly she glimpsed a shimmer of frenzied, red zig-zags, tiny, jagged bolts around his head; then waves floating toward her like heat off a desert floor. Anna had rarely sensed such wrath. She thought of a snake seeking a warm body of its prey. There was something else underneath his rage—anguish. Anger always covered grief. Unless she probed deeply enough, outrage was always good camouflage for sorrow.

"You've also lost someone to drugs," Anna said softly. It was not a question.

For a moment, Yamasaki struggled to speak. He made a choking sound as if sinking into quicksand. He again took off his glasses but not to clean them. He laid them aside on his desk and buried his face in his hands. His shoulders did not shudder, so she knew he was not weeping. He was just terribly bereft.

Anna struggled not to take on this man's pain as her own. It was physical, a stillness in their shared heart, hopelessness in the chest. Catching her breath, Anna tried to detach from the man's suffering. She remembered all the cold cases when she'd had to investigate whether the opioid death was an accidental overdose or suicide. Very few opioid fatalities left a note. Maybe each time they took their painkillers, some part of them hoped for final release, a kind of opioid roulette.

Families and friends of each person who overdosed often pleaded with Anna to reassure them that it was a mistake, not a purposeful leave-taking of all those who loved them. If inconclusive, opioid deaths were the most haunting. Those who survived a loved one's suicide would always be racked by the guilt of wondering if they could have done more or could have even stopped the inevitable.

"I'm sorry," Anna too often had to tell the survivors. "We just don't know if it was suicide or an accidental overdose."

"We'll never know," they'd respond. "It will take a whole other life to figure this out."

A whole other life, Anna thought now as she sat in silence with Yamasaki. She knew what toll an unsolved murder took on a soul. And yet, murder like her sister's hit-and-run was more clear-cut, since it clearly was not Lizzie's choice. She was an innocent.

"I . . . couldn't . . . save her." Roger Yamasaki finally lifted his face from his hands and gave Anna a look so full of longing, she knew he was not thinking of her. "Don't you see? I've got to try and save others . . . so many dying for just a brief high or hope . . . young people who don't believe there is any world left for them to live in, old people who believe their lives are over . . ."

In her mind's eye, Anna clearly caught an image of a slight, elegant woman. Her body was a sliver of bright light, but her oval eyes sought Anna's from another world, begging her to solace this man who sat hunched and broken.

Tell him I'm here, the woman's voice was a wisp, her image shimmering like distant heat lightning. *I didn't mean to leave him.*

"Your wife," Anna whispered tenderly.

The man laid his head on the table and sobbed inconsolably.

Anna bowed her head to shake away the inner vision of this troubled soul. She wished she and everyone were trained to develop their intuitive birthrights, to be open to contacting those who had passed. Spirits often tried to visit, bless, and remind those left behind that we are not so alone. Anna had often wondered what this world would be like if other dimensions were sometimes revealed to us—like the parallel universes physics theorizes.

Would we grieve so long? Would we be so horribly lonely?

Anna's parents had dismissed her childhood visions of her late grandmother who visited her or a favorite lost dog who often ran through her room at night. Instead, her parents tried to convince their two daughters that Catholics controlled the universe—and any supernatural visions were best left to qualified, officially canonized saints. Her mother's favorite heroine was the Ecuadorian St. Mariana of Jesus, who had lived in her sister's house and from whose blood a lily bloomed. St. Mariana's death miraculously ended epidemics and earthquakes. But St. Mariana did nothing when Lizzie was mercilessly struck by a car, leaving only sharp, white flecks of paint to litter her back. No lilies bloomed from Lizzie's blood. Was St. Mariana any solace to all those dying from this opiate epidemic?

Anna couldn't say any of this to Roger Yamasaki. Maybe if she were a nun or a social worker instead of a detective, she could be more of service to him. They might talk about life and death and what came next. But Anna had learned to keep her sixth sense secret, even if sharing her insights might give comfort. Now, she couldn't even confide in Rafe the inner knowledge that Roger Yamasaki was no murderer. Rafe would remind her she was often wrong, and they needed to double-check his alibi.

At last, the man lifted his head, hastily wiping tears from his cheeks.

Anna leaned across the interview table and held Roger Yamasaki's eyes. *She's still with you*, Anna wanted to assure him. But all she could say was, "You're not alone."

Roger Yamasaki cocked his head, suddenly studying Anna. "No?" he asked, his voice husky with emotion.

"No," Anna assured him softly. Then she added all she could officially say. "You're free to go for now. Take care."

Back in the office, when she caught up with Rafe at lunch, she lied. "Didn't get anything more from Yamasaki."

Rafe nodded. "Figured as much. Like Yamasaki, Toni Fleishman's rehab alibi also seems to check out for the attack on Eleanor Kiernan."

Anna noted Rafe, by habit, offered her half of his pastrami sandwich. She didn't like the salty, stringy meat, but she gratefully took it. Otherworldly contact always left her exhausted and starving.

"Well," Rafe said, his mouth full. "Remember, Eloise and Hugh Cushman alibi each other for the time of Cushman's murder. And for the night Eleanor was attacked."

"We'll interview them next," Anna said and saw her partner's face fall.

"You're the boss," he shrugged. "But Eloise Cushman is hardly the type to drive a getaway car for her son to attack Eleanor Kiernan. She'd just hire someone to do her dirty work. She's high-society, fifty-something, more a Balayage Blonde. Two-hundred and fifty dollars a pop per treatment."

"Surprised you know that fascinating styling fact." Anna tried to tease him, but Rafe just shrugged again. He was obviously not happy about yet another interview.

"We're just spinning our wheels here, Anna," he sighed. "Cushman's family is out of the frame."

Anna persisted, "Did the Cushmans or anyone at Fortura have any inkling there was a new will . . . like Kiernan claims?"

"The family vigorously denies it." Rafe finished his half sandwich and was eyeing Anna's enviously.

She did not hand it to him. "Hungry," she explained. "Just broke my Keto diet."

"Dessert?" he asked. "I've got homemade carrot cake with cream cheese frosting."

"Be gone, prince of darkness!" Anna shook her head but was happy her partner was again offering her his husband's culinary delights.

"Okay." Rafe made a show of chomping his carrot cake muffin. "If the family or anyone at Fortura knew a revised will gave Eleanor controlling shares, it would give them strong motive to get rid of Cushman *and* her."

"Then why wouldn't the Cushman family also go after Toni Fleishman, Cushman's biological daughter?" Anna asked. "Unless they don't know about Toni yet."

"Yeah, and the fact Cushman might have left Fleishman a small fortune in his new will, not just the current allowance for her rehabs filed under philanthropy."

"You got the photo of Toni from her fashion days?" Anna stood up from her desk. "Let's show it to Cushman's ex-wife and stepson to get their reaction. I'm guessing Toni wasn't among those present when they read the will. She may be Cushman's secret."

A rap on the glass of the office walls showed Captain Dimitri scowling at them. He made an impatient motion with his hand as if to say, "Get on with it!"

"We're moving too slowly," Rafe muttered. "Our first-time real murder case, and we've just got more questions than answers."

"So, let's interview the family," Anna said, glad Rafe didn't protest.

If they didn't uncover something fast, Anna knew they might find themselves demoted back to cold cases. It had been almost a month since the murder. She thought about going to her murder board and eliminating some more of the suspects. Jackson Poole and Jasmine Wolf were already gone. But taking down Eloise and Hugh Cushman, Yamasaki, and Toni Fleishman might look like they had really made no progress. Anna firmly believed the real murderer was still tacked up on their bulletin board, taunting her failure to find the truth.

XV

ANNA

May 26, 2019

I t took some time to navigate the hills and one-way streets to get through rush-hour traffic to the Cushmans' home in Seattle's elite Magnolia Bluff neighborhood. A maid ushered Anna and Rafe into the vestibule of Eloise and Hugh Cushman's spacious home overlooking the Salish Sea. Anna noted both Cushman's ex-wife and stepson were dressed more for an early summer fete than an informal investigation. Eloise wore a striking red linen dress, which showed off her ample cleavage, and scarlet high heels—no stately silk float and cashmere drapes for this trophy ex-wife. Her face was creepily serene from countless Botox treatments. *Who would willingly ply one's lips with toxic botulisms from spider or snake venom?* Anna wondered.

Her son, Hugh, was casually decked out in a richly patterned sweater, slacks, and Italian sandals.

"Welcome, detectives." Eloise greeted them. "You're just in time for dinner."

"Thank you, but we're on duty . . . we can't . . ." Anna began, but Eloise dismissed her with a wave of her perfectly manicured hand.

"Nonsense," Hugh said. "It's well past your quitting time. Our cook has been working all afternoon for this dinner party. Might as well enjoy a beautiful meal while we talk. Plus, I'm starved, aren't you?"

Dinner party! Anna glanced at Rafe in alarm, hoping her partner would insist on a professional interview and not be drawn into dining with suspects. But Rafe was already following Hugh and the tantalizing scents wafting from the kitchen.

"We appreciate this little 'at home' visit," Eloise Cushman said as she took Rafe's arm. "So much more civilized than a police station."

Reluctantly, Anna followed, scrutinizing Cushman's former spouse for any anxiety or avarice in Eloise's expression. She couldn't tell. *Thanks a lot, Juvederm.* Anna recalled what little she'd gleaned about Eloise and Hugh Cushman. The ex-wife was well-known for her charity work and philanthropic, but sometimes erotic, parties. She was a staunch conservative Republican, active in the arts. The Cushmans had donated a whole wing to a local cancer center and were big donors to a local art museum—but no support of any rehab centers.

Hugh was another matter. With his well-born conceit and rather tentative career as a tennis pro, he would have a good motive to kill both his stepfather and Eleanor Kiernan for any disinheriting change in Cushman's will. By now the will had been read, and it predictably gave his controlling shares to his son and ex-wife. Cushman had only left his sailboat, airplane, and Friday Harbor beach cottage to Kiernan. She wasn't, as she'd claimed, in the succession line at Fortura for shares to give her ultimate power.

"Let me introduce you to Cook." Eloise was at ease and in her element, as she almost danced into the kitchen to greet the cook with a Parisian peck on both of her cheeks.

In the adjoining dining room, Hugh was navigating between the liquor cabinet and bar with equal familiarity, though he did seem to move with an unnaturally deliberate gait for a young athlete. Maybe he'd gotten a head start on cocktails.

Unlike Rafe, Anna refused to take an offered seat at the cozy nook in the elaborate kitchen. She stood, notebook in hand, trying to maintain some formality to their interview. It surprised Anna when Rafe amiably nodded to the cook as if he knew her.

"Hello again, Mrs. Salvatore," Rafe said. "I see the family has inherited one of Mr. Cushman's greatest legacies."

The woman preened under Rafe's compliment as Eloise purred, "I tried to steal Cook away from Leo for years . . . now she's all *ours*."

Anna admired the way Rafe was ahead of her in tracking the cook's move from murder victim's employee to his possible murderer's employment. She nodded at her partner in appreciation.

Leonard Cushman's cook scurried around her ample kitchen, whipping up a feast. Eggplant lasagna, caprese, and panna cotta. Anna knew the Italian custard dessert was Rafe's favorite. She despised eggplant, with its spongy texture and weird, moldy taste.

"I haven't had anybody to cook for since . . . well, since the death," the cook said. "Please, officers, help yourself to an hors d'oeuvre."

She was surprisingly slender, quick, and efficient, with a stained apron and silver curls so tight they pinched her temples.

"It smells wonderful, Mrs. Salvatore," Rafe smiled. "The family is lucky to have you."

The cook beamed at his compliment. "Yes, I'm happy to be of service to them, especially after their loss."

"We just have a few more follow-up questions." Rafe sampled a prosciutto slice from the savory antipasto plate already on the counter and nodded to Anna.

"Of course, Mr. Bartelli. I'm also all yours." The cook practically bowed to Eloise lingering in her kitchen. "And theirs."

Anna was irritated when Mrs. Salvatore shooed Eloise into the dining room to join Hugh for cocktails. Unlike Rafe, Anna had little patience for chitchat, especially when it also involved food. Besides, Rafe had already interviewed Cushman's cook at the crime scene. At the butcher-block cutting board, Rafe now even served as sous-chef for the cook as she diligently rolled dough for the lasagna noodles.

Who makes their own pasta these days? Resignedly, Anna perched on a wooden stool, watching her partner slice tomatoes for the lasagna. She glanced at her watch. She was itching to interview the ex-wife and stepson to see if their mutual alibis held up for the night Eleanor was attacked. Forensics had found the blood on Kiernan's Scottie dog's teeth was B negative—not a match for any of their Fortura suspects or Toni Fleishman. Blood analysis from Schick Shadel revealed Toni Fleishman's blood type was not the same as her father's, the rare AB negative. DNA saliva samples they'd taken were pending.

The DNA from the torn pant leg the dog had snagged, though somewhat degraded, was not a match with any persons of interest. Not yet. All they had was a set of unknown prints from the dog's collar. The detectives hoped to get from Eloise and Hugh voluntary blood, fingerprints, and DNA samples to rule out Eloise and her son from their inquiry—or to more firmly include them. Such a request was better done in person with recalcitrant suspects, especially since they had no evidence yet to garner any warrant for the Cushman exes. Both Eloise and her son had lawyered up with Fortura's Bart Adams.

Rafe stopped slicing at the cutting board and telegraphed to Anna with a slight nod to let him take the lead with Mrs. Salvatore. "Have you always worked for the Cushman family?" he asked casually.

She smiled. "Mr. Cushman fought to get me in the divorce," she said proudly.

Rafe laughed appreciatively. "It must be good to continue a family tradition."

"Yes, Mrs. Cushman and Hugh do appreciate good food," the cook agreed with a toss of her silver curls and a hearty thump of her rolling pin as she again attacked the dough. "Even when they were going through their divorce, this family never fought like savages over their dinner table. They were polite and never raised their voices. Hand me the paring knife please, Detective Bartelli," Mrs. Salvatore said.

As Rafe handed the cook the slim kitchen knife, Anna noted how expensive and sharp it was, even as she sliced through rubbery mozzarella. It was like cutting up an albino's corpse.

Rafe prompted the cook. "Mr. Cushman and his ex-wife and stepson often argued?"

"Oh, like any family, they argued most about money." Mrs. Salvatore shrugged and rolled up her sleeves. She didn't bother with the pretense of a white chef coat, just a summer cotton shift of yellow pansies. Again, she leaned into the rolling pin and flattened the dough into a satisfyingly thin layer. It took some effort, but the cook was in good physical shape. It must be a prerequisite for Cushman's employees.

"Ever hear them arguing about Mr. Cushman's plans for a new will?" Rafe asked.

For just a moment, the cook hesitated, fingering her golden crucifix necklace. She seemed to be considering carefully before she replied. "Am I under oath, officers?"

"No . . . not yet," Rafe said quietly.

"Well, I cannot lie. There was . . . some talk, yes, of a new will . . . but I don't eavesdrop on my employers," Mrs. Salvatore said. She hefted the layers of pasta into a rectangular glass baking dish. "I'll need those tomatoes now, Detective."

Anna leaned back against the counter, now appreciating her partner's ability to get this vital information from a cook she would have dismissed as irrelevant. They never would have gotten this vital info if Eloise and Hugh hadn't been banished to the dining room by Mrs. Salvatore. *Rafe always says, "Don't just follow the money. Follow the food."*

"Here you go." Rafe finished his cutting board chore and let the cook gather his small mountain of juicy, red slices into her waiting saucepan. Rafe said very lightly, "You didn't mention a new will in our first interview."

"It wasn't my business to blab about Mr. Cushman's private affairs." Mrs. Salvatore sniffed, moving onto the custard. "Especially on the day of his death." Mrs. Salvador again fingered the gold cross necklace on her bosom. "But now, it's all . . . well, nicely settled."

Settled? Anna thought.

She wondered if Cushman's ex-wife and stepson hired Leo Cushman's cook to keep her silent about any new will—to transfer her loyalty to them, instead of the victim.

"During the divorce . . . when they argued, did Leonard Cushman ever threaten to cut off anybody in his family?" Rafe asked, keeping his voice very soft so it wouldn't carry into the dining room where Eloise and Hugh were enjoying a second round of dirty martinis.

Mrs. Salvatore swirled heavy cream in the saucepan. "Can't let the cream curdle," she cautioned.

"Panna cotta is my favorite dessert," Rafe confessed, coming to peer with the cook over the gas stove. "Ever thought of opening your own restaurant?"

Mrs. Salvatore beamed. "Mr. Salvatore and I have always dreamed of it! In fact, the Cushmans are investing in our restaurant plans."

"Leonard Cushman left you money for your own place?" Rafe asked.

"No," the cook said quickly. "Mrs. Cushman and Hugh are investing—" Suddenly the woman stopped, caught her breath, as if realizing she'd said too much.

"Ready?" Rafe precisely placed the small porcelain custard cups into their waiting water-bath roasting pan. The cook poured the pale, hot liquid into each one without a single spill.

As Mrs. Salvatore set the saucepan aside, Rafe drew out a crinkled, blurry photo of Toni Fleishman from an old *Seattle Weekly* spring fashion spread. "One last thing, please. Do you happen to recognize this woman?"

Squinting, with a smudge of flour on her cheek, the cook was obviously relieved the questioning had shifted to someone else. She glanced quickly at the photo. Then she said firmly, "No, never seen her before."

All the air escaped Anna's chest. *Is she lying?*

"Look again, please," Anna said. "We need to identify anyone who visited Mr. Cushman, especially the night he died."

Obligingly, the cook studied the photo for a long time. "No clue," she declared. "Poor dear, she looks like she's starving."

They'd also have to send the photo to the maid to see if she recognized Toni Fleishman. Anna had been sure Toni was the unknown woman who'd called upon Leonard Cushman the night he was killed.

Rafe gave Mrs. Salvatore a winning smile. Then he gingerly lifted the roasting pan of custard cups into the huge oven. "How long?" he asked, as if his only purpose now was kitchen assistant.

Gratified, the cook nodded. "I'll set the timer. Of course, panna cotta is best refrigerated overnight, but we'll have to make do. Cocktails, detectives?" Mrs. Salvatore smiled brightly and tapped Rafe on the shoulder. "Thanks for your help." As she washed some dishes piled up in the sink, the cook added, "By the way, the more I think about his late-night visitor, the more I think she was a businesswoman, well-dressed. Maybe someone Mr. Cushman worked with. She had a very nice leather briefcase. I offered her a coffee. She asked if I had any kombucha. Vile stuff. Why anybody drinks such sour—"

"And did you give her a glass?" Rafe asked.

"No, I had Cecelia, the maid, bring some up to Mr. Cushman's office."

"Ah," Rafe nodded as if the information were inconsequential. "Good to know. Did the professional woman give her name? Was it perhaps Eleanor Kiernan?"

"No, not Eleanor. I know her. This other young woman was in such a big hurry . . . and I had something simmering on the stove." Mrs. Salvatore nodded to Rafe with a tempting smile. "Brussel sprouts, sriracha style."

"Yuuum." Rafe nodded.

As Rafe escorted Anna from the kitchen, she whispered, "Well done! So, there *was* a new will. Eleanor was right."

"Maybe so," Rafe whispered. "And was the blonde visitor a private lawyer . . . or a lover?"

In the dining room, the maid was setting out the fine china, engraved napkins, polished silverware, and wine glasses. Hugh, obviously feeling his gin, gallantly pulled back a chair for Anna. Employing all her self-control, Anna refrained from rolling her eyes. She did allow herself one glass of white wine.

Eloise raised a Riedel goblet generously filled with Masseto Tuscan Red. "*Salut!*" she said. "We'll have leisurely cocktails while we wait for Mrs. Salvatore's lasagna."

Though Rafe had gleaned vital information about Cushman's will and new details about the late-night visitor from the cook, Anna was not able to squeeze in a single question during the endless cocktails and eventual meal. She did glean from the Cushmans' seemingly offhanded remark they'd been together at home watching a film the night Eleanor Kiernan was attacked. Then they all, even Rafe, talked ceaselessly about the delights of "real" Italian lasagna and a caprese with local vinegar and "divine" olive oil Eloise had discovered in Tuscany.

If Anna had paid closer attention to the chatty food discussion, she would have picked up a detail Rafe later seized upon to help them in the case. But it escaped her. Instead, Anna surreptitiously studied the Cushman heirs.

Eloise had the most frightening fingernails she'd ever seen. Bold fuchsia, curved, and tapered long, seriously dangerous, as if her lethal acrylic manicure could double as a murder weapon. Occasionally, she tapped those knife-like fingernails against her wine glass, like unconsciously calling a board meeting to order. Anna would have to find out if she was now a major player on Fortura's board, if this dinner would ever end. She was trapped in some endless period piece mystery series that should have been a short film.

"Now I remember why it was so hard for me to stay in shape when I lived with my stepfather and his amazing cook." Hugh delicately dabbed his mouth with the linen napkin.

"I hear we have panna cotta?" Hugh asked Mrs. Salvatore, who was scurrying in with dessert and champagne.

A framed photo of on the nearby veranda revealed a clumsy, chubby little boy, probably the brunt of bullying and ridicule at recess. Was his fledgling and rather modest professional tennis career compensation for this or to prove to his critical stepfather that he was fit? He was too husky for a tennis pro. In his late 20s now, Hugh appeared both spoiled and insecure. Anna wondered what kind of father Leonard Cushman had been to Hugh. His quick claiming of what had most assuredly once been his stepfather's head-of-the-table seat betrayed both the young man's arrogance and his ambition. But Anna perceived Hugh didn't sit easily on the throne. He seemed depressed and anxious, as if his stepfather would rise from the dead, denounce, and send Hugh to his room for a time out. Or a workout.

Perhaps Anna's uneasiness and frustration over the non-interview triggered her second sight. She never knew what would suddenly grant her access to knowing another's secrets. When she tried to purposefully access something hidden about a suspect, her intuition often failed her. Her sixth sense was a fickle partner.

As the Cushmans talked about their most recent European vacation and its culinary highlights, Anna endured the eerie detachment that often accompanied her strongest visions. Flickering behind Hugh's head were quick images like a faint, stuttering video.

Hugh Cushman, dressed in a black hoodie and running pants, crept up the stairs to Eleanor Kiernan's home office. He was surprised that her door was ajar and quickly let himself in. As if following him from a great distance, Anna watched as Hugh stealthily crept up behind Kiernan in her office. She was absorbed by her research; she didn't hear Hugh. But her dog did. Growling, Brodie circled the intruder.

"Brodie, shhhh!" Kiernan said distractedly. "Just raccoons."

Hugh crouched, hiding behind Eleanor's desk. Though low to the ground, the Scottie was a formidable opponent. His strong, hunting-bred jaws clenched around Hugh's right ankle. Hugh covered his mouth to stifle a painful shout. Kiernan was about to turn around to glimpse her attacker. Dragging the dog along, Hugh lurched toward Kiernan and raised a large flashlight, slamming the back of her head—not once, but twice—as she fell to the floor. Savagely, Hugh grabbed Brodie's thick collar. He struck the Scottie's hind legs with the flashlight. The little dog let out a startled whine and let go of his captor. Limping, bleeding, his pants right leg torn, Hugh ran out the back door.

There she was, as his mother had always been—waiting for Hugh. In the car. She had so often waited in vain for her son to succeed at anything. But this time, Hugh had done it! He'd killed the heir his stepfather had threatened to choose over them.

Anna shook her head and the faint images dissolved. Their motive was clear: there was a new will somewhere, which disinherited Eloise and Hugh Cushman. Did this mean Hugh had also killed his stepfather and stolen the new will?

Anna took a breath and kept her head bent. It didn't help to know something this incriminating if Anna couldn't prove it with factual evidence. Certainly, she couldn't tell Rafe her suspicions. Fuming, Anna fingered her elegant, champagne flute with its unsampled fizzy froth.

"I'll ask Cook for seconds on dessert," Hugh said. Pushing his chair back with an audible scrape, Hugh stood up from the dining table. He tilted slightly, grabbing the table for balance. "Too much of my father's excellent wine," he explained with a smile.

And never enough of his stepfather's money, Anna thought.

Hugh was obviously favoring his right leg where Anna believed Kiernan's dog had bitten him. Anna resolved to find a way to prove Hugh's guilt in the attack on Kiernan and perhaps Cushman.

As Hugh walked into the kitchen, Anna considered maybe the limp was enough to get a warrant. The Cushmans wouldn't agree to give up any physical evidence without a warrant—maybe not even then.

Anna fiddled with the cell phone in her pocket, pretending to take a call. "Excuse me." She almost bolted from the dinner table.

No one noticed her exit. In the vestibule, Anna made a whispered call to the coroner. "Sorry to disturb you, Horace," she began, imagining he was multitasking over his microscope as they spoke. "Any DNA updates on the fabric you found on the dog's teeth?"

"Working on it."

"What about those prints on the dog's collar?"

"Already told you, no print match for anybody you've interviewed so far. No one in the system or Fortura's records. Why? You got another suspect in mind?"

"Cushman's stepson, Hugh," Anna said *sotto voce*. "He's limping as if he's been injured. Dog bite?"

"Maybe," Horace said slowly. "But the guy is a tennis pro, right? Injuries are an occupational hazard. We'll need more than his limp for DNA or blood samples." He rang off.

Anna was now grateful Rafe had accepted the dinner invitation in lieu of a proper interview with Eloise and Hugh Cushman. There would be wine glasses and silverware to lift fingerprints for their coroner. Horace wouldn't ask how she got the prints if they helped solve this case.

As Anna returned to the dinner table, Hugh was safely seated. Again, the conversation devolved to recipes and Italian cuisine. Mrs. Salvatore made a quick appearance to deliver a lengthy dissertation on the importance of making one's own pasta. Anna surreptitiously stared at Hugh's champagne glass. It was full again. Anna resolved to somehow secretly pocket Hugh's dinner knife and slender champagne flute. When it was empty, the crystal would be clouded with his fingerprints.

XVI

ELEANOR

June 1, 2019

She wished Thomas had spent another night so he'd be here this morning when Detective Crane came for a follow-up interview. But Thomas was out of town on a big case. Eleanor had begun to rely upon Thomas in a way she'd never counted on another man—not the overshadowing Leo and certainly not her inconstant brother. Her own father was inattentive and absent, even before he fell to his death at forty-one. As an independent widow, Eleanor's mother had thrived, supported by her family's old money and her academic ambitions.

"History is written by men," Eleanor's mother had always taught her. "His-story. But it's the women who truly change things. Make sure we survive."

With her mother's mantra and her own keen mind, Eleanor had never given marriage much thought. Any man who came close to proposing was dismissed with some excuse. Eleanor had been more content with brief affairs or long-distance relationships. Frankie had often teased his sister. "You've got Brodie," he said. "What man could compete with him?"

As Eleanor waited for Detective Crane to arrive, she scooped up the companionable Scottie in her arms and let him take his usual throne on her lap. She noticed Thomas had taken the liberty of moving her favorite rocking chair nearer the bay window for a better view of the city. It was where he read case files and the *New York Times* those days he had stayed over as her caretaker. Eleanor grinned when she saw his slippers—blue suede moccasins—tucked under the couch. Of course, Brodie had chewed the slippers mercilessly as his way of claiming this man. Thomas didn't seem to mind.

Eleanor was torn whenever she asked Thomas for advice. The head injury made Eleanor doubt her own instincts. She was more cautious. Losing both Leo and Frankie had left Eleanor feeling more alone, adrift, than any time in her life. Also, since she was still on mandatory administrative leave, she had no daily job to distract her from any anxieties. Work had always been Eleanor's refuge and centered her.

She missed the clean order of her lab and the camaraderie of her assistants as they tested some new formula. Surrounded by people and familiar but rigorous routines, Eleanor was grounded, in service. Whenever she and her team discovered some new drug or vaccine, Eleanor had believed she was part of some higher purpose. But now she profoundly regretted what she, Leo, and the Fortura researchers had spawned when they'd created this opiate that was now killing as many as it healed.

Even before the knock on her door, Brodie leapt off Eleanor's lap and ran, barking his baritone, deep-throated rumble. He sounded like a much meaner and bigger dog. Eleanor peered through her reinforced door's tiny peep hole and opened the door for Anna Crane. With one foot, Eleanor gently eased her diligent dog away from Anna's knees. The detective wore casual black slacks, a red cotton cardigan, and a lightweight, black fleece vest—Patagonia, expensive, but had a precise, hand-stitched patch on its shoulder.

Eleanor was pleased the detective came alone without her partner. It was fairer to meet as equally capable women. Leo had always told her that in business, any transaction required shrewd bargaining; biology had taught Eleanor there were parasitic or predator-prey relationships, but then, sometimes there was the miracle of symbiosis. As she welcomed Anna into her home, Eleanor hoped the two of them might find some way of working together. This young officer seemed the most open to believing all Eleanor had sworn happened the night of Leo's murder.

"Good morning," Eleanor said, noticing how Anna easily leaned down to pat and ruffle Brodie's scruffy ears.

Eleanor made a mental note that she really must trim her Scottie again. The white fluff around his dear face was scraggly. Brodie sniffed the intruder, then suddenly sat at attention as if awaiting a treat.

"I always carry them in my pocket." Anna reached into her vest for a bone-shaped biscuit. "Pumpkin and cheese. Grain-free, okay?"

"Perfect." Eleanor nodded and invited the detective into the living room. "You've got your own dog?"

"I wish," she smiled and took a seat in Thomas's rocking chair. "Someday."

"You just carry dog treats around?"

"Standard gear for a detective."

"And postmen."

"It's usually the dogs who go postal."

While she was quite self-possessed, the detective appeared to be uncomfortable in Eleanor's house. Maybe she thought it too upscale or pretentious, this expensive Tudor on Queen Anne hill.

It surprised Eleanor her dog took up his post next to the other woman's chair, not Eleanor's. He was probably holding out for more treats.

"You said you had more questions, Detective Crane," Eleanor began.

"Anna . . . please," the detective insisted amiably.

Eleanor didn't remember this casual style of speaking from their first interview. Then she'd been suspicious, more of an antagonist. Now, the detective was almost sympathetic. Eleanor had to wonder if her head injury had made her require pity. She straightened up in her leather chair, an unconscious hand pushing her hair to cover the scar on her skull. "How can I help you . . . Anna?"

For just a moment there was a studied silence between the two women as they assessed each other. Eleanor was determined to hold her ground if Anna were trying to trick her into some confession now that she wasn't quite herself after the injury. Anna was closely observing Eleanor. Their silence was at first tense, but as they continued their quietude, there was an unexpected ease, as if they were carrying on a silent conversation.

Eleanor had the distinct impression Anna was scanning her in some way she couldn't resist but only sense. It was a faint familiarity, as if the detective could somehow tap into Eleanor. Or maybe it was the Tylenol, which accounted for this slight drain and dizziness. Even over-the-counter drugs diminished Eleanor's energy.

At last, Anna nodded, as if they'd reached some unspoken agreement. Her dark brows unknit; her expression shifted from scrutinizing to collegial. Her beautiful black eyes changed as swiftly as weather.

"We believe we've found out who attacked you," Anna began quietly.

Eleanor leaned forward, alert, almost afraid to hear. "Who?"

She had her ideas of her attacker, mostly centering on someone at Fortura who wanted to finally get rid of her plans to hold the company accountable. Thomas was convinced her attack was unrelated to Fortura power politics and more about anti-drug activists. But Thomas was also obsessed with his agency's opioid crisis case.

Again, Anna studied Eleanor intently, almost contemplatively. "We've arrested Hugh Cushman for your attack," she said.

"Hugh! He would never hurt me," Eleanor protested. "How do you know this?"

Eleanor noted Anna hesitated, either because she didn't want to reveal her evidence against Hugh or she had none. Just suspicion. Like her suspicion Eleanor had murdered Leo. Eleanor wouldn't allow this to detour Hugh's life. When Leo had married Eloise, he had adopted her son, Hugh.

"I don't believe it.!" Eleanor burst out loudly. "Hugh Cushman is my godson. Has been since he was a teenager."

Brodie ran to her side, leapt onto her lap, and sniffed around for another possible attacker. "Hush." Eleanor soothed her dog, whose back hackles were raised, electric white snarls. Eleanor calmed her dog, gazing at Anna.

"My dog would surely have recognized Hugh . . . not attacked him."

"Dogs know when their people are in danger from predators," Anna said simply. "It's the wolf in them."

Taken aback, Eleanor held her dog tightly. It was impossible the boy she'd adored could do her any harm. The idea was preposterous. Heartbreaking. Eleanor's head throbbed with disbelief, allowing the opiate of denial to kill the pain.

Anna continued, tentatively. "We've finally matched Hugh's fingerprints to those left on the collar of your brave little Brodie here."

At the sound of his name, Brodie jumped off Eleanor's lap and again took his post next to Anna. She reached into her pocket and offered him another biscuit.

"Those fingerprints could be from another time Hugh visited me . . ."

But even as she defended her godson, Eleanor knew suddenly the detective might be right. If there really was a revised will and Hugh had seen it, he had every motive to want her gone. A terrible thought hit Eleanor. *What if Hugh also killed his stepfather and had stolen the will?*

"We took Hugh's fingerprints at the station when we had cause to suspect him. They do match Brodie's collar," the detective repeated. "Hugh is in custody. But we'll need you to press charges against him."

"I just can't . . ." Eleanor shook her head. "Leo would never forgive me for sending his stepson to prison."

While Leo had never really cherished his ex-wife, avoiding her as often as possible, he was devoted, in his own distracted and distant way, to his stepson. He'd always told Eleanor he regretted having no biological child. Leo promised he had left some money in his new will to a fund for foster children to help educate them about opioids, but Eleanor assumed this was his guilty conscience or his attempt to placate Eleanor after her brother's overdose.

"Hugh is just a lost kid," he'd often tell Eleanor, as if his stepson were a teenager.

Eleanor knew Hugh had a history of anxiety and depression and had never really made his mark as an athlete, either in school or professionally. Eleanor remembered a scene of jogging with them in Volunteer Park. Hugh tried to keep his lead and Leo at first let him, as if they were in a race. But right before some imaginary finish line, Leo had sped up to a bursting sprint eclipsing his stepson.

"I can't help it, Ellie," Leo had confessed with much chagrin after their jog. "I can't help but beat Hugh, even though he's just a boy."

Eleanor had shrugged. "Do you always have to win, Leo?" she'd asked, not even expecting a reply. They both knew the answer.

Anna leaned forward in her rocking chair to press Eleanor. "Not holding Hugh accountable won't do him any good," the detective said. "He could have killed you."

"Hugh wouldn't dare . . ." Eleanor struggled. "He's . . . he's too much a momma's boy."

Anna calmly folded her hands in her lap as she said, "We think it was Eloise Cushman who drove the car to help Hugh escape."

"Eloise Cushman driving a getaway car?" Eleanor tried to laugh. "Impossible!" Yet she thought, *She drives her son in every other way. Why not this?*

Anna was gazing at her. "Please do consider pressing charges against him . . . and his mother. They intended to kill you. Was it to keep you from inheriting Fortura's controlling shares? They claim they are innocent, with no motive, because there is no new will."

Eleanor didn't know if she should lie for her godson when it would invalidate Eleanor's claim that Leo had made a new will. Her head thudded with pain. Eleanor wished Thomas were here to advise her. Eleanor's own criminal lawyer told her the detectives had a strong case and a lot of evidence against her, but it was circumstantial.

"I don't have to explain my decisions to you, Detective." Eleanor stood up and called her dog back to her side. "After all, you'll probably be testifying against me if I do end up on trial for Leo's murder. Won't you?"

"We're investigating many other suspects."

Anna's expression suggested Eleanor was correct. Though her trial was on hold, it was a possibility if Leo's murder was unsolved. Though she'd been attacked, Eleanor might be their most convenient suspect.

"My godson would never harm me." Eleanor stood, her voice firm, but she fought off a wave of nausea so urgent she had to grab the armchair for balance.

"You're in danger yourself if the Cushmans aren't—"

"No! I won't destroy Hugh's future and our relationship by pressing *any* charges. Find someone else to blame."

Her offense succeeded in startling Anna. The detective was suddenly less self-assured, as if Eleanor had hurt her feelings. *Ridiculous! I'm the one who should be offended.*

Anna pursued her more cautiously. "What if Hugh Cushman is also responsible for the murder of his stepfather? The man who mentored you . . . the man you say left all his Fortura shares to you instead of his family?"

"How would Hugh know about my stiletto?" Eleanor crossed her arms.

But even as she spoke, she wondered if Eloise and her son, like most Fortura employees, knew about the knife in her lab desk. It was no secret. Perhaps Leo had even bragged about giving it to Eleanor as a gift.

Overwhelmed, Eleanor vehemently shook her head. It was monstrous to even consider any of Anna's accusations. "No!" Eleanor repeated with a definitive nod of her head. "I will *not* send Hugh or his mother to prison." Unsteadily, Eleanor moved toward the front door. "Good day, Ms. Crane."

The detective rose from the rocker and for a moment she lingered, eyeing Eleanor with a return to her earlier wariness. She quickly recovered her professional demeanor, like camouflage.

"I suspect there's much you're not telling me," Detective Crane said. She studied Eleanor, her dark eyes penetrating. "There are a few more things . . . and I'd like to come back again after you've had some more time to process—"

"You think I'm not in my right mind?" Eleanor snapped. "I assure you, Detective, I am. My decision is final. Hugh is *not* going to prison. And neither am I."

Eleanor closed the door quickly. Her skull throbbed with the predictable, dull, and insistent pain. It made her head feel so fragile, broken.

Only then did it hit Eleanor that someone to whom she'd shown kindness—a boy she'd known since he was an awkward adolescent, a young man who'd cheerfully tackled the chore of peeling onions for paella in her kitchen when she cooked for the family, her once beloved boy—might really be her attacker.

It's what detectives often said: "Always someone you know." Someone who doesn't wish you well. Someone who plans and longs for your death. Friends and family and other intimates were the most dangerous.

Why get close to anyone?

XVII

ANNA

June 5, 2019

"I'm not going to ask how you knew it was Hugh Cushman's prints on the dog collar," Rafe grumbled as he handed Anna a homemade biscotti. "Or what you and Horace did to get such inadmissible evidence . . . *before* Hugh Cushman even got printed at the station."

Anna nodded, acknowledging his criticism, relieved at his return to their morning ritual. But she was, like Rafe, frustrated about the case, which was dragging on. Eleanor Kiernan adamantly refused to press charges against her stepson and the ex-wife, and the couple was released.

"I'm just going to stay mum with Dimitri so we can take credit for solving at least one case," Rafe said. "Even if we can't fully prosecute the Bonnie-and-Clyde crime spree. You'd think with all their money, the ex-wife and stepson could have hired someone to take out Kiernan."

Rafe was right. They could at least mark the attack on Kiernan solved if not prosecuted. Their captain was now muttering about handing their murder case over to a "more competent and experienced" team. But the street-drug fentanyl case was ongoing with even more of the drugs—with the lethal lure of false brand-name labels—hitting the streets. Captain Dimitri couldn't spare any of his more experienced detectives for the Cushman murder.

"Doesn't it concern you that Eleanor is in danger?" Anna asked Rafe.

"So, it's 'Eleanor,' is it?" Grimacing, her partner walked away—no lingering for their usual morning chat. Rafe stopped, shook his head. "*She's* your partner now? And no, I don't fret about her at all. Kiernan has you—and the FBI guy—as her bodyguards."

His comment stung Anna. Maybe Rafe had picked up on the thing she'd tried to hide from him and from herself—her unsettling fascination and sympathy with a suspect. Anna tried to dismiss this connection with Eleanor. It was probably because they'd both lost an only sibling, Anna reasoned. It was possible to feel orphaned and more abandoned by the loss of a sibling than a parent.

Am I attracted to her?

It had been so long since Anna had been truly enamored by anyone—not since her first boyfriend in college, who'd turned out to be gay. Anna didn't count casual sex with transient partners. This thing with Eleanor felt more of an obsession, like the gravity compelling other planets into their orbit.

Anna was disturbed she was circling closer to her suspect and losing her necessary detachment. This was the biggest sin in any investigation. Psychologists who counseled detectives would call this bond a simple "transference," an emotional misdirection or magnetism, not real intimacy. But that diagnosis didn't really explain restless nights when Anna tried to fend off unsettling dreams about Eleanor: the two of them somehow together on small planes, traveling to unexplored territory, with weather close, warm, and inescapable as humidity—the body's climate change.

Anna had never had an affair with a woman; if she ever did, she thought it might be someone like Eleanor Kiernan. This growing awareness of her own surprising erotic openness made Anna wonder if investigating her own sexuality would now be as bewildering and unsolvable as the mysteries facing her as a detective. Anna worried this unexpected doorway was a sensual detour, perhaps an imprudent experiment—a brokenhearted alliance.

Anna blamed herself for her unruly heart. Her romantic interludes with men had always ended in disaster: abandonment, affairs, betrayal, sometimes even boredom. Besides, Eleanor Kiernan was obviously straight and involved with her FBI handler, who was as much a guard as her Scottie dog.

Just what I need, Anna warned herself, *an unrequited love affair*. Launching into a new romantic realm where she could get hurt by *both* men and women? *No, thanks!*

If she and Rafe were confiding in each other, Anna could have told her partner about these emotional struggles. He would be the first to understand. After all, he'd also been with women for many years before finding his husband.

"Welcome to the wonderful world of gender fluidity!" Rafe would only congratulate, certainly not deter, her.

Because Rafe was so devoted to his husband, he'd always encouraged Anna's brief but intense romances. But if she ever told him about this obsession with their prime suspect, he'd have to report her to the captain. She'd be thrown off the case, perhaps dismissed from live investigations for good. Maybe they wouldn't even welcome her back to cold cases.

At the door, Rafe coolly informed Anna, "I'm solo today, working on another angle."

"What angle?"

"You know, the big clue *you* missed at the gourmet dinner with the Cushmans," he reminded her, not keeping a critical tone from his voice. "What Mrs. Salvatore told us about the cigarette in the candy dish on Cushman's foyer table."

"Oh . . ." Anna sat up straighter in her worn desk chair. She'd forgotten all about the unfiltered cigarette disdainfully snuffed out in the glass dish. It had taken forensics a long time to identify the lipstick on the cigarette. "Okay, thanks." Then Anna was compelled to add, "I'll run it by Eleanor."

"Of course, you will." Rafe laughed, a knowing expression on his face. It was not so much judgment as dismay. Just as Anna well knew her partner's "tell," Rafe knew hers. "You'd never make a poker player," he'd once teased her. "You don't know how to bluff."

WHEN SHE CALLED AGAIN TO SEE Eleanor Kiernan, Anna was greeted with a cold announcement. "I hope you're not here again to try and persuade me to press charges against Hugh and Eloise?" Eleanor was alluringly aloof, dressed in a flowing rose-gold silk caftan. "And please don't treat me again like a victim. I'm certainly *not*."

Surprised by Eleanor's accusatory tone, Anna summoned her professional demeanor like a shield. "Thanks for taking time to see me again," Anna kept her voice steady, "Just a few quick follow-ups."

This time as she entered Eleanor's living room, Anna focused on anything but Eleanor. She noted how spare the interior design was, except for the comfy rocking chair. Anna spotted a large pair of blue moccasins under the rocker. Must be where her lover took up residence. The only real color in the room was a large painting—abstract slashes in scarlet and purple resembling a hallucinatory Jackson Pollack. An even messier mind had painted this miasma.

"My brother's," Eleanor said, when she noticed Anna studying the canvass. "Frankie painted it in rehab."

Anna said nothing. She refused to lie and say something nice about the painting. It was pure, unprocessed pain—not yet art. She wondered why Eleanor made such a disturbing painting the focus of her living room. It must haunt her home every moment. Home was supposed to be a retreat, not a reminder of regrets and self-recrimination. Anna had promptly donated all of Lizzie's belongings to Goodwill. She'd kept only one memento—Lizzie's Australian fire opal earrings.

Anna took her seat in the rocking chair, facing Eleanor on the divan.

"I'll get right to the point, Ms. Kiernan," Anna said, determined to keep the interview brief and any hint of her own sympathy fiercely in check. She tried to throw Eleanor off guard. "Last time we met, I didn't have time to tell you that the Cushmans' cook, Mrs. Salvatore, acknowledged she'd heard talk of a new will . . . just as you claimed."

Eleanor leaned forward eagerly. Her defenses dropping. "So, Mrs. Salvatore is working for Eloise now? Shifting alliances. Will she testify about a new will? Did she see it? Witness it?"

"Mrs. Salvatore is not saying." Anna shrugged. She was more in control now. Professional. Aloof. "And another thing . . . do you know who in the household or anyone in Cushman's close circle smokes unfiltered Lucky Strikes?"

"Leo is . . . was . . . rabidly anti-tobacco," Eleanor said. "Wouldn't ever allow smoking in his house."

"The cigarette was blotched with lipstick," Anna added. "Not *your* shade."

Anna silently cursed herself for letting Eleanor know she might have noticed the cool, blue-toned, red lipstick Eleanor favored. Anna recognized the brand and even the color. She'd once chosen it herself, but only for date nights—Jane Iredale's subtle "Natalie" shade of blackberry and rose, its sweet taste of Tahitian vanilla.

"I certainly don't smoke," Eleanor said.

"It took us some time to include other persons of interest and get their DNA. But we've identified the DNA from the lipstick smear."

"Whose is it?"

"Toni Fleishman's."

Eleanor let out a little gasp. "I told you, Detective, I always thought she was involved in Leo's murder."

"Toni Fleishman is his biological daughter," Anna continued placidly. She was pleased Eleanor was truly startled and pressed her advantage. "Seems she found out from one of those ancestry DNA tests. Did you know?"

Anna felt slightly guilty at Eleanor's shock. The woman held her head with both hands as if to silence some inner roar.

Fighting off a desire to offer any empathy, Anna was silent. *Eleanor's world must be upside-down with all her losses. I've made it worse.*

"But . . ." Eleanor's shook her head. "Leo always told me he had no biological children," Her brows kit, face falling open. "Can't believe he wouldn't have confided in me."

"You thought you were his only close relationship?" Anna asked, then had to add, "Toni Fleishman was the single 'Find My Friend' on his cell phone. Perhaps he was trying to call her as he lay dying?"

She waited for Eleanor to compose herself. The dog leapt into Eleanor's lap, anxiously licking her face.

"Brodie," Eleanor said softly, her voice choked. "It's okay." It obviously wasn't.

Anna continued, even though Eleanor's eyes were brimming. "Cushman didn't know he had a daughter until a few years ago when Toni Fleishman found him. She asked him to help pay for her repeated rehabs."

"No wonder Toni hates me . . . not only because of Frankie . . ." Eleanor said, her eyes widening. "Toni must have thought I was also getting all Leo's attention instead of her." Eleanor took a deep breath. "Leo did tell me he was planning to fund programs for addicts in foster care. I just thought it was his guilty conscience about all the teens dying from overdoses, like those fentanyl deaths."

"Yes, we're tracking that . . . all the kids overdosing now."

Eleanor gazed thoughtfully at Anna. "You know, one of our employees found some of those lethal pills stamped with Fortura's brand on the streets. Before I was put on leave, I'd launched an in-house investigation to see if any of our labs might be the source."

"Good," Anna nodded. "I'll let our department working on the case know."

Captain Dimitri would be impressed she'd stumbled upon this lead in the fentanyl case. It would distract him from criticizing her for their unsolved Cushman murder. Anna opened her notebook and took a quick note to ask the lead detective to get a search warrant for Fortura labs.

When she glanced back up at Eleanor, she saw the woman trying to hide tears streaming down her face.

"Do you . . . do *you* think Toni killed Leo . . . I mean, her own father?" Eleanor asked.

Again, Anna kept her distance, but her throat tightened at the sight of Eleanor's grief. The woman's tears made her seem so suddenly defenseless. Anna fought the instinct to offer her a handkerchief like the one she'd given Roger Yamasaki when his dead wife's spirit hovered near him. Suddenly more unwanted images flickered inside Anna's mind:

Leo Cushman and Eleanor Kiernan leaning back, laughing, their tousled heads together, skimming the waves as they heeled his sailboat into the wind.

Anna realized she was intuiting Eleanor's own memory. Of course, Eleanor was still mourning this man who had both helped make and destroy her. How terribly sad to believe Leo Cushman was killed by his own daughter. But Eleanor's

whistleblowing about her mentor had also been a kind of intimate destruction.

Anna waited again for Eleanor to gather herself. Then
she said quietly, "The rehab center claims Toni Fleishman was
there the night of the murder. But Toni could have escaped.
Most addicts do. The cook did not recognize her photo. But we
believe Toni was at Cushman's home the night he was murdered
or sometime shortly before. Toni chain-smokes Lucky Strikes.
Unfiltered. We just needed her DNA to prove it."

"Where is she now?" Eleanor hastily brushed the tears
from her cheeks.

"We have an alert out for her. She's missing—maybe
relapsed and back on the streets." Anna sat quietly for another
moment, letting Eleanor take it all in. Then she concluded,
"Did you know Cushman confidentially left Toni a generous
monthly stipend in his original will? The one just enacted,
leaving the Cushmans all his Fortura shares."

"Like I said . . . the Cushmans and I are not talking right
now." Eleanor shook her head. Eleanor straightened her
slender shoulders and clasped her hands together in her lap.
Closed again. "Any day now, I expect they'll fire me, unless
someone finds the new will."

Anna felt another pang of sympathy for Eleanor. *To lose her
brother, her mentor, her adopted family, and now her job. It's enough
to destroy even a strong, accomplished woman like Eleanor.* Anna
hoped Eleanor had the resilience to weather all of this—and
this fall, if they found more incriminating evidence, a possible
murder trial, unless Anna could prove Eleanor's innocence.

"Let's talk about the future of the company *without* you in
the picture," Anna said.

"Well," Eleanor responded thoughtfully. "Without me
taking control at Fortura, there will be no lawsuits fairly settled
and no one held accountable for the opioid crisis. It will just get
worse and kill so many more people, especially now that Fortura

has developed our own version of fentanyl." Eleanor sighed and gazed at Anna, her lovely violet eyes taking her in. "I need your assistance, Anna," Eleanor said. "Guess I always have."

Her words struck Anna more deeply than she would admit. Eleanor's vulnerability was both disconcerting and compelling. "What do you need, Eleanor . . . from us?"

"You know I'm working on my own investigation. Thomas is helping me. When Leo called me that night, he also said he'd set up a trust fund for his lover, Jasmine Wolf, and her tribe, among other beneficiaries. I first assumed Leo's lawyer was Bart Adams, his corporate lawyer. Now, I think it was another private lawyer outside of the company—someone who could keep such a big secret as a new will."

Anna nodded slowly. "Yes, the cook also said there was another visitor to Cushman's home the night he was killed. Mrs. Salvatore described this woman as very professional, carrying a briefcase."

"Must be Leo's private lawyer!" Eleanor exclaimed.

"Maybe so. Makes sense he would go outside the company for a personal will."

It struck Anna she was now engaging Eleanor in her musings, the way she used to include Rafe. In a way, she and Eleanor were now in a kind of partnership—tense, unpredictable, dangerous, and professionally inappropriate—but an alliance. Anna sensed it in the way Eleanor Kiernan was engaging her. The two women sat in the shadow of Frankie's chaotic painting, studying each other.

"What if . . ." Anna thought a moment longer, then continued. "What if . . . the outside lawyer also found Cushman dead and fled the scene with the new will? That would be why it wasn't found in his safe. But then, why wouldn't the lawyer come forward with the revised will? It's her legal responsibility."

Eleanor stood up and crossed over to Anna, touching her hand lightly.

"You *do* believe me, Anna?" Eleanor asked; her tone was intimate, exuberant. "That I'm innocent."

The woman's slight touch threw Anna into a tumult of emotions and unwanted images:

Eleanor frantically feeling for a pulse in Leonard Cushman's wrist, dashing around his bedroom, knocking over the wine glass, desperately searching the open safe.

Eleanor resting her head on Thomas Filson's shoulder as they lay in bed, her tousled, but perfectly cut, short red hair glowing against his dark chest. They are laughing, Eleanor's legs wrapped around his.

Eleanor in a sauna, the hiss of steam clouding her nakedness.

The flickering, fast images overwhelmed Anna with their vivid and visceral intensity. She grasped the rocking chair arms to steady herself, trying to catch her breath, to keep hidden all she unwillingly witnessed in Eleanor's cluttered aura. The swirling, jagged images reminded Anna of Frankie Kiernan's hallucinatory, unsettling painting. She realized Eleanor kept this painting's chaos on her wall because it mirrored her own inner world. No wonder, with her mind so jumbled by these haunting memories, Eleanor kept her home and her lab Zen and well-ordered, almost like someone with an obsessive-compulsive disorder.

"Are you okay?" Eleanor's touch was now almost tender, warm.

"Fine . . . I'm fine." Anna leaned away from Eleanor's hand. The last thing she needed was to feel any more connection to this woman whose mind was so scattered and whose pain drained Anna's energy. "Just my usual low blood sugar."

"Let me get you something to eat." Eleanor quickly went into the kitchen, calling back. "I'll make an omelet."

Anna was glad to be left alone. She stood up from the rocking chair, instinctively dropping into the physical calm and centering of her martial art training. Horse posture—knees slightly bent, palms circling her naval. Thirty-two circles clockwise. Thirty-two circles counterclockwise. She dropped her center of gravity like roots deep into the earth and let the flow of her own inner core return to protect her from anyone else's energy. Her martial arts teacher had trained Anna to defend against any physical, as well as energetic, intrusions on her own energy. But this training was less of a defense against her own impulses than another's physical attack.

Anna knew Eleanor had not meant any trespass against Anna by a simple touch.

Her mistake was in opening herself to Eleanor. Anna had allowed herself to imagine, to get too close, when she really needed to keep her distance. Any attraction or desire always made Anna too susceptible to others. Rafe was right. She must now shut down her second sight, especially toward what her partner believed was still their prime suspect. She must ground herself and step back to see more clearly. Step *way* back. Separate. Anna resolved to investigate without any more intrusive and unsettling intuition—or longings.

By the time Eleanor came back into the living room with a perfectly cooked mushroom, gruyere, and avocado omelet, topped with a spring of rosemary (probably from her own herb garden), Anna was again sitting in the chair. Not rocking.

"I have some garlic parmesan bread from Bakery Nouveau," Eleanor said. "I could toast it for you."

"No, thanks, I really must get going . . ." Anna said and obligingly picked at the omelet, though she was not hungry.

She was relieved she'd contained whatever wild energy or attraction had overcome her. Now, as she considered Eleanor, she felt only a dull numbness. It struck Anna that shutting down her keen senses and acute sensitivity—of knowing what should perhaps not ever be known—this nepenthe must be why people got addicted to opiates: to stop the pain, the doomed hopes, the angst, and futile desires.

Eleanor took her place opposite on the divan. She leaned forward. "I'm so grateful to you for believing in my innocence."

"Well, we'll have to prove it," Anna said quickly, but noted Eleanor smiled at her use of the plural pronoun.

"*We* will." Eleanor nodded.

It was one of the first things Eleanor Kiernan had said to Anna when they arrested her on Cushman's stolen sailboat. An eerie echo. Anna shoved the memory aside.

"There's someone who might know the lawyer Leo hired to draw up his new will," Eleanor said.

"Who?" Anna asked, relieved they were back on the solid and safer footing of just investigating others together.

"Jasmine, the head receptionist at Fortura," Eleanor answered. "For years, Jasmine and Leo have been lovers. On and off again. Leo is . . . or was . . . not one for fidelity. But he trusted Jasmine. Or Jackson Poole, Leo's executive assistant. He'd see everything. Leo often confided in them both. I've tried to ask Jasmine and Jackson about Leo's new will, but they won't tell me anything. You could officially question them again."

"They both have solid alibis for the night of the murder," Anna said. "Poole was working late, and Jasmine Wolf was at a family tribal gathering."

But Eleanor's suggestion might be very helpful. She'd ask Rafe to double-check Jackson Poole's alibi. Anna had suspected Jasmine and Leonard Cushman were lovers. He might tell a lover what he couldn't tell his own family.

"Thanks so much for the lead," Anna said abruptly, standing to go, leaving half of her omelet uneaten. Anna wanted to call Rafe and ask him to meet her at Fortura to again interview the receptionist and executive assistant.

"There's something else . . ." Eleanor Kiernan said, but haltingly, as if she were searching for words. "Something about . . . well, something else I found out . . . about *you* . . ." Eleanor smiled rather guiltily. "After all, I'm also a professional researcher."

Anna's chest tightened, as if Eleanor had knocked the wind out of her. Anna did not want Eleanor taking a keen interest in her. It would get past all of Anna's defenses. Even now, Anna felt her hard-won protection and any detachment toward this woman falling off as if Eleanor were psychologically undressing her.

"I didn't mean to pry . . ." Eleanor explained apologetically. "But then, you were prying into *my* life so I—"

"What is it?" Tension thrummed at Anna's temples.

"I asked Thomas to do some digging into your sister's hit-and-run."

The room spun as if Anna were the one with the closed head injury. "It's an unsolved case," Anna said woodenly. "Doubt you know something about it that I don't. Spent years trying to figure it out."

"Must be terrible for you . . . a detective," Eleanor said sympathetically.

The concern in Eleanor's expression made Anna want to bolt. But she couldn't move away. *Does the FBI have access to something I don't?* Anna was torn between informing Eleanor that her sister's murder was none of her business—and the equally strong desire to reach out and take Eleanor's arm fiercely and demand more info.

Panic seized Anna—thickness in her tongue, hammering in her head, and shivers along her jittery arms hanging limply at her side. Broken boundaries. This was what happened when she worked outside the norms, when she listened to her intuitions and allowed them to distract her, when her heart dominated her head.

Even as Anna cursed herself, she asked, "What is it you think you know about my sister's death that I couldn't find out?"

Her voice was as cold as her trembling body. Anna's breathing quickened and she didn't want to hear what she knew was coming next: Something awful about her sister. Something that would forever change the way Anna remembered and even mourned her sibling. Waiting for Eleanor's revelation, Anna realized this bone-deep dread was what Eleanor must have endured—always waiting for the phone to ring, for the message that her twin was dead. But Eleanor had always known about Frankie's fatal weaknesses. Anna had not yet really recognized her sister's.

"The restraining order was never formally filed, so Atlanta cops probably wouldn't have told you about it," Eleanor said so gently, as if her voice could lessen the blow, as if she understood what she was about to say would forever shadow and shatter Anna's sibling bond. "It was originally issued . . . *against* your sister."

XVIII

ELEANOR

June 9, 2019

"You made a serious mistake talking to Detective Crane without me here with you," Thomas informed Eleanor as they cooked dinner together in her spacious kitchen.

Eleanor bristled at his presumptive tone. It reminded her of the corporate lawyer, Bart Adams, chiding her for talking to the police without his permission. "I can handle my own affairs, Thomas," she frowned. "You don't always have to be here."

Taken aback, Thomas was quiet a moment, then said in a softer voice, "That info on the restraining order against Lizzie Crane. It was just between us."

He seemed slightly hurt as if she had somehow betrayed him. "You said you didn't want to be my private investigator." She reached out a conciliatory hand to touch his face. "Besides, I much prefer you in my bed and kitchen."

Eleanor had proposed a simple summer meal of pasta tossed with summer squash, red bell peppers, and her favorite local sausage served with a *mista* salad. A Mediterranean diet was more her style. But Thomas was determined to experiment with a rack of lamb and a well-reviewed Robuchon recipe for *puree de pomme de terre*.

"Don't be such a snob." Eleanor sniffed at the suggestion. "Why not just call it mashed potatoes?"

"Because he's a French chef." Thomas grinned, giving her his most persuasive peck on the cheek.

"Julia Child didn't put on such airs," Eleanor said. "Besides, it's too hot tonight for heavy mashed potatoes—"

"You don't like hot and heavy?" Thomas wrapped his arms around her.

His hair was even curlier after their shower, the scent of her favorite wild peppermint soap lingering on his dark skin. He was a subtle companion, settling into her domestic routines with the ease and unobtrusiveness of a thoughtful guest. Thomas never overstayed his welcome, and he had a sixth sense about when to give Eleanor the solitude every introvert required. Thomas was much more outgoing than Eleanor, but he was also often traveling on a case—a schedule that suited Eleanor well.

Now that she was still on mandatory administrative leave and not allowed into the lab every day, Eleanor was apprehensive and a little uncertain about her purpose in life; she had more time to herself and enjoyed Thomas's distracting visits. He never presumed she was free or would drop everything to see him. In a way, Eleanor had met her match for both limited intimacy and fond detachment. But she worried Thomas might prove, like most people, to be unreliable. He might betray her, as had her twin brother, by some unhealed wound that drove him to self-destruct. Eleanor was always on the alert for the man to reveal the character flaws demanding his banishment. Whenever Eleanor allowed any hint of dependence on Thomas or a long-term attachment, she'd remind herself, *None of my affairs last very long.* It was her history. Her story.

"I told Anna . . . Detective Crane . . . that you were . . . well, my handler."

Thomas's smile widened. "Does she know just how much I handle you?"

"Stop it!" Eleanor swatted him with a dish towel. "If I give in to lamb and mashed potatoes, will you agree to strawberry rhubarb pie?"

"Deal," Thomas said as she handed him the potato peeler. "No," he held up his hands in horror. "We cook them in the skins."

Eleanor shook her head and took out a homemade crust she'd kept in her freezer for her favorite pie. "What does the FBI think about your so-called handling of me?"

"I tell them it's an in-depth background check," he said, preparing to steam the delicate potatoes.

"No, really, do they know about . . . well, this? You and me?"

He sighed. "They wouldn't approve."

"Do you think we're also making a mistake?" Eleanor had to ask. "I mean, our being together when you've got this big opioid case?"

"It's not like *we're* addicts," Thomas teased. He gathered up his fingerlings and dropped them into the boiling saucepan. With an affectionate wink, he said. "The only thing I'm addicted to is your cooking." Leaning down, he scratched Brodie's ears. "And your dog."

Brodie barked, awaiting any scraps as Thomas pulled open the oven door and basted his rack of lamb with more garlic and onions. Brodie pranced around the kitchen. "Leftovers, big boy," Thomas promised him.

"So why do you think it was a mistake to tell Anna Crane what you discovered about her sister's hit-and-run?" Eleanor insisted.

"It was in case you needed some leverage with the detective. Didn't seem to me you needed to use it—not yet anyway."

Eleanor raised her Japanese ceramic paring knife from the perfectly ripe strawberries. "It wasn't about leverage," she admitted. "I just thought . . . Anna and I were working together so well to find out who might have killed Leo. Brainstorming."

"The detective was just doing her job, Ellie," Thomas said dismissively. "The two of you are not really working together. She might yet pin Leo's murder on you if she can't find the real killer. She's a novice under a lot of pressure to convict. You can't trust her."

Eleanor frowned. Again, she didn't like Thomas or any man deciding who she could trust. Today's criticism or caution was the first time Thomas had overstepped his boundary. Stoically, she stripped the rhubarb stalks and said nothing.

"Remember, your Anna Crane seriously studies aikido. She may just be using your own energy against you, the way a martial artist fights—and a good detective." As if sensing her displeasure, Thomas added, "Listen, a cop will tell you anything to gain your trust. It's their training—"

"Is that what you're doing with me?" Eleanor demanded. "Sleeping with me to gain my trust . . . maybe get even more information for your opioid case? I've given you everything I had."

Quickly, Thomas was at her side, again wrapping her in his arms. "You've given me so much, Ellie. It's not about my case. It's about . . . well, about us. Our future."

Eleanor pushed him back enough to gaze directly into his eyes. There was an openness in his expression she'd not seen before, even when they made love. His defenselessness and even a hunger for her made Eleanor feel both drawn in and yet frightened. Her brother had sometimes regarded her this way—with a longing for something she couldn't give and didn't possess.

Suddenly Eleanor flashed on a scene from high school. Their mother had just moved them from Palo Alto back to her Boston roots. In the new school, Frankie hadn't made friends as quickly as Eleanor. Frankie was usually the more social of the twins. But Boston, with its strict hierarchy of class and money, didn't offer the easy access of the West Coast. With her academic talents in chemistry and biology, Ellie quickly joined the nerdy but successful students. Frankie drifted from soccer to theater, searching for his peer group.

Every time they'd started a new school, the twins would take lunch together until they each always found friends. But in Boston, Frankie wasn't thriving. With his long red dreadlocks, dated Grateful Dead T-shirt, and battered, black, high-top sneakers, he didn't fit in with the Ivy League-bound scholarship set. One day in the cafeteria, Eleanor had found a place at a table with others working on a complicated genetics project. She'd glanced up, slightly irritated, when Frankie expectantly approached with his lunch tray. There was no seat for him.

Eleanor didn't invite her brother to join the other advanced-study students. Frankie didn't belong, and he knew it. Her brother shrugged and walked away to sit alone, but not before Eleanor clearly saw his face—hurt and hungry.

After her denial, Frankie was most often alone, as if he were forsaken and exiled. Now Eleanor wondered if this was when his addictions began. *Was I the first to break the twin bond and trigger his forlorn love?* If so, he'd certainly taken his vengeance on her—leaving Eleanor forever alone, completely confused about how to be truly intimate with anybody else ever again.

"Future?" Eleanor now leaned away from Thomas, who gave her time to take in his question while he tackled a huge slab of cold Irish butter. "I don't think about the future, not after Frankie."

"That's obvious when you tried to make your ridiculous getaway after Cushman's murder," Thomas said. "It was reckless. You're always a flight risk," he muttered.

It was what her mother had told her. Eleanor tried to laugh off the accusation. But she knew Thomas was right.

"It's your gut instinct," Thomas continued. "To escape . . . if you think you're going to get caught . . . by a cop . . . or a lover."

Eleanor was uncomfortable with this conversation and all it might demand of her. She tried to tease Thomas out of his pique. "Listen," she smiled. "There is no future for us living together when you have a cat who would eat my little pup alive."

Thomas's great love was his Manx cat, ill-named Mortimer. Feral and robust, the snub-tailed creature was barely domesticated. His tan-and-black fur was luxurious and yet matted from prowling his Capitol Hill neighborhood terrorizing songbirds and other felines. Mortimer belonged more on the savannah than cozy city streets. Once, Mortimer had almost killed a toy poodle. With his fierce jaws, her Scottie might have a chance against Mighty Mortimer, but not if the Manx leapt onto his back, attacking a slower and shorter creature. It would be a bloody safari for Mortimer.

"What if I don't want to live together?" Thomas insisted. "What if I like living alone, just as you do?" He smashed the steaming hot potatoes savagely and folded in the melting mountain of butter.

"Too much butter," Eleanor scolded him.

"Someone's got to fatten you up." Thomas defended the buttery swirl he whisked round and round. The prospect of his favorite comfort food always softened his mood.

But Eleanor shook her head when he added even more pats of butter to the whipped topping. "Looks like a food coma."

"Truce?" he offered. "We can table the future for now. Let's eat."

"Will you share the oven with my pie?" she smiled, despite herself.

"Yup." Thomas checked and triumphantly moved aside his aromatic rack of lamb.

As they set the table together and sat down to their feast, Eleanor returned to the subject of Detective Crane. "Listen, Thomas, I only confided in Anna what you'd told me because I was grateful to her. She figured out who attacked me. I wanted to give her something in return."

"She was just doing her job." Thomas sighed. "It wasn't for you."

"I think Anna has always believed in my innocence," Eleanor insisted. "Did you?"

"What're you, psychic?" Thomas snorted. But he changed tone, seeing Eleanor's determination. "So, how did Crane take the news of a restraining order against her beloved sister? If she didn't know about it, she was also probably in the dark about a lot of things her sister was up to in Georgia. Long distance makes for easy denial." He poured them both more Merlot. "Did you tell Detective Crane the other information I found out about her sister's priors?"

"No," Eleanor said quickly. "She practically ran away when I told her about the unfiled restraining order. I dared not tell her anything else. You're right about Anna not clearly seeing her sister's faults." Eleanor hesitated. "I often didn't want to see my brother's."

Chagrined, she remembered all the times she'd believed her brother's assurances he was at last clean only to find Frankie was stealing from her again. Or calling Eleanor in the middle of the night, desperate for her forgiveness, when she knew what Frankie really wanted was another loan, another fix. Anna didn't seem to know about her sister's real troubles—the dark descent of a sibling from which there was little rescue.

"I just feel bad for Anna," Eleanor said as they finished supper with satisfied sighs. "Sibling woes also run in her family."

The oven timer dinged, and Eleanor strode proudly to her kitchen to prepare a generous slice of her strawberry rhubarb pie for them. Her family always enjoyed it warm with sour cream.

"For someone who you say is clear-eyed and really percep-tive," Thomas said, "your detective friend is blind to people closest to her. So . . . just don't get too close to her."

"She's not really my friend," Eleanor protested.

But Thomas was right again. She'd begun to think of Anna Crane as someone she could trust, someone who might, after they'd solved Leo's murder, be a distant friend. Unless, of course, the detective made the mistake of convicting Eleanor, to solve her case.

"Well, she did give you the good advice any friend would," Thomas softened. "Like me. She's right . . . you *should* press charges against the Cushmans for attacking you."

"Not *this* again." Eleanor put down her fork and pushed away her favorite pie. "I told you, Thomas, just like I told Anna . . . I'm not going to press—"

"Listen, if Lizzie Crane's boyfriend, who first issued and then withdrew the restraining order . . . for god's sake, Ellie, he must have really feared her! A big, strong dancer terrified of his ballerina ex-partner? Why? What did he think she could do to him?"

Eleanor raised her shoulders. She wished he'd stop pressuring her.

"And what do you think the Cushman ex-wife and stepson can do to you? If they finally find this new will you say Cushman made . . ."

"Eloise and Hugh wouldn't dare again—"

"Now, who's in denial, Ellie?" Thomas had again adopted his clipped professionalism of his FBI-agent persona. "If you get Fortura controlling shares, then you're even more of a target! The Cushmans know they're being watched, but what's to stop them from hiring someone else to attack you next time? Big Pharma is pitiless. They have millions of deaths on their hands. What's one more?"

Eleanor was silent, sullenly staring down at her abandoned dessert. Unconsciously, her hand went to her head. It was aching again now that she had tapered off the Tylenol. It was possible Anna would, indeed, track down Leo's new will; then what? Would Eloise and Hugh really go after her again?

For the first time since her attack, Eleanor allowed herself to feel fear. It was as if her body—what she had long believed was a humble wheelbarrow for her beautiful brain—suddenly demanded all her attention. Her jaw and hands trembled, her stomach tilted sideways, and her heart pounded so furiously that it echoed in her ears. Of course, her nervous system joined in her body's percussion with the urgent, aching drumbeat of flight-or-flight. Eleanor couldn't hear herself think.

It hit her. *People I care about want me dead.*

Eleanor finally felt the blow that had broken her skull.

Before her brother died, Eleanor had believed she could never survive without her twin. Now, she had to wonder if the reason she didn't press charges against the boy who had attacked her was because she believed she deserved his rage. She was in Hugh's way, just as she had always been in Frankie's way. Or maybe she thought life would be easier if she could exit and join her brother in another life.

But Eleanor no longer wanted to follow Frankie. With a fierce flush of life force, her body told her, *Stay here. Right here!*

She grasped the dinner table for balance as Brodie leapt onto her lap with an anxious whine, and Thomas came over to hold her tightly.

"Yes," she whispered, her voice shaking. "I will. I will press charges."

XIX

ANNA

June 12, 2019

" I doubt they'll ever see a day in prison." Captain Dimitri scowled by way of congratulating Anna and Rafe on the charges filed against Eloise and Hugh Cushman. "Not with their high-paid lawyers and now limitless wealth."

Eloise and her son were out on bail. They'd fervently dismissed the detectives' questions about any new will or any culpability for Leonard Cushman's murder.

"Then why did you attack Eleanor Kiernan?" Anna had demanded when she and Rafe had formally arrested the Cushmans.

"We didn't," Eloise insisted with a forbidding glance at her son. Since they'd been charged with the crime, she did all the talking. "Your evidence won't hold up in court."

The Cushmans' criminal defense team did all the maneuvering, entering a plea of "not guilty" for them both. Their attorney claimed Hugh's fingerprints on Brodie's collar were from an earlier visit to Eleanor. He also claimed the wound on his leg was from a random dog bite when he was jogging. By the time forensics was able to examine Hugh's scrupulously cleaned wound, any dog-bite DNA was too old and too degraded. As for Eloise, the only evidence that she drove the car away from Kiernan's home post-attack was from a near-sighted neighbor without his glasses. He couldn't identify the Cushmans in a lineup.

Anna was determined to track down the new will Eleanor and the Cushman's cook claimed did exist. It would give the ex-wife and stepson a motive for their attack on Eleanor and perhaps also on Leonard Cushman.

"Now, get back out there." Captain Dimitri dismissed his detectives with a snort. "Find me more evidence. Close this frigging murder case."

The Fortura elevator dinged on the top floor. Pausing in the busy lobby, before the ostentatious spray of summer flowers—a huge arrangement of purple hydrangea and pink rhododendrons punctuated with snapdragons—Anna touched Rafe's elbow.

"Remember, early on, I suspected Jasmine was Leonard Cushman's mistress," she said nonchalantly.

"Yeah, yeah, one of your ESP hot flashes," Rafe snorted. "And I just got my haircut at a psychic barber in West Seattle."

Stung, Anna flinched. She wasn't confiding much in her partner anymore, certainly not any suspicions gleaned from the sixth sense she had shut down ever since her unsettling visit with Eleanor. Though she was a little lonely for herself, Anna had adamantly refused to listen to any insistent inner voice. Everything was by the book now. Nor would she ever tell Rafe Eleanor's disturbing revelation about the restraining order initially issued against her sister right before Lizzie's death.

Anna had made several calls to the Atlanta detective who'd handled Lizzie's hit-and-run case, but he'd not yet called her back. Anna dreaded what else the Atlanta cop might have kept from her about Lizzie, perhaps out of sympathy for a fellow detective. She couldn't believe her little sister had anything to do with her own demise. But she questioned why there was a restraining order issued against Lizzie and why it was withdrawn.

As they approached Jasmine Wolfe at the reception desk, Anna let Rafe take the lead.

"Thanks for granting us this follow-up interview," Rafe began.

It was obvious Jasmine Wolf wasn't delighted to see them. Nervously, she motioned them into a side conference room and took her seat at the very end of the table.

Politely, Anna and Rafe took the plush chairs she offered them, a respectful distance from Jasmine. Again, there was a pretentious spray of grandiose flowers. The stand of tall sunflowers obscured the shy receptionist from their view. Anna had the image of this table as a kind of violent battlefield with so much floral camouflage that people hid from each other, planning to pounce—predator-prey relationships at Big Pharma.

"I've already told you everything I know, detectives," Jasmine Wolf said, her hands folded before her on the gleaming table.

"Not quite," Anna said, her voice calm. "You never mentioned Leonard Cushman was your lover and had drawn up a new will including you and your tribe."

Jasmine let out a little gasp, and Anna noticed her hands shook. "That was confidential," she protested. "I don't think Leo's new will is filed."

So, Eleanor was right! Anna almost leapt forward and her slight movement startled Jasmine, who retreated behind the bright wall of sunflowers.

If this were a soccer game, Anna would have been called offsides. She noted Rafe was surprised, refusing to exchange a knowing glance with Anna, as he would if they were working closely together. Anna didn't like pursuing this woman, who was as sensitive and alert as any lone gazelle. A new will, if finally found, would be contested by the surviving Cushmans, who had the power and money to make Jasmine's life miserable.

Surely, she'd lose her job. Anna had noticed the photos of an adorable toddler in a corduroy jumpsuit on Jasmine's desk. No husband. If this boy were Leo's, he would be an heir—a rival for Hugh.

Jasmine stared at her hands and said nothing. But her face was clouded with swiftly shifting emotions, as if she struggled with herself. At last, the receptionist met Anna's gaze.

It seemed to take all of Jasmine's courage to say, "I couldn't witness the new will . . . because, as you obviously know Leo, Mr. Cushman, told me he included me and my tribe in it. They'd say we exerted undue influence on him."

"We?" Anna pursued. "Where is the will now? Who did witnesses it? Do you have a copy? We can get a warrant."

"I don't know what happened to it." Jasmine ducked as if escaping a blow. "I don't know who witnessed it."

Anna knew the receptionist was lying. She hoped Rafe sensed it too. Had someone put pressure on Jasmine to deny any revised will? Why wouldn't she want to help bring it to light if it helped both her and her tribe?

The Quileutes, whose reservation perched precariously at the far northwestern tip of the state, were proud coastal peoples. Their elders had refused to return to their ancestral whale hunting at a time when the gray whale was again under siege by pollution, boat traffic, and other tribal hunting. They had also refused the mixed blessing of casinos. The tribe was long known by outsiders for its popular La Push cabins nestled on some of Washington's most pristine beaches.

Anna often stayed in their rustic but well-designed A-frame lodges when she wanted to escape from the city. A robust fireplace, the shush of the timeless Pacific, brave tide pools of purple starfish and rose-colored sea anemones—they were all Anna needed to restore herself after a particularly daunting cold case. But ever since the bestselling *Twilight* series was set near the Quileute Reservation, they had been besieged by tourists. Most locals, like Anna, had trouble getting booked into their cherished La Push cabins.

In fact, Anna wished she and Jasmine were at La Push now, sitting before a beach fire, instead of navigating this battle scene of a corporate conference room. On her Native ground, Jasmine might be more trusting.

"Let's say, hypothetically, that Leonard Cushman was, as you told us before, very generous to you and your tribe, like with the grant he once gave your father for a Quileute tribal canoe." Anna leaned forward to peer past a stray sunflower. "Why *wouldn't* you want the new will found?"

For just a moment, Jasmine took a breath as if to simply answer. Then, she crossed her arms and sat back defiantly. "I . . ." she stopped. "I can't say more."

Whether it was instinct or intuition, Anna didn't know. She suspected Jasmine was trying to protect someone but not herself. It wasn't about her love affair with Leonard Cushman. He was gone. It was someone who was very much alive—and as at much at risk as Jasmine. Her child?

Rafe downshifted to a sympathetic tone, even sitting back behind the flower arrangement to give Jasmine the illusion of refuge.

"Just one last quick question, and we'll be out of your way," he said. "Mr. Cushman had a visitor late the night he was killed. A professional woman with a briefcase. Someone his maid didn't recognize and for whom his cook had served kombucha. Do you know if your CEO was seeing anyone else? Another affair? After all, he was found naked."

Instantly, Jasmine blushed, and Anna could see Rafe mistook this for pain or jealousy. But Anna recognized it as something much more primal—pure fear. She jumped in before Rafe could continue.

"We think his visitor might have been another employee or a lawyer," Anna said, purposely not glancing at her partner.

If Anna had, she would have seen Rafe's resentment, as if impatiently waiting his turn again at jump rope. "*Not* a lover or prostitute. Would you know any lawyer outside of the company Mr. Cushman might have hired to revise his will?"

Jasmine collapsed behind the sunflowers, head bent, hands again clenched. "You'll probably find out anyway, when you get your warrant . . . or a subpoena," she murmured. "My cousin knows she has a legal responsibility to finally file the new will."

"Your cousin?" Anna encouraged. *Is this who Jasmine is protecting?*

"Ruby Wild Eagle, my cousin." Jasmine nodded. "Leo . . . Mr. Cushman wanted to hire someone outside the reach of his family and of Fortura." Jasmine glanced around anxiously, as if expecting an ambush from some company spy hidden at the table. "Ruby delivered the revised will to Mr. Cushman the night he was killed, but she didn't meet with him for very long. Ruby had to get right back to the rez."

Anna knew it was a four-hour drive to the Quileute Reservation, which meant this lawyer would be driving half the night to get home. What was the hurry? Was she afraid?

Then she understood. Jasmine's face revealed both discretion and a kind of weary despair. "Your cousin . . . did Leo Cushman meet her dressed in his robe? Not exactly the right attire for legal business," Anna said softly. It was not a question.

It was an acknowledgment Anna understood only too well why a professional woman would not want to linger with a client known for his wayward affairs. She liked Leonard Cushman much less now for his assumption such an intimate summons and expectation would surely be answered. If Cushman had once been Jasmine's lover, perhaps even fathered her child, how arrogant to assume he might also seduce her cousin.

"Did Leonard Cushman have a thing for . . ." Rafe blurted out. "Well, for women like your cousin . . . and you?"

If Anna could have reached Rafe, she'd have kicked him under the corporate table. Anna had to stop herself from frowning at her partner. But she realized Jasmine had caught her upset. Her knitted brow suggested she shared it.

Rafe, a gay man with such remarkable sensitivity, was so clueless when it came to another man's misuse of power. He had griped about how much instant press the #MeToo movement received when gay men had long-suffered denial, prejudice, and death during the AIDS crisis. Several of his friends were afflicted with the ravaging disease, courageously fighting it daily with cocktail drugs their insurance companies stingily doled out.

It always comes back to drugs.

The prospect of another argument with Rafe after this interview filled Anna with dread. Maybe she'd avoid mentioning it.

But Jasmine surprised the detectives with a sudden soliloquy. "Yes, Leo Cushman and I had an affair," she said firmly. "Yes, he especially liked women of color. It's why Ruby wore a wig. Blond. To ward off any advances. But when my cousin saw Leo waiting for her at the top of the staircase wearing only his robe, Ruby was smart enough to just drop off the will on the table in his vestibule. It was already witnessed. Finalized. Then, she left."

"She's on the rez now?" Rafe asked. "With the new will?"

Jasmine gave a curt nod, then stood up and adjusted the one limp sunflower, so it stood tall again with its sunny spray. "Ruby drew up the will as a favor to me, not Leo. Tribal people know *not* to get messed up in white people's business," she concluded. "Never works out well for us. No matter what they promise. No matter the contracts or the wills. White people have shown us—their treaties are made to be broken."

Anna hid her faint grin. They'd just been lectured on history, racism, and sexual and corporate politics by the person they'd expected was the most powerless. No wonder Jasmine had fared well at Fortura. By the time she was finished, and if the new will was ever found, she'd probably run the company.

XX

ANNA

June 11, 2019

"**D**on't gloat. And I'll let you choose our music all the way to the coast." Rafe nudged Anna as they headed to the Quileute Reservation to track down Ruby Wild Eagle.

The tribal lawyer who had drawn up Leo Cushman's revised will was hiding out in her small community, demanding they meet her in person. Anna didn't mind the long journey. At last, she and Rafe were on the same page and their investigation was revitalized with this new lead. Any revised will would give the Cushman ex-wife and stepson strong motive for murder. They would not escape justice, as they had with their attack on Eleanor.

"I never gloat." Anna smiled, relieved to return to their usual banter after the weeks of disagreements over this case. "I'll even endure more Mozart."

On this remote ride along the rocky beaches and ancient forests of the Olympic Wilderness, any radio station they tried to tune in was so full of static, it was as if announcers spoke in tongues. Rafe happily plugged in his Spotify playlist of *The Magic Flute*.

"You've never actually heard the whole opera." Rafe grinned, cranking up the volume of Mozart's fantastical music, as he took the winding roads with one casual hand on the steering wheel. "Now, we've got the time and my own car's great sound system."

When they'd first been paired up as detectives, Rafe had given Anna season tickets to his beloved Seattle Opera, only to discover, accidentally, she'd given them to one of her chorale mates. Anna always invited her partner to salsa and sometimes even swing dancing at her favorite Seattle clubs, Havana and Monkey Loft. Rafe usually begged off any dancing together. They compromised on off-duty time together going to karaoke nights at Seattle's popular dive bar, Ballard's Water Wheel. They'd been surprised to discover Rafe's baritone and Anna's mezzo-soprano made for a tolerable duet. They once received a standing ovation for their karaoke rendition of Marvin Gaye and Tammy Terrell's, "Ain't No Mountain High Enough."

Most reassuring to Anna was Rafe's reclaiming of their easy camaraderie. Both loved road trips. This was the longest drive they'd ever taken together. They were on duty and getting paid overtime. Though the weather was tricky with this early summer thunderstorm, the farther they got away from Seattle, the more relaxed they were. Their camaraderie was inspired by the companionable fog, the abiding calm of primordial forests, and the percussive patter of rain.

Her partner had promised Anna a bit of a detour just dipping into her favorite rainforest, the Hoh. Mozart's soaring violins and mischievous piccolo runs were a bright soundtrack to the haunted darkness of the Hoh. Though temperate, the Hoh this late afternoon was like a dramatic descent into time—old-growth Sitka spruce and hemlock cloaked and hidden with the mysteries of moss and rare ferns, its mist-shrouded cedars bowed by relentless Pacific winds and fourteen feet of yearly rainfall.

For several hours, rain audibly pelted Rafe's Prius, and

Anna's weather alert app had predicted hailstorms. But there was no wireless signal now, so they were driving blind through the storm. Rarely encountering another car, they paused to stretch and take in the turbulent Pacific's whitecaps at Ruby Beach, where on a clearer day they could have seen Destruction Island. Then they headed due north along the rugged coastal highway past the Hoh Indian Reservation toward La Push.

Even in June, it was so chilly on these wild coastlines that Rafe snapped on a little heat. From her many vacations on the reservation, Anna knew the Quileute called their homeland's incessant rainfall "liquid sunshine."

Listening now to Rafe singing along with Papageno's triumphant, rapid-fire, "Pa-pa-pa-pa-pa-pa-papapapapa," Anna wished she knew enough opera to properly take Papagena's part. The perky duet was growing on her. Or maybe she'd just heard it so many times, its comedic musical stutter was charming.

"How much longer?" Anna asked, trying to keep any eagerness from her voice.

"The opera or the drive?" Rafe grinned. "Relax." He hummed along with the duet. "We'll get to Forks in about an hour. There's a diner at the turn-off famous for its fruit pies. Another quick detour for dessert?"

"What?" Anna had to shout over the sudden pelt of hail. Icy stones bounced *rat-a-tat-tat* on their hood, leaving a few visible dents in the metal.

"Damn!" Rafe swerved to the side of the road to wait out the hailstorm. Obligingly, he lowered the volume. Then he shocked Anna by saying, "Okay, enough Mozart. You can put on your playlists now. Almost at the diner. I'm hoping for banana cream pie."

"Hmmmmm." Anna happily considered her dessert options. But she would argue they turn toward the Forks diner tomorrow on their way back from the rez.

"Best pies on the coast. What's your favorite?"

Though not a foodie, Anna did love a good piece of homemade pie. "Key lime," she said, remembering her mother's masterpiece: not too sweet, blissfully tart on the tongue. "But nobody makes it right outside of the Keys. Or my mother's kitchen."

"How about strawberry rhubarb, fresh now, or sour cherry?"

"Dunno . . ." she mused. "I'll know when I see the pies."

Anna was busy shuffling through her cell phone's Spotify playlists, nothing on her mind but fruit pies when the premonition struck her. A jolt straight up her spine as if her backbone were one of those carnival high strikers of heavy sledgehammer and bell. *Ding! Ding! Ding!* She heard the shrill sound of a struck bell painfully echoing in her ears. Cupping both ears with her hands, Anna shoved back in her seat.

"What?" Rafe laughed. "My music too loud?"

He didn't hear what she saw.

Their car swerving crazily to avoid an elk leaping out in the darkness. The sickening thud of a flailing body as it broke the windshield. Propelled forward, Rafe's head rammed against the windshield with a terrible crack. Everywhere the bloody smear and blur of fur, jagged glass puncturing Rafe's forearm and his face. His airbag didn't inflate. Hers did.

But when Anna anxiously checked her partner, he was fine, fiddling with the speaker's volume dial. Rafe didn't even notice Anna's stricken expression, how wide her black eyes were as she steadied herself, one hand flat against the dashboard.

"Hey, here's our turn—and our pies." He pointed to the huge green sign: "Forks: Population 3,175, Vampires 8.5."

A gaggle of tourists in red-and-yellow slickers were snapping selfies in front of the famous sign. Their bus had a banner: "Twilight Tour."

"Perfect," Rafe said. "It's twilight. Look out for werewolves and vampires."

"And fans with fangs," Anna murmured.

She was desperately trying to keep up some semblance of normal banter with her partner. But her vision still seized her. This premonition she couldn't share with Rafe, even if it might save his life. She wouldn't ruin their road trip truce with any more of her forebodings. Firmly, she pushed away any more disturbing images.

Her mood darkened. Anna tried to focus on the same world everybody else inhabited, except perhaps the fantasy fans. She'd read the *Twilight* author had never even visited the Quileute Reservation before she'd chosen its sculpted beaches for her novels. Perhaps the author simply discovered that the Quileutes believed their ancestors were descended from wolves. Anna wondered how the tribe regarded all these white people showing up to worship werewolves—imaginary creatures—when the actual gray wolves were finally returning to their native lands and being gunned down by some outraged ranchers, cattlemen, and state wildlife officials. Wolves, like many tribes, were endangered.

Like the cash-rich casinos for other tribes, these zealous *Twilight* tourists were another mixed blessing. Anna wondered if the Quileute people, with their traditional hospitality, would welcome or resent these hordes of *Twilight* fans? How was this small, one-mile reservation handling such an influx? Perhaps it was another form of cultural appropriation—but it was also a chance to survive in such a far-flung homeland. As the tourists trundled back into their *Twilight* tour bus, Anna was relieved, remembering the tribal police had reserved a two-bedroom beach cabin tonight for her and Rafe. Otherwise, they'd have to camp in this intense storm or drive back to Seattle at night.

Her frightening premonition made Anna resolve tomorrow morning that she'd insist on taking the wheel for their long drive home. Perhaps the precaution could change her terrible omen and avert the accident. She glanced over to check the light on Rafe's dashboard, which showed his car's airbags were on.

"No time for pies now. Tomorrow, Rafe." Anna tried to keep her voice light, but her hands were trembling. Obviously, her determination to shut down her sixth sense did not work. There was no use controlling second sight. It had its own rules. Maybe this premonition was so imperative, it needed to bypass her conscious will.

Rafe shrugged. "Okay, Anna, but promise me. Pies for breakfast tomorrow?"

"Promise."

As they drove along the switchback curves of Second Beach, Anna was struggling between two worlds: one of the so-called real and the other the surreal chaos of her second sight. This beach of hunchbacked islands—where for thousands of years, the Quileutes buried their ancestors—always whispered to her with a supernatural authority, *We're here*.

The reservation's wild horses weren't here, but the free-roaming elk from the Roosevelt herd were. An elk cow and her spindly calf grazed now along the roadside. Anna stared at the mother, wondering if this one might catapult against their car in the gloaming.

As if she could fend off any doom, Anna plugged in her phone's playlist. Lauren Jauregui's upbeat, "More Than That," brightened her mood. Anna joined in the chorus, practically shouting the lyrics. Rafe gave her a grin and hummed along.

As they pulled into the reservation's ocean-side resort, Anna's breathing steadied at the sound of the surf, the modest tribal center with its rouge-colored rounded roof, and the familiar beach cabins stoically facing Pacific winds. The welcome sight of James Island with its spindly, twisted trees atop the pyramid-like ridgetop, restored Anna's equilibrium. They had arrived safely, even in the dark and fierce storm.

The stalwart tribal sheriff with his bandanna headband and long braid welcomed them with the graciousness of Quileute tradition.

"Ruby Wild Eagle will let you interview her as long as I'm present," Sheriff Woodman said. He led them to a beach cottage, with its stylized red-and-black wolf painting adorning the door. The cabin was so close to the surf that their voices were almost drowned out as they sat on the spacious porch in redwood deck chairs.

"Did you catch our gorgeous sunset tonight?" Sheriff Woodman asked as he poured the detectives hot coffee from his large thermos.

Anna hadn't drunk coffee in years, but she sipped the rich, dark brew, wondering why she had ever given it up. It revived her. Rafe was asking about what pies their tribal diner was offering tonight for supper. He and Sheriff Woodman chatted amiably while they waited for Ruby Wild Eagle to join them.

When the lithe woman arrived, Anna noted how much she resembled Jasmine—same luxurious black hair and oval eyes. Unlike her cousin, Ruby Wild Eagle had an edginess. She was quite beautiful but wary. She appeared jittery, poised for flight—more like a hummingbird than an eagle.

Anna noted Ruby had her own drink—a bottle of ginger kombucha—perhaps like the drink Cushman's cook had ready to serve his visitor. Ruby took her seat in the farthest deck chair away from the detectives.

"You've found me, officers," she said, her voice all but lost in the winds. "What do you want?"

Anna was taken aback by the woman's directness, not the polite exchange of pleasantries she'd usually enjoyed with the Quileute. Maybe to become a tribal lawyer, Ruby Wild Eagle had to give up her traditional hospitality. Anna hesitated, figuring out how best to interview her.

"We want to see the new will you apparently drew up for Leonard Cushman," Rafe answered with such simplicity and equal directness that it eased Anna's awkwardness. "We also want to know what you witnessed when you visited him the night he was murdered."

Ruby Wild Eagle glanced at the sheriff as if for reassurance. She might fly off the deck and disappear into the fog-shrouded night.

"It's all right, Ruby," Sheriff Woodman soothed. "You're not in any trouble. Tell them what you know."

It was only then Anna realized how young this lawyer was—probably only a few years out of law school. She'd certainly negotiated difficult tribal contracts but probably none of them involved a cold-blooded murder.

"Jasmine sends you all her best," Anna said, knowing that inquiring about family was a vital foundation for any real conversation with tribal people. Usually only white people rudely got down to business without these polite dialogues. "She told us to trust you."

"How is my cousin?" Ruby Wild Eagle relaxed a little, her shoulders softening, but her dark eyes were narrow, alert.

"She's sad," Anna said. "You know Jasmine cared about Leonard Cushman."

Anna's honesty had the effect of settling Ruby down. Anna wondered what Ruby thought about her cousin having an affair with a man like Cushman, who had invited a wisely resistant Ruby Wild Eagle up into his bedroom at the top of the grand staircase. Anna could see it now: Leonard Cushman clad in only a rich, paisley robe, awaiting the tribal lawyer in her protective blond wig—there only for business.

"When I heard Leo Cushman was murdered, I decided it was too dangerous to file his new will," Ruby declared. "Not until *you* people found his killer. It was the only way to protect Jasmine and—" Ruby stopped, crossing her arms across her chest.

"Did Leo Cushman leave an inheritance to Jasmine . . . and her child?" Anna asked quietly. "Is the boy his?"

Ruby Wild Eagle was determinedly silent, gazing out at

the whitecaps visible even in the darkness. There was turbulence, with a storm settling in for the night. Her expression was thoughtful, as if considering all she might be allowed by law and relations to say.

"You'll probably demand a DNA sample from Jasmine's son," Ruby Wild Eagle said, at last. "So . . . yes, James is Mr. Cushman's biological child."

Anna nodded gravely. "And Leo Cushman wanted Jasmine, his son, and your tribe taken care of."

"Leo Cushman wanted so many things." Ruby Wild Eagle frowned. "And so does his family. We must protect ourselves from such greed . . . not just for money, but for the future."

"I understand," Anna said quietly.

"You really don't." Ruby Wild Eagle shrugged and then added, "I've gotten texts threatening Jasmine and me, warning us to tell nobody about the will."

"*We* can protect you." Anna tried to assure her, but even she doubted a small tribe could be spared the attacks of a corporation like Fortura or a litigious family like the Cushmans, who would contest any new will. Not when their profits were threatened.

"Forward me those texts," Rafe said. "I'll track them down."

"It'll be a burner phone." Ruby hunched her shoulders. "I'm not leaving the rez until you catch whoever killed Mr. Cushman. I'm safe here. I wish Jasmine and James would come back to the rez for their own safety."

Ruby Wild Eagle was on her own ground. She sat up straight in her rocker, staring out at the waves—a solace, a territory inseparable from her seafaring people. It was as if all those ancestors buried in the nearby old-growth trees of James Island anchored her. She knew how to paddle treacherous waters.

"Mr. Cushman asked me to draw up a new will because he believed his changes would never be honored by any company lawyer," Ruby continued. "Or by his board of directors or his family. He needed an outsider."

"Makes sense." Rafe asked, "Can we see the new will? Was it properly witnessed and notarized?"

Ruby Wild Eagle hesitated, seemingly offended by his rapid-fire questions. "I may just be a tribal lawyer, Detective, but I know the law. It's all witnessed and legal."

Ruby Wild Eagle stood up, closed her kombucha bottle cap with a firm twist, and was about to leave. Sheriff Woodman deftly touched her elbow to halt her escape.

"Just give them the will, Ruby," he advised. His craggy face and his composure steadied the young lawyer. "Only a few more questions and you're free."

With a sigh, Ruby leaned against the deck railing and gave the detectives a nod.

"Who witnessed the revised will?" Anna asked, keeping her voice calm and steady. She was worried Rafe's interrogation had offended this young woman, who had such a burden placed on her slender shoulders.

Again, Ruby Wild Eagle hesitated, as if realizing what she would tell them might change everything. She gazed out the beach at low tide, as if longing for the shelter of the driftwood, broken branches silhouetted by moonlight.

Instantly an image formed in Anna's mind—a pale and slick young man, someone who had threatened and terrified Ruby Wild Eagle. The calculating, angular face floating before her second sight was shocking. Anna recognized him and her inner world expanded.

Why didn't I see this before?

"There were two witnesses to Mr. Cushman's will," Ruby Wild Eagle said, her voice tense with fear as she finally fled. "The first was his tennis buddy, sworn to absolute secrecy. And the second was his executive assistant, Jackson Poole."

Rafe jumped up from his rocker. "Poole? We've got to question him again."

"He has a firm alibi from the Fortura janitor working at

the headquarters all night," Anna cautioned, but she, too, felt a jolt of adrenaline. They would have to prove with evidence both Ruby Wild Eagle's claim and Anna's intuition. "The will? We'd like to see it now, please, Sheriff."

"Ruby will fax it to your captain for safekeeping." Sheriff Woodman stood up and stretched as if he had much more important matters to attend to than a rich man's last will and testament. But his parting words belied his suddenly tense body language. Obviously, he didn't know if these young detectives could be trusted, since his tribal lawyer was receiving death threats. "We'll keep the original copy until it's all faithfully resolved. Ruby will stay here for her own protection. Jasmine and her son, too, if she comes home."

Sovereign ground, Anna thought. How wise of Leonard Cushman to work with a lawyer under another tribal court and police jurisdiction. Even a slick corporate lawyer like Bart Adams couldn't touch this will. She and Rafe must work within this nation's rules.

Sheriff Woodman didn't smile. His tone, like his stance, was formal. As he accompanied them to their car, he added, "Our tribe appreciates another canoe grant in Mr. Cushman's revised will. We've already chosen the tree. A two hundred year old cedar from Haida forests up in British Columbia. An elder tree."

There it was—a man's life value was measured by an old-growth tree. Better a tree carved into a canoe to carry a whole tribe than paper shares in a company killing people. Sheriff Woodman had promised to fax Captain Dimitri on his landline. Anna knew Dimitri would immediately put out an APB for Jackson Poole. It was too late for them to drive back to Seattle tonight. Even if Rafe asked, Anna wouldn't risk it after her pre-monition. She could tempt Rafe to stay with a salmon supper at the reservation's popular diner. Maybe they also had good pies.

"Do you think Poole also has a key to Cushman's house?" Rafe asked, as he and Anna ate their perfectly poached king salmon feast. It was almost the diner's closing time, and Rafe had noticed with disappointment all the homemade pies were sold out.

"Yes, there was no sign of forced entry," Anna answered. "Poole was Cushman's executive assistant. He saw everything Cushman did. He witnessed a new will that left controlling shares to Eleanor Kiernan. Did Cushman leave nothing at all to Poole after all his years of service? If so, it might give Poole motive, opportunity—"

"The guy also had access to Kiernan's stiletto in her lab desk, right?" Rafe said. "Means. Murder weapon."

Anna frowned. "But the other blood smudge on the knife handle doesn't match the samples Kiernan gave us from Poole's chart. His was type A positive."

Rafe nodded. "Bummer about the blood. Our lab didn't take any DNA on Poole, did we? Never swabbed him. But I'll bet you it was Poole who texted Ruby Wild Eagle and threatened her. I'll find out. And we'll haul in Poole for an interview when we return." Rafe sat back in the booth, yawning. "What is it about the ocean? Always rocks me to sleep."

"Not me," Anna sighed. Ruby's revelations were so vital, her mind was buzzing. She'd not get good sleep tonight. She cursed herself for drinking the sheriff's strong coffee; it was like mainlining caffeine.

In their beach cabin, Anna listened to her partner's hearty snore rumbling from the next bedroom. The intimate surf was so loud, it seemed to slap at the foot of her twin bed. A rising tide. She must sleep if she were to be fit to safely drive them the four hours home tomorrow. Anna expected insomnia or the recurring nightmare of her sister's hit-and-run. She didn't expect to drift off into the bliss of six seamless hours of sleep.

When she awoke to a foggy dawn, she wrapped a well-worn Pendleton wool orca blanket around her shoulders and put on the kettle for more coffee. There were no teabags on the kitchen shelves. Fiddling with the paper filter, she almost missed Rafe's dashed-off note on the counter. Fortunately, she could decipher his hurried handwriting:

Off to Forks—pies for our breakfast. Back soon!

"No, Rafe!" she shrieked. It was dark; he was driving without her. Could she stop what she dreaded was going to happen?

Anna ran out of the cabin in her pajamas. But she was met on the path to the tribal office by Sheriff Woodman.

"Your partner . . ."

For a moment Anna thought he might wrap his arms around her. His face was blank with pity. "A bad accident on the road to Forks before dawn. Elk leapt into his car. He's alive, been airlifted to Harborview. You can borrow my deputy's car to drive back to the city. He'll pick it up this weekend when he goes to Seattle."

Anna barely had time to thank the tall, angular man. Weeping, she raced back to the cabin. She gathered her partner's clothes into his neatly organized overnight bag. As soon as she had a wireless signal, she'd call Rafe's husband to get to the hospital, where she would join them as soon as possible. As she dressed, she wavered between worry and rage. If she'd confided in Rafe her premonition—and if he'd listened—would that have saved him, just as her sixth sense had once stopped her sister from committing suicide? But Anna had only temporarily averted Lizzie's death.

She should have been in the car with her partner, as her vision foretold, when it struck the elk on the twisting, reservation road. What good was it to be forewarned about an accident she couldn't clearly understand or prevent? Her gift of foresight was useless against someone else's fate. *So why listen to it?*

During the endless drive home, Anna denied herself any accompaniment, just the gray underworld of rain, the hum of engine, and the clank and rattle of something loose in the backseat. No music. No magic. No duets.

Solo.

XXI

ELEANOR

June 14, 2019

"I'm really sorry about your partner," Eleanor said to Anna, as she invited her into a well-lit kitchen. "Will he make it?"

"We don't know yet." Anna's face was uncharacteristically pale, her eyes shadowed.

Another summer storm shuddered the windows overlooking a drenched city. Marine fog seeped into every crevice and corner like resident ghosts. Eleanor hoped the fragrance of her homemade pie baking in the oven, the copper kettle cheerily boiling, and the eager attentions of Brodie would offer some solace to this woman whose lips were tense with grief and regret. It struck Eleanor that, after all the weeks of being a prime suspect herself in Detective Crane's murder investigation, Anna was the one who now appeared guilty. Anna had not been driving when her partner was blindsided by a leaping elk. Yet the detective had told Eleanor on the phone when she asked for another visit today that the accident had been her fault. She offered no other explanation.

"We have Cushman's new will," Anna said as she distractedly took a chair at Eleanor's small kitchen butcher-block table.

"Yes, I know," Eleanor nodded, a rush of relief and gratitude that this woman had believed her and followed Eleanor's lead. "Jasmine told me her cousin drew it up for Leo to keep it safe." All Jasmine had said was that Eleanor was left controlling shares in Fortura. Eleanor hoped Anna would reveal more. "What now?" she asked the detective. "Can you stay for tea?"

Anna's nodded absently and fiddled with a tea cozy on the kitchen table. Her dark hair was strangely shorn and haphazard, as if the detective had cut it herself in some mourning ritual. Eleanor had to wonder why Anna Crane had chosen such a hard-hearted job when she was obviously so sensitive. As the detective shifted uneasily at the table, Eleanor couldn't help but imagine how she'd style this woman, as she often did her few friends. With Anna's attractive curves, full lips, charcoal eyes, and a long-ago broken nose, Eleanor would let Anna's luxurious curls fall free from its disciplined ponytail; she would also purge Anna's closet of these boring black slacks, shapeless jackets, and sensible walking shoes that gave the quite feminine woman a look of self-imposed but not quite successful androgyny. Why did Detective Crane hide her generous breasts and obvious grace?

If Anna had asked for her Pygmalion skills, Eleanor would have marched Anna down to Green Eileen, the local outlet for Eileen Fisher's consignment castoffs. Those beautiful, recycled fabrics would agree with a detective's salary but also nicely drape and distinguish Anna as a woman with natural style and sophistication. Eleanor wondered if the detective was Cuban, Italian, or Black Irish, like her own family ancestry.

Under Eleanor's scrutiny, Anna bowed her head, her shoulders hunched. "We're all dearly hoping Rafe . . . Detective Bartelli . . . will recover . . ." Her voice broke.

"Oh, dear," Eleanor put down her spatula and quickly crossed the kitchen to embrace Anna.

"Don't . . ." Anna evaded Eleanor's arms. "Don't touch me . . . please."

Taken aback, Eleanor retreated to her loudly whistling kettle. Anna covered her ears and bent double until Eleanor plucked up the kettle to stop its shrieking.

"Sorry . . . sorry," was all Eleanor could think to say, feeling at fault for their last interview and her snooping about Anna's private life. Thomas was right; she should never have used the disturbing information he'd confided in her with Anna. The woman was so suddenly fragile. Again, truly surprising for a cop.

"I'm sorrier still I blurted out about the restraining order and your sister," Eleanor said. "It wasn't my right to know—or to tell."

Anna lifted her face, tears welling in her expressive eyes. So dark. Obsidian. She brushed tears away quickly, obviously struggling to regain her composure. Eleanor wondered if Anna and Detective Bartelli were lovers, though she'd assumed he was gay.

As if sensing Eleanor's question, Anna whispered, "Rafe is like a brother to me."

"Yes," Eleanor echoed, her voice low. "Losing a brother can break your heart more than losing any other man."

Anna covered her face with both hands, her elbows on the kitchen table. Eleanor wondered if she had many friends or if perhaps, she, like Eleanor, was also aloof from others. It was the curse of keen intelligence and a life-long close sibling bond. Families could be like cloisters, a barrier to any other intimacy.

Anna lifted her face from her hands, her brows knitted in despair and something else—a new resolve. "Please tell me *everything* you found out about my sister."

Eleanor crossed over quickly and laid a light hand on Anna's sleeve. "Are you sure this is the right time to . . .?"

"Yes," Anna said and shrugged off Eleanor's touch. "I need to know."

"Well," Eleanor began slowly, retreating to the stove, "the restraining order against your sister was first issued because she'd been stalking her ex-fiancé, also a dancer, and attacking his new girlfriend. Your sister made threats by text and phone, alarming the couple so much that they'd moved to a new apartment."

"No," Anna said. "Lizzie wouldn't ever . . ."

"I'm so sorry to tell you all this, Anna. There's no police record because Lizzie's ex-fiancé and his girlfriend decided not to press charges and withdrew the restraining order."

Anna shook her head in obvious dismay. "How did I *not* see my sister was descending into such . . . madness?"

"I know all about denial," Eleanor said softly. "We just can't see the people we love with complete clarity. My brother . . . your sister."

Eleanor would have attempted to embrace Anna but sensed she was in too much shock to be solaced. She kept vigil close by her, while Anna recovered herself. Eleanor was surprised by her trust of this woman who had first pursued and accused her of murder. *Should I get this close to someone I really don't know?*

"Thomas will help us," Eleanor offered. "Maybe he can talk to the Atlanta cop again. Maybe another call from the FBI will—"

"Or a visit from me," Anna said firmly. "The cop can't issue a restraining order against a fellow detective."

Eleanor busied herself with steaming half-and-half for her double espresso. For Anna, she brewed a ginger-chamomile blend. Anna placed a hand over the teapot as if for warmth and stared past Eleanor out the kitchen window. She watched a hummingbird flit and dart at the feeder.

At last, Anna took a deep breath and explained, "I'm here again because my captain and the DA asked me to follow up . . . just two final questions." Anna's voice gained strength as she summoned her professional demeanor.

"Of course," Eleanor said, as she swirled the steamed cream in her coffee. She settled herself across the table from Anna.

Abruptly, Anna stood up, teacup in hand. Leaning against the counter, Anna dutifully said, "First. now that you've pressed charges, the Cushmans are out on bail. I'm sure your lawyer told you. Their trial is set for late fall. Will you be a witness for the prosecution?"

This request startled Eleanor. Of course, Thomas had warned her she might have to testify against the Cushmans about their attack on her, but Eleanor didn't realize it would be in just a few months. She'd hoped for more time for her head to heal.

As if reading her mind, Anna said quietly, "Hugh and his mother will always be a danger to you, especially now that the new will has been officially filed and you will soon have controlling shares in Fortura."

Anna was right. With the discovery of the revised will, Eleanor was immediately under legal attack not only by Leo's ex-wife and stepson but also by the Fortura board, who were vigorously contesting the new will. They all insisted it was drawn up by a lawyer whose tribe had a vested interest in it. They stated Leo Cushman was blackmailed by his mistress, Jasmine Wolf, into leaving her and her child some of his fortune.

Bart Adams had demanded a paternity test for Jasmine's son. The Cushmans claimed Ruby Wild Eagle, as a tribal lawyer, had an undue interest in drawing up this new will. They insinuated Jasmine had been in league with Eleanor to convince Leo to cut off his ex-wife and stepson. Like with most families who contested a will, this legal wrangle was a mess. Jasmine Wolf, with her son in tow, had left Fortura to join her cousin on the Quileute Reservation. Eleanor had written Jasmine an email pleading with her to come back to the company, now that Eleanor was in control—at least for the time being.

No thanks. No disrespect.
Not my world anymore.
Is it yours?

The question haunted Eleanor. She was not yet allowed back at work, awaiting the board meeting to officially recognize her controlling shares. Eleanor planned to settle long-stalled lawsuits with those who'd lost loved ones to overdoses. She had used her own money to hire Ruby Wild Eagle to help her with restitution legal affairs, once Eleanor was in control. But the Fortura board and many stock-owning employees intended to stymie Eleanor at every turn. They would fight Eleanor and try to find a way to outmaneuver and oust her, even with her shares. Fortura had proven to be a Houdini when it came to being held accountable, though the Justice Department was closing in on them. Eleanor took some credit for this.

"We'll never really win big against Big Pharma," Thomas had advised Eleanor just last night as they lay in bed together, Brodie nestled between them. Her dog snored more than her lover.

"We . . ?" Eleanor smiled.

She wrapped her legs around him. She was getting used to having Thomas spend almost every night now. It was no longer about him helping her recover from her injury; it was a tacit understanding that he belonged here.

"Even the FBI is having a hard time, with all our resources, bringing them to justice. While you're waiting to get back to work, Fortura may try to file for bankruptcy and hide its billions in offshore accounts. The Cushmans may yet avoid any personal accountability." Thomas had switched off the night light, tucking Eleanor into his arms.

"So, will you testify against the Cushmans, Eleanor?" Anna's soft question brought Eleanor back to her kitchen.

Before she could answer, the ding of her oven timer reminded Eleanor her pie was at last done. She pulled open the oven door and the delicious scent of hot crust wafted out into the kitchen. She'd made this good graham-cracker crust from scratch especially for Anna, who had obviously lost weight since her last visit.

"It's key lime," Eleanor announced, as she sliced Anna a large piece of the pale cream pie, frosted with coconut.

Anna nodded politely when Eleanor presented her with the pie, but she hesitated as she at last reluctantly sat down again at the small table. Anna fiddled with a slice of lime atop her creamy pie, then obediently took a small bite. Her expression suddenly changed from disinterest to delight. "You're the only other person who's ever matched my grandmother's key lime pie," Anna marveled.

"Most people make it too terribly sweet." Pleased, Eleanor watched Anna devour her dessert. "Seconds?"

"Yes, please." Anna held up her plate.

It was the first time Eleanor had ever seen Anna really smile—a surprisingly warm and yet shy expression, as if she reserved it for very few. She wished Anna might someday include Eleanor among her friends. Eleanor realized that since Frankie's death, she had become more open to intimacy. First Thomas, and now Anna. Thomas had gingerly suggested he might take up some more space in her bedroom closet now they were practically cohabitating.

"I made this pie crust for you from scratch." Eleanor surprised herself by bragging. She certainly didn't need to impress Anna. "It looks like you haven't eaten in days."

"Unlike you, I can afford to lose weight."

Brodie padded over to Anna and leaned into her as if protecting her from the gloom of another summer rainstorm. Eleanor took another moment to enjoy her own slice of pie. The right mix of sweet and sour tingled on her tongue. "To answer your first question, yes, I will be a witness for you at the Cushmans' trial." She took a breath. "Someone does need to hold them accountable. What's your second question?"

Anna nodded. "Thank you for having the courage to testify. Second question. Did you know Jackson Poole was a witness to Leonard Cushman's new will?"

Eleanor sat back in her kitchen chair, startled. "Why on earth didn't Jackson come forward with that evidence after Leo died?"

Now Jackson's sudden disappearance from Fortura made more sense—and why he never answered her calls about when she could return to work. "If Jackson witnessed Leo's revised will . . . well, he's such a snoop, he'd have also ferreted out all the details—" Eleanor's face flushed. "You think *he* had something to do with Leo's death?"

"Yes," Anna nodded firmly, "the will left Jackson Poole nothing. No shares, so no leverage against you and your plans for Fortura. We've tracked down a text he sent threatening Ruby Wild Eagle. Poole has escaped our attempts the last few days to find and bring him in for questioning."

Eleanor nodded. Jackson Poole possessed everything of which they'd accused her: Leo's keys; access to the stiletto in her lab desk; and he'd witnessed and probably secretly read Leo's revised will. "Didn't you ever consider him for Leo's murder?"

"Poole had an airtight alibi from the janitor that night. We didn't really think he had a strong motive. But since Poole's disappearance and our new suspicions, the janitor has recanted his alibi. Said Poole paid him a bundle to lie. Except for the fact he's left town, as you once did, we don't have any other real evidence against him. He's the wrong blood type for the smudge and the DNA we found on the stiletto."

"What blood type is Jackson?" Eleanor tried to remember. She should have known. "I gave you the list from our medical records, right?"

"Type A positive," Anna answered. "The other blood smudge on the knife is type O. So, it can't be Jackson Poole. And it doesn't match the DNA profile for Poole you provided to us from your 2014 Fortura clinical trials."

Eleanor leapt up from the table so quickly she knocked over her chair. Instantly, Brodie was by her side, barking. "Brodie, shhhh," she said, patting his head. "Anna, come with me!" Eleanor called out as she ran up to her office.

Jerking open the filing cabinet Thomas had so neatly righted after her attack, Eleanor searched for "Frankie and Eleanor: Genetics file." Years ago, as an experiment to see if she had the same genetic potential for addiction as her twin, Eleanor had paid a thousand dollars to a local company to sequence Frankie's genome and hers. She'd been astonished to discover her blood was two types: O *and* A negative.

After some deep dives into cutting-edge research, Eleanor found she'd acquired some of her twin brother's blood while they were in the womb, including Frankie's genomes in his blood cells. Since twins receive nutrients in the womb from their mother's same blood vessels, they could be born with a mixed blood type. It was weirdly comforting to Eleanor that Frankie was not only her fraternal twin but also his blood and his DNA were mixed with hers. They were even closer than twins. They were what scientists called, "chimeras"—after the Greek myth of the female, fire-breathing monster, part-lion, goat, and serpent. It was not lost on Eleanor, ever the researcher, the word, "chimera" was also defined as an illusion, impossible to achieve. Certainly, a long and devoted life together with her twin was a fantasy.

She pondered how to explain to Anna this complex science. "Listen," she said. "Jackson Poole was diagnosed just three years ago with leukemia. AML. We all pitched in to help him through a stem cell transplant, since he had no family here."

"Yes . . . so?" Puzzled, Anna waited patiently for Eleanor to explain.

"A stem cell transplant is a brutal miracle, but it worked. Saved Jackson's life. He even just got to know and correspond with his European donor, a woman from France!" Eleanor grabbed Anna's elbow for emphasis, as she led her to the front door. "A stem cell transplant patient receives the matched donor's healthier cells. Jackson's blood type—and even some of his DNA—was completely altered to become his donor's. Whatever evidence you found on the stiletto would be his *donor's* blood and DNA."

"I don't quite get it," Anna admitted.

"Look, Jackson made sure he had an alibi. He knew his blood type and DNA wouldn't be requested by police if his alibi stood up and you believed his frame of me." Eleanor shook her head. "Of course, even if Jackson found out I gave the police those Fortura clinical trial blood tests and DNA profiles, he'd believe he was safe. Jackson knew the blood sample was from my 2014 study. It wouldn't show his *new* blood type and DNA."

"So, it would be a perfect crime. Poole knew he could commit a murder, and, if we collected blood and DNA from the scene, it would only match his female European donor."

"He's a chimera!" Eleanor declared. "Listen. We don't know Jackson's new blood type or DNA. But I can find out his DNA, even though he's run away."

Anna nodded thoughtfully. "Yes, I've read something about homicides when DNA and blood evidence identify the wrong person. Maybe a twin or someone who is a stem cell transplant recipient. No one ever told us about Jackson's leukemia. I did notice he was remarkably pale."

"Maybe Jackson didn't think he'd live long enough to get what he believed he deserved from Fortura and Leo. Maybe he was desperate . . . or just got greedy." Eleanor ruffled her dog's ears. "Brodie, stay! Good boy. I'll be home soon."

Anna had to run to keep up with Eleanor, who raced to her car and shouted back, "After his stem cell, Jackson told me he also sequenced his new genome. Just for fun, to celebrate his new DNA and blood. I don't have access to that genome info, but I'll bring you something from Jackson's desk . . . his fountain pen or Rolodex, which will certainly have Jackson's new DNA. I went with him to one of his transfusions after his stem cell transplant. Maybe Human Resources updated Jackson's new blood type in his files. I've got access to Fortura's database from my office computer." Eleanor opened her car door. "I'll go to my Fortura office—the security guard will let me in if it's just a quick visit—and then I'll meet you at the station."

Eleanor's car screeched out of the driveway, barely missing the green recycling bin on the curb.

XXII

ANNA

June 14, 2019

As Anna and Eleanor strode into the Seattle police station together, Captain Dimitri called out to them. "Crane," he shouted. "Come!"

When Eleanor, carrying a thick Fortura file and a coffee cup in a plastic baggie, attempted to follow Anna into the captain's office, he signaled her away.

"Close the door," Captain Dimitri snapped as Anna entered and stood at attention before his cluttered desk. "I know you've lost your partner. But now you're teaming up with a suspect?"

Anna saw Eleanor had taken a seat at Rafe's empty desk. "Eleanor Kiernan has updated blood analysis and new DNA info to share with us on Jackson Poole," Anna insisted. "A really big new lead."

"I put out an APB on Poole, as you asked. But why are you sharing evidence with *her*?" Captain Dimitri bellowed. "It's against all the rules . . . what the hell, Crane?"

Anna steadied herself to face his fury. Instinctively, she adopted the poise and stance of her years of aikido training.

Allow the assault, lean into the aggressive energy, shift, and rebalance it, to use against the attacker. Now, she had to summon aikido's ancient strategies for self-defense with her boss. She breathed deep, planted her feet, and stepped slightly away, to let his rage move right past her.

Anyone watching would have seen the sputtering captain fall forward an inch, gripping his desk for balance. Eleanor was witnessing the encounter, probably like a silent movie through smudged glass. She wouldn't exactly know what she was seeing but could only sense Anna had somehow gained the upper hand with this angry man. He suddenly sat back down in his office chair, as if invisibly shoved.

"Out!" Captain Dimitri growled, dismissing Anna. "Get rid of her. She's playing you. Kiernan may yet stand trial for murder, for God's sake. I'll team you up with another more experienced partner, who can teach you to investigate the right way."

The right way, Anna thought. *Not my own way.*

She had struggled with such advice all her life. Anna stood stoically in front of Captain Dimitri's desk, unwilling to leave.

"You don't want to even hear any new evidence?" Anna asked her captain, who was rummaging through his towering pile of file folders as if she weren't there.

Captain Dimitri didn't meet her gaze, but he did answer. "No," he growled. "Not until you've got something real to show me. Not your endless suspicions. But bring in this Poole guy, if you can find him."

Anna straightened her shoulders and left his office. She fought the desire to slam his glass door. It might break. Besides, she didn't want to wait around for Captain Dimitri. With Rafe fighting for his life, she would soon be teamed with another detective, probably older and officious—someone Dimitri expected to break her like a wild filly.

She didn't have to ask Eleanor to follow her quickly out of the office. Eleanor had obviously observed Anna's dressing down. It must be familiar to her. Eleanor was waging a similar fight against the Big Pharma execs, mostly male, who refused to accept her authority.

"I'll drop off Poole's updated blood labs and coffee cup for forensics," Anna said as Eleanor followed her out of the office. "They can compare his DNA and blood with what was found on the stiletto. Meet me in the parking lot so we can take one car."

"Okay." Eleanor nodded and left the station.

In his lab, Horace was in a tolerably good mood. "Whatcha got? More secret and inadmissible evidence?"

"Possible break in the Cushman case. Can you give me a DNA analysis on this, stat?" Anna asked. She handed the coroner Jackson Poole's coffee cup. "And here are updated blood labs on Jackson Poole to match with the murder weapon."

"You owe me again, Crane." Horace pretended to scowl but took the evidence bag.

Anna could see he was intrigued. Horace always liked a flashy finish to any murder case. He promised to call Anna with the results.

In the parking lot, Eleanor was waiting, alert and engaged, an expression Anna always admired in any partner.

"So, where are we going?" Eleanor smiled faintly and took her place in the passenger side of Anna's old car. She strapped on her seat belt, as if Anna were a race car driver.

"Anywhere but here," Anna confessed. "Do you have any idea where Poole might run? A friend or lover?" Anna glanced over at Eleanor. "Poole certainly didn't hesitate to tell us all about *your* San Juan hideaway when we were looking for you."

"I've got a hunch," Eleanor said, reaching out to touch Anna's arm. "Take the tunnel."

Her tone and touch were so easy and intimate, Anna was surprised by her own quick, physical reaction . . . a slight uptick in her pulse and flush in her cheeks. Again, there was warmth, like humidity clinging to her skin—and an image of traveling with Eleanor in a small plane over piney forests strangled by kudzu. There was a surge of affection like an ache in Anna's heart.

No, I don't want to know this! Anna scolded herself. Unlike her second sight, which Anna had little success in shutting down, she was accustomed to denying her senses, her body's unruly attractions. Her body, unlike her heart, was more disciplined.

Anna pursed her lips, cursing the downtown traffic and slick hill. She had always preferred a stick shift for better traction on these rainy streets, especially at stop lights on steep inclines. But she'd traded her old Saab for a used Prius. On this steep downtown hill, her car stuttered as she slipped backwards at the stop sign. An SUV behind her honked.

"Once Jackson brought a date to an office party . . . a woman . . . can't remember her name," Eleanor said. "Vanessa somebody."

Eleanor fell quiet, gazing out at the crowded city streets. Only Seattle tourists used umbrellas. Even the most polished businessmen and elegant women preferred Gore-Tex. It always amused Anna to see fashionable females in slickers and impossibly high heels. Now they navigated through the new and expensive tunnel replacing spectacular views of the Salish Sea along the historically unsafe but long-cherished Highway 99 viaduct.

"Did you talk with this Vanessa . . . do you know where she lives?"

Eleanor tilted her head thoughtfully. Then with a start, she said, "Somewhere on Lake Union . . . on a houseboat. She talked about how hard it was to get her grand piano down the floating docks and up the spiral staircase. She did seem overly possessive of Jackson. More a caretaker than a girlfriend."

"In Poole's personnel file, did he list next of kin, someone to contact in case of an emergency?"

"Yes," Eleanor said. "That's my take. But let me double-check it with Jasmine." She plucked her cell phone from her purse.

"Jasmine Wolf?" Anna was startled. "I thought Jasmine had quit Fortura and was back on the Quileute rez. For refuge from all the legal battles over the will."

"I'm trying to persuade Jasmine to come back to work as *my* personal assistant. Even if I don't go back to Fortura, I want someone with her integrity. You know Leo's new will left a trust fund for her son, but Jasmine wants to keep working."

"Yes, Ms. Kiernan?" Jasmine's voice was clear, even on the cell phone speaker. No static. Professional, yet warm.

"Can you still get access to Fortura's personnel files? I need to find out if Jackson Poole listed somebody named Vanessa for his emergency contact?" Eleanor directed politely. "I'm sure you have friends in Fortura's HR."

Within minutes Jasmine rattled off, "Vanessa Garrison, 206-864-9960. 5700 Fairview Avenue, Houseboat Number 20."

"Thanks, Jasmine," Eleanor said, a note of satisfaction in her voice. "This is why I need you by my side."

Eleanor hung up but not before Jasmine cautioned, "Be careful if you find Jackson. He always bragged in the break room about spending time at the shooting range. He has a license for a handgun. That's why my cousin was so afraid of him."

One hand on the wheel, the other instinctively reaching to make sure her own gun was holstered, Anna left the long tunnel and took the exit for Lake Union. As she wove through the lakefront neighborhood down to the row of houseboats, Anna wished Rafe was still by her side. If she found and arrested Jackson Poole, if she could prove his guilt by matching his DNA and blood to the stiletto, her partner would also get full credit for solving their first case. If it were Rafe partnering with her, instead of Eleanor, Anna would not have to deal with unsettling emotions with this woman so near her.

Even now, Anna's mouth was dry, and she worried she might say something inappropriate, some signal betraying any more than a professional alliance with Eleanor. She was too aware of Eleanor's light but lovely perfume—some floral, perhaps tropical, harmony. Plumeria? Anna opened her window to let the scent waft out into the rain.

"Here we are," Eleanor said excitedly, leaning forward in her seat as they miraculously found a parking spot in the narrow, gravel lot.

"We should get forensics back soon. Might give us sufficient cause to arrest Poole if he's here. I've given the coroner your phone number too. Please wait for me here in the car," Anna directed Eleanor. "You can't be any part of this arrest. I've let you in too much already."

"Don't *you* need backup?" Eleanor insisted.

"No, my captain won't authorize it. We don't even know Poole is here."

Anna jumped out of the car. She knew she was making a rookie mistake in not calling for backup if she even suspected Jackson Poole was hiding here in a houseboat. But she'd already made so many mistakes with her captain, who distrusted her instincts and this alliance with a suspect. Anna barely trusted herself anymore. This time, no one else must get hurt.

Running down the floating dock between rows of bright, pastel houseboats, Anna hunched low to hide her approach. The dock tilted and swayed sideways. Anna shifted her weight automatically, her aikido skills compensating for the slippery wood.

Behind her, she heard a sudden patter of footsteps. Anna unholstered her gun and realized Eleanor was close behind. "No, Eleanor!" Anna hissed. "Told you to stay in the car."

"I'm with you!" Eleanor fiercely insisted and caught up with Anna on the narrow dock. Eleanor almost lost her balance, and Anna instinctively reached out to steady her. "If Vanessa

Garrison recognizes me," Eleanor said, "she'll let me in . . . maybe even tell me where I can find Jackson."

Anna seriously doubted Jackson Poole's girlfriend would squeal on him, but she allowed Eleanor to follow her. "Stay behind me," she instructed.

The dock was like a slanting sidewalk, undulating under their weight. Rain drizzled and raised little whitecaps on the lake, rocking the houseboats. The dock creaked, and Tibetan wind chimes tinkled. Their sonorous, baritone gongs reminded Anna of the companionable croaks of bullfrogs in Florida marshes. Anna had always wanted to live on a houseboat, but they were too expensive on her salary. Several of these floating homes had sailboats parked at their decks.

At Houseboat Number 20, a calico cat perched on a window box of red hydrangea and pansies, his amber eyes tracking them as if he were on rat patrol. Anna rang the doorbell, which echoed a snippet of opera. Again, Anna thought of Rafe.

No answer. But Anna heard footsteps on the other side of the door. Next, a quick tug of a window curtain, a pause, then the scrape of something outside on the houseboat's wooden dock. She knew without seeing it—a kayak.

"Stay outside, in case he runs," Anna ordered Eleanor. "Call 911 for backup!"

This time, Eleanor did as Anna asked. Quickly, she dialed 911 and then took up a position between houseboats, while Anna ran around the houseboat to its dock. A thin man in a red slicker, hoodie hiding his face, slid a sleek kayak off the deck into the water. Poole wore no life preserver, just a huge backpack, and he wielded his tall paddle like a weapon.

"Jackson Poole!" Anna shouted, racing toward the small dock. "I'm arresting you on suspicion of the murder of—"

He was bent over, slightly off balance, one leg almost in the kayak when Anna reached him. On the rocking dock, Anna struggled to halt his escape, stomping on his boot, and twisting his arm behind his back. Poole cried out in pain but kept diving toward the kayak, towing Anna along with him. There was suddenly nothing solid for her to haul him back onto the moss-strewn deck. Together, they toppled into the lake.

The splash of cold water was a bracing slap against Anna's face. Anna held Poole's arm as he fought her off, struggling in the waves, his other arm clamping down on her head to drown her. Anna twisted and struggled underwater to escape Poole's grip. He was wiry, but strong, holding her underwater. Desperately, she frog-kicked up toward the surface but again, he blocked her, plunging her back into the dark, dank waves. Suddenly, she was sinking. Out of air.

XXIII

ELEANOR

June 14, 2019

"Where's Anna?" Eleanor shouted, as Jackson hoisted himself out of the cold lake and onto the dock. "You can't let her drown!"

Panicked, Eleanor poised to dive in after Anna, when suddenly the blunt barrel of a gun was shoved into the small of her back. In the distance, she heard sirens. She needed to stall Jackson long enough for the police to arrive.

"She's dead," Jackson said matter-of-factly. "Saw her last breath. You'll be dead, too, if you don't *move*." He punctuated each word with a painful jab of the gun deep into her ribs. "We'll take my car."

"You don't need me, Jackson." Eleanor's heart thudded so loudly she could hardly hear her own words. Anna had been underwater way too long.

Eleanor scanned the surface of the lake to see if Anna had possibly surfaced. Nothing, just the lolling waves and a jet skier zooming by. Fighting back tears, Eleanor again considered diving in after her. But Jackson shoved her away from the dock's edge and back into the houseboat.

"She's gone," Jackson repeated. "I will kill you too—nothing left to lose. Now, move!" He hoisted the backpack over his shoulder and shoved her as the sirens shrieked closer.

"Just run, Jackson." Eleanor wouldn't budge. "I'll only slow you down."

Jackson struck her with his pistol. She winced at another sharp pain to the wound in her head that had not yet healed.

"Want *another* head injury, Eleanor? Your beautiful brain will be worthless."

Reluctantly, she did move as he pushed her along the unsteady dock between houseboats. Surely somebody would see she was in trouble—a man forcing her. But there was only the wide-eyed calico cat watching their progress down the slippery dock toward the gravel parking lot. *Where are the cops?*

"You drive," Jackson Poole ordered Eleanor as he took up his position in the passenger seat. "Boeing Field. No heroics."

As she drove out of the parking lot, she saw in the rearview mirror the flashing lights of police cars finally arriving at the houseboat. Too late. In a flash, Eleanor realized Jackson's plan. Of course, Leo's private plane was always parked at Boeing Field, ready for them to fly off to San Francisco, Portland, or the elegant Roche Harbor in the San Juan Islands for lunch or a corporate meeting. Jackson also often accompanied Leo on these short jaunts, but Leo had never taught his executive assistant to fly—not as he had Eleanor.

On the freeway, Eleanor tried to figure out a way to delay their takeoff. "I'll have to go in and file a flight plan with the tower," she said, when they pulled into the airstrip parking area.

"Bullshit," Jackson sneered. "I've flown with Leo enough to know the tower guys don't care where we're going. We could be running a drug trafficking ring, and they wouldn't notice." He laughed bitterly. In his most commanding voice, he called the Fixed Base Operations guys. "Two November-one-two-three Alpha Bravo out for takeoff."

As the plane was towed out to the runway, Eleanor cursed Leo for paying the mechanics and ramp guys so handsomely that they always had his private plane fueled and ready to go. There were no security guards she might somehow signal. Nobody paid any attention to Jackson propelling her forward, the gun digging into her ribs as he walked her across the tarmac to Leo's sleek blue-gray plane. Eleanor slowly climbed into the luxurious cockpit of the Cirrus. A surge of panic set in. Jackson was desperate enough to kill her; but just like Leo's sailboat, Eleanor had never flown Leo's plane without him beside her in the cockpit. The sunny, cloudless weather meant she'd not have to get any coordinates from the tower to fly by instruments.

"Skip the preflight check," Jackson ordered her as he stripped off the backpack to quickly stow it in the cockpit. "Let's go!" He waved the gun threateningly near her temple.

Eleanor engaged the engine, going through the start-up procedure in a kind of numb, practiced routine. But her mind was preoccupied with the terror that, once they were airborne, she'd have no way to stop Jackson without endangering herself. When they landed, wherever they landed, she would be a liability. Jackson wouldn't hesitate to kill her as he had Leo—and now Anna. Like he said, *"Nothing to lose."*

The propeller jerked once and then spun in a fast, silver blur as the plane let out its loud, but smooth hum. The plane shuddered sideways, and Eleanor saw a large, plastic baggie fall out of the pocket of Jackson's backpack. It was full of small blue pills, all stamped with the Fortura brand. Instantly, Eleanor recognized these must be the illegal fentanyl-laced street drugs killing teenagers and scoring drug dealers millions. She made a quick mental note to tell Anna to issue a warrant for Fortura labs. Then, Eleanor remembered. *Anna is dead!*

Rage, like hot bile, rose in her throat. "You!" she shouted at Jackson Poole. "You're dealing fentanyl, using Fortura labs! You're a monster—killing kids!"

"*They* take them." Jackson shrugged as he strapped on his seatbelt and adjusted his wireless headset. "Just get us up and out of here!"

Angrily, Eleanor switched to the tower frequency on her headset as she asked for taxi clearance.

The disembodied voice of the busy flight tower, "November-one-two-three Alpha Bravo cleared for takeoff."

After a short taxi, they were aloft. As they soared over the Seattle skyline, Eleanor glanced down at South Lake Union with its boat traffic and a scattered kayak class. She stared hard at Anna's watery grave, hoping she'd somehow managed to survive. A wave of emotional nausea hit Eleanor when she banked and leveled the plane.

"So, where are we going?" Eleanor asked.

Jackson didn't answer. Instead, he glared at her. "Of course, Leo left you this goddamn plane   in *both* of his bloody wills," Jackson said. "*You* were always the favorite."

Glancing across at Jackson, she recognized his envy and jealousy over Leo's expensive toy that he could never copilot. "Where do you think you can run?" Eleanor asked, trying to keep her voice calm as she dutifully scanned the instrument panel.

Jackson demanded, "Head north toward the border. I'll let you know where to land when we get there."

Eleanor wondered if Jackson was working with some drug ring operating at the border. She decided she might stall and gain some advantage by admitting, "Listen, Jackson, this is my first time in the cockpit without Leo. Wind's up. It might get a little rocky."

"Higher!" Jackson demanded. "Faster!"

They lifted into the steel azure glare embracing their curved, glass cockpit like a waking dream. This was usually

Eleanor's favorite moment, when the sky eased inside the plane, as if they were lost in a floating bubble. But now, her hands trembled on the throttle. She studied the busy computer screen, noting the 120 knots.

"This plane practically flies itself," Leo had often taught her. "The avionics is connected to satellite for weather info. And GPS shows you all the nearby airport locations if you need an emergency landing."

Eleanor dearly hoped Leo was right. While she'd done reasonably well with all the flying school lessons, she was not an ace pilot. She'd always been nervous when temporarily taking over the pilot controls. Eleanor didn't have enough experience as a solo pilot now to do anything but keep flying north. She took a shallow breath, her mind racing. She had no idea how to pilot a plane while also trying to disarm her dangerous passenger. There was nothing to do but steady her hand on the throttle and side yoke.

As they flew over the twisting emerald tributaries of the Salish Sea, Eleanor was unexpectedly dizzy and struggled to focus. Lightheaded, she felt a warm trickle of blood in the back of her skull after the blow from Jackson's pistol. He'd ripped open her head wound again. As they entered turbulence and thunderclouds, the plane bumped and thudded against the clouds like a silver cork.

"We're losing altitude," Jackson said, a note of panic in his voice. "What's wrong with you? Fix it. Don't try anything stupid, Eleanor."

"It's just some chop, Jackson," she muttered, but Eleanor wasn't so sure she hadn't done something wrong because of her disorienting head wound. Suddenly, the plane dropped and lost altitude. Thunderclouds loomed ahead. Lightning flashed in the distance.

"Leo should have made *me* his copilot. Not you!" Jackson muttered.

There was so much anguish in his voice Eleanor stared at him. Jackson Poole was much thinner than Eleanor remembered as he sat shivering in the cockpit, his clothes soaked from his dive into Lake Washington . . . his drowning of Anna. He had a beach towel from his trunk wrapped around his thin shoulders like a mummy. Jackson glared at Eleanor, his face flushed and his expression furious.

"*You*," he growled at Eleanor. "It's always you."

Eleanor gazed ahead at the storm clouds, her face creased with emotion, her skull throbbing with familiar pain. What if she blacked out? Eleanor summoned all her stamina to stay conscious and alert. She managed to level the plane again.

Keeping her voice very neutral, she said, "But it was you, Jackson, not me, who killed Leo. You let yourself into his home with your own key copy. You'd witnessed the new will. Nothing left for you . . . no shares in the company as Leo surely promised you." Eleanor glanced at Jackson quickly to study his face. It was frozen.

"It was an accident," he murmured. "I didn't go there to kill Leo. I was devoted to him. Like you, Eleanor." He fell back in the seat, shaking his head. "But he found out about the fentanyl . . . and called me to come over. He even threatened to turn me in. Can you believe it? *He's* the criminal, not me."

Eleanor faced him, her eyes bright and pained. "But you stole the stiletto from my lab desk," she said in a low voice. "It was *all* premeditated."

"No!" Jackson shouted. "I just took your knife with me because . . . because I needed some protection. You know Leo. He's stronger than I am after my transplant. Ruthless."

"You seem pretty ruthless yourself."

Poole stared straight ahead. A full, excruciating minute passed and then he began to speak in an almost child-like voice. "I risked everything to cover up Leo's dirty work, his bribery of doctors to overprescribe our drug. I set up his illegal lobbying with the FDA and reps in Congress. And he was going to turn *me* in for my little fentanyl side deal?" Jackson sighed, his face seized with disbelief. And sorrow. "And then, after everything . . . all the years . . . he asks me to witness a revised will . . . and for me, *nothing*!" Poole stopped, his eyes filling. "Leo never thought he might die . . . he didn't know the first thing about dying."

"Not like you, Jackson," Eleanor said, her voice soft, a whisper. "You know all about dying, don't you, Jackson? You barely survived."

Jackson bent double, sobbing, shoulders heaving.

Despite her fear, she reached out a consoling hand. But misinterpreting Eleanor's touch, Jackson roughly thrust her aside. "I'll shoot you!" He screamed so loudly her headset vibrated. "I will!"

Eleanor shrank away from him but there was little distance between them in the cockpit. "You won't make it without me," she said. "You need me to pilot this plane."

"I won't make it in prison," he countered, scowling. "I'll be some big bad boy's bitch, just like I was for Leo."

She knew the truth of it. Jackson was handsome but frail, perfect bait for hardcore rapists and gangs. He might have survived leukemia but would not survive prison life. Irrationally, Eleanor allowed a surge of compassion for this young man who, like her, had also given Leo Cushman so much of his life, only to probably end up paying the most for her mentor's crimes. Jackson was right. Leo probably would have turned him in for his fentanyl dealings. If the Justice Department finally indicted Fortura, Leo might have even let his executive assistant take the fall. Maybe the reason Leo completely cut Jackson out of his new will was to give himself plausible deniability.

The thought sickened her. But Eleanor heard Leo's voice coaching her to keep flying, keep Jackson Poole talking to distract him. The late summer sun glinted off silver wings as the plane edged toward San Juan Island.

"Are we landing on Friday Harbor?" Eleanor asked.

"No . . . on Waldron," Jackson retorted, recovering himself from any emotion now except rage.

Eleanor frowned. Waldron was one of the many islands dotting the Boundary Pass waters between Washington and British Columbia. From there, anyone with a motorboat could steal across into Canada, as she'd once planned when she made her escape. Even if there was a tiny airstrip on Waldron, it wouldn't be attended. The island was isolated, inhabited only by the few who could afford a retreat to private beach cottages—perfect for Jackson's drug-running trafficking.

"Canada, Jackson?"

After a beat, he said, "Got dual citizenship, so BC won't be so quick to extradite me. After we land, I'll be long gone. You can fly yourself home or wherever the hell you want . . . it's *your* plane," he spat out.

Eleanor knew Jackson would never let her leave the little far-flung island alive. Pulse quickening, she tried to focus on flying, but her hands were clammy and slick on the throttle. Sweat trickled down her brow, again blurring her vision. She understood her fate: Jackson had killed Leo and Anna. He would kill her too. She was out of options. Terror overtook her. Her body trembled.

But suddenly there was Leo's voice again, clear, and forceful as if he'd spirited into her headset. *Pull the chute!*

No, I can't! Eleanor stopped herself from protesting out loud. *Too dangerous!* She didn't have the skill to execute such a drastic plan.

You've trained for it. Leo's voice was insistent. *It's your only option left.*

Stealthily, Eleanor glanced up at the large, red handle in the cockpit's ceiling. Leo had insisted she learn the Cirrus parachute system. "It's a chute for the plane, not the pilot," Leo had schooled her. "If you're really in trouble, don't hesitate to use it. You'll wreck the plane on landing . . . chances are, you'll survive. But it'll be a wild ride!"

A tilt-a-whirl ride was perhaps the only way Eleanor could sabotage Jackson's escape and try to save herself. The tumult might dislodge Jackson from his weapon and free her as his hostage. But she didn't know how to land if the chute worked and if the impact would worsen her head wound. *Too risky!*

Eleanor noted they were now over San Juan Island's Roche Harbor, the last airport before the border. It was trickier than Friday Harbor, with a shorter, tree-lined landing strip, heavy crosswinds, and unforgiving, turbulent water on either end of the runway.

It's my only option!

Gathering her courage, Eleanor took a deep breath and abruptly cut the engine.

"What the hell?" Jackson yelled as the plane dramatically dropped altitude toward Roche Harbor airport. "We can't land yet!"

He tackled her with both hands, pushing her down in her seat as she tried to lift herself up to reach for the chute handle. The memory of Jackson forcing Anna down into the lake, her arms clutching the waves, desperate for a handhold, gave Eleanor a surge of furious strength. She smashed her elbow into Poole's face and heard the sickening snap of a broken nose. Yelping in pain, Jackson released her, cradling his bloody face.

"Damn you, Jackson!" Eleanor yelled and grabbed above for the chute handle.

It was heavy, at least a forty-five-pound pull. She had to hold her other wrist to brace it as she jerked the handle down with all her might. She heard a roaring *whoosh*, and the chute's small rocket deployed, jerking the plane suddenly vertical, nose down, swiftly losing even more altitude. Pilot and copilot smashed backwards into their seats as the Cirrus dove straight for the water. With a thunderous *thwack* and jolt, the plane descended at dizzying speed. Across Eleanor's chest, the thick strap was so heavy and tight, Eleanor had to gasp for air. Blood rushed to her head. Next to her, Jackson was strung up, puppet-like, in his seatbelt. She didn't see any gun.

Another bone-rattling yank upward leveled the plane. The yellow-and-orange parachute billowed. Attached by long cords at the tail and the nose of the plane, the chute floated above the cockpit like a bright kite, catching the crosswinds.

"With the chute you're not flying anymore . . ." Leo had warned her, "you're falling. It'll be crazy scary . . . descending 1,700 feet per minute. Try to aim for touchdown on water, not land. Less chance of fatalities."

The plane was shuddering and tipping sideways over Spieden Channel toward the Roche Harbor Airport. Eleanor caught sight of a police boat, zooming out underneath them, blue lights flashing.

"No!" Jackson screamed groggily as he regained consciousness. He grabbed for the throttle. But there was no control, only descent, as the plane dropped precipitously, lunging toward the waves.

Instinctively, Eleanor crossed her arms in front of her face to prepare for the crash. The Cirrus hit the water in a gigantic splash like a falling meteor. Her body slammed sideways against the cockpit door, but she had the wit to use the nearby emergency hammer to smash open her window. Icy cold water surged inside. Jackson, conscious, punched her in the chest. Popping open his own cockpit window, he dove into the inflatable lifeboat. It fit only one person.

"QUITE A SIGHT, THE PLANE'S PARACHUTE," Sheriff Conway drawled as Eleanor lay painfully inside the screeching ambulance. "Rich tourists at Roche really enjoyed the dinner show. Especially your fight with Poole over such a tiny lifeboat."

The back of Eleanor's skull exploded, and Eleanor dreaded what an MRI might reveal about yet another head injury. But she could move her legs and arms, so no paralysis. "Jackson?" she asked.

"There was already an APB out for him, so we recognized him right away," Sheriff Conway said. "He's been airlifted down to Harborview. Broken legs."

Eleanor took a painful breath. Her ribs were wrapped in a tight bandage, and she could tell she was on heavy opiates because her injuries did not hurt. Yet.

"Did they give me Neocodone?" She hoped the pills were not laced with fentanyl like those Jackson had made in the Fortura lab. "What pills did you give me?"

"*Not* those we found floating in a backpack washed up with your parachute," Sheriff Conway said drily. "Those are evidence."

The ambulance rounded a long curve, and Eleanor sat up so suddenly, it made her head spin. Before she blacked out, she managed to ask the Sheriff, "Anna Crane? Detective? Did she . . .?"

"Captain Dimitri says . . . call him," Sheriff Conway frowned.

XXIV

ANNA CRANE

June 28, 2019

Rafe adjusted his hospital bed to a ninety-degree angle to greet Anna. His expression was so welcoming and warm, it was as if they'd never argued.

"Hello, stranger," he said and motioned with one arm, encased in a bright red cast, for her to sit beside him. "I hear you drowned."

Anna grimaced. The memory of drowning in those dark, oily waters haunted her. She'd awakened many midnights these past two weeks, breathless. What she'd never tell Rafe was what had really happened underwater. Out of air, she'd watched her last breath, a burst of loud bubbles, escaping to the wavering light above. Still, she sank. Blackness. Frigid cold. Arms wide, her body at last let go, lungs naturally breathing water. Deep draughts filled her lungs, almost soothing, like a memory of the womb. But then, a familiar face appeared, calm and steady, with a faint smile.

"Lizzie!" Anna sang out, her tone muted.

An amused, fond voice she'd so longed to hear again, whispered, *"Not your time."*

Her little sister embraced Anna, lifting her up to blinding sunlight at the surface of the busy lake. The chop and slap of waves on Anna's face forced her to gag. Harsh air hurt her lungs, shocking her back into breathing.

"Got ya!" someone shouted.

A red kayak banged against her back, then someone gripped her belt and hauled her up onto the flat of his boat bed.

"Hold on!" the young man shouted and paddled mightily toward shore.

"I was lucky," was all Anna told Rafe. "Lucky a kayaker witnessed me struggling in the water with Poole. The guy had to make a choice—save me or stop Poole."

"Good choice." Rafe grinned, but his voice was serious. "You drowned, I was snoozing in the hospital, but Poole got nabbed."

"It was Eleanor who got him, not me," Anna insisted.

"But we get all the credit. Heroes, right?"

"My daddy *is* a superhero!" Rafe's five-year-old son, Nate, shouted, perched on the other side of his father's bedside.

Rafe's husband, Terrance, eyes glazed from lack of sleep, held Rafe's hand, which was studded with IV tubes, his eyes fixed on the monitor, as if willing Rafe's blood pressure to stabilize. Terrance tried to smile, but it cost him. He'd been told the next few weeks were crucial to Rafe's recovery from a punctured lung and spleen, a broken leg, sacrum, and skull fracture. One of Rafe's eyes was patched with a huge white bandage. His brow was crisscrossed with stitches and blotched in purple and black bruises.

"Your stitched face looks just like a Rorschach test," Anna said.

It wasn't his skull fracture affecting his memory, it was the pain medications. She was worried Rafe might get addicted to the Neocodone, so she had consulted Eleanor about weaning him off the opiate as he got better.

"For those in such pain, like your partner," Eleanor had assured Anna, "opiates are therapeutic. Long-term use is the problem. Keep me posted on his progress, and I'll keep watch with you."

Keeping watch. Anna gingerly touched Rafe's swollen arm, studying the graffiti-like drawings on his plaster. "I see Nate is illustrating your cast again," she said.

"It's his cartoon strip." Rafe laughed. He pointed out a purple sea serpent spiraling up the plaster. "Better this than the tattoos he's hoping to get himself someday too soon."

"Even kids have tats now," Anna said.

"Nate thinks my scars are almost as cool as tats," Rafe said, grinning. He pointed to the six-inch white cicatrix crawling across his forehead. "Looks like a slug inching across my face." He scowled, which only made the wound more vivid.

"I love slugs . . . Seattle's mascot," Terrance said.

Rafe grinned at his husband and son. "How 'bout you two go get me some contraband sweets downstairs at the cafeteria? Anna will watch over me. Always does."

As Terrance and Nate left the room, Anna traced her partner's disfigured brow with a quick and gentle finger, then sat back in the chair, somewhat embarrassed.

She'd seldom touched Rafe, only an elbow bump in close quarters or a playful pat on the back. She steeled herself for the flood of images often accompanying any intimate physical connection. Her sixth sense was working overtime since her drowning. Sometimes near-death encounters opened one's native sixth sense even more fully. She'd often glimpsed her partner's aura to decipher his mood or health, but she'd never witnessed the tumult of his emotional imagery—prismatic colors echoing in her mind's eye like a shimmering blue-green hologram.

Rafe hoisting his newborn son up to the fluorescent surgical lights, his face joyful, streaked with tears she'd never seen in him; Rafe and his husband holding hands at the opera; Rafe singing loudly on a dark, crooked road, the crash of a large body against his wind-shield, animal screams, glass shattering, an aria still quavering. The mineral smell of blood and oil.

It didn't surprise Anna there were no images of her and Rafe together. Here she was, right here beside him, where she should have been the early morning of his accident. She should also be injured and here in the hospital alongside him.

"Glad you're here now," Rafe said in a voice so soft, she almost didn't hear him.

Had he read her mind, somehow sensed her visions? After all his complaints about her sixth sense, his distrust of it, Anna could see a rosy warmth around his heart, the violet glow around his head—as if his near-death had also opened Rafe's own intuitive eye.

"You've changed . . ." she said softly, "You understand."

"It's just the opiates," Rafe shook his head, but there was the slightest smile.

Rafe lay back in his bed as he tried to rearrange his broken arm and leg underneath the thin bedsheet.

"Can I help?" Anna asked.

"Just sing to me, Anna. Your voice is good as any painkiller."

Anna took a deep breath. "Sing what? I don't know enough opera."

Rafe struggled to sit up and took a ragged breath. "'Ain't no mountain high enough . . .'" he began, his voice thin as a reed.

"'. . . to keep me from youuuuuu . . .'" Anna took up the melody, her rich, full-bodied voice lifting his raspy baritone.

Their duet was strong as they once were together, broken-hearted as they had become, fragile as their futures. But their voices rose above the rush and chatter in the hospital hallway, the noisy monotone of machines was now only rhythmic beats, a background to their harmony. They didn't have to finish the song because without their karaoke stage, they didn't remember all the words. But it was enough to just sing the chorus over and over until Anna's voice failed her.

She blurted out, "Oh, Rafe, it's all my fault . . . the accident . . . I never told you . . . I saw it coming but didn't warn you." Tears stung her eyes.

"You couldn't tell me," Rafe said, "because I wouldn't listen." He patted Anna's hand, straining his IV tubes. "I'd stopped listening to you, Anna. That was my fault." He tried to grin, but his lips were chapped and split. "I've had a lot of time to think, stuck here in the hospital." He hesitated, his soft, brown eyes studying her.

In his expression she read the same deep affection for him, for all their work together, for what they had yet to achieve. Anna knew it might be months before Rafe was recovered enough to return to their work. Meanwhile, she'd been paired with an older, gruff, and boring detective who barely tolerated her. He was a good cop, but Anna suspected he was also an alcoholic. They got along professionally—tethered, but not simpatico. She only trusted him with administrative details. Lately, she'd considered requesting a transfer if Rafe didn't return or perhaps even leaving the force. But she didn't know what she would do instead.

Rafe continued pensively. "From now on, I promise to listen, Anna. Your sixth sense is maybe just another word for what other cops call 'gut instinct,' right? And hey, I've got my own premonition now."

Anna grinned. "What do you see, dear precog?"

"I see us asking the captain to make us lead detectives on a special task force to investigate the fentanyl case." Rafe struggled to sit up in his hospital bed, his eyes gleaming, his face gaining more color. "You were the one who broke the Fortura lab ring that Poole was running. Why not take the lieutenant's test so by the time I come back, you'll have the power you've earned?"

"*We've* earned," she corrected him.

"Right! We've solved our first active homicide. Poole is pleading guilty to get a lesser sentence. Our captain got a lot of credit for our good work. So . . . go for lieutenant, Anna."

"Let's think about it."

"Hell, you'll probably make captain someday." Rafe laughed then continued more seriously. "Listen, Anna, my husband and I play a game . . . maybe it's our form of intuition. It certainly requires seeing the future."

"What's your game?"

"Whenever we face a big decision about our lives, we ask, 'Who will we *become* if we do this?' Like when we were deciding whether we should adopt. We had to ask, 'Who will we become together if we are parents?'"

"You made the right decision," Anna said, smiling. "You are the best parents I know. And I got a beautiful godson out of the deal."

"And Nate got you." Rafe let go of her hand to reach out for her shoulder. It was an awkward movement, and his cast bumped against her with an audible clunk that made them both burst out laughing.

It was the signal for Anna's offering. "Here's the pie you risked your life for," she announced, relieved to detour their conversation away from any talk of her promotion and perhaps their separation. "Banana cream!"

Rafe clapped delightedly, if awkwardly, as Anna reached into her satchel and presented him with a whole pie, a plastic knife, and paper plates. It was perfectly chilled, with banana slices arranged like a smiley face on top of the whipped cream.

"What is it with us and pies?" Rafe laughed. "Think we're addicts? Did you make it yourself?" Rafe delightedly reached for the pie and cut them two huge pieces.

"Eleanor Kiernan's recipe," Anna answered, diving into the delicious confection.

"The two of you are getting together now . . . off-duty," Rafe said. It was more an observation than a question.

"Not yet," Anna said evasively.

For a moment, Rafe looked like he might pursue his partner, but then he again attacked his big slice of pie. "You'll spill when you're ready. You always do."

For a few moments both Anna and Rafe fell into a companionable silence while he devoured two pieces of pie. She ate one. Then they were interrupted by a nurse taking vitals. The robust nurse bantered with Rafe, and it was obvious Anna's partner had charmed the medical staff. She missed him by her side and realized she could never leave him and their partnership.

"Hey, did I ever tell you the meaning of my name?" Rafe grinned.

"Short for Rafael?" Anna guessed. "Right?"

"Right, my Italian father's ancestry. But my mother was Norwegian, so she gave me the Norse nickname. Rafe means 'council of wolves.'"

"Whoa!" Anna said. "I like your mother."

"What I'm trying to say, Anna, is I work best in a hierarchy, a pack, even if Dimitri sometimes ranks me as a beta guy. But you, Anna"—Rafe gave her an admiring glance—"you're an alpha female, a natural leader. Even when you try to fit in, you stick out. So, why not lead? Take the lieutenant's test."

"Dunno." Anna mind was spinning with everything Rafe was suggesting.

"I'll follow your lead." With his good hand, he grabbed his son's Magic Marker, bright pink, and drew in bold, jumbo letters a heart with the initials: RB + AC. "You're the bleeding heart," he quipped as he sketched his drawing into the top of his cast. "I'm the arrow."

XXV

ELEANOR

September 1, 2019

On a cool, sunny morning, Eleanor sent a text to Anna.

Just saw news Poole took a plea.
Tea at B. Fuller's Mortar & Pestle in Fremont?
Near statue of Stalin.

When the women met outside the tiny teashop, Eleanor noted Anna's smile lit up those wide eyes with warmth.

"Well, you look none the worst for drowning," Eleanor said. "Let's celebrate your afterlife."

"'We must laugh, and we must sing.'" Anna nodded.

"Indeed." Eleanor was delighted to hear this favorite quote unexpectedly redeemed from when she'd used it in her brother's obituary. She missed Frankie every day, but Eleanor had grown used to his companionable silence, like a family ghost.

As they entered the teashop, Eleanor noticed Anna had traded her sensible black slacks and stolid shoes for a more flattering style: white-gold hoop earrings, which nicely offset her periwinkle chambray blouse, crisp dark jeans, and low-cut boots. Anna's face was lovely with the suggestion of makeup.

"Nice lipstick." Eleanor smiled. "Jane Iredale?" Eleanor wondered if Anna's casually sophisticated outfit today was carefully chosen to impress her. She wondered how things were going for Anna without Rafe at work and if it were as difficult for her as Eleanor had found navigating the Fortura board's politics, even when she was, briefly, a major shareholder. Without her partner, the detective must feel lonely. Eleanor certainly was.

"Do you miss him?" Eleanor asked. "Rafe?"

"Every day. Every case," Anna replied. "But Rafe will be back at work in January. We believe . . ." Anna hesitated; her face suddenly shadowed. "We *hope* 2020 will be a much better year for us all." Anna seemed to shake away some disturbing thought.

Eleanor's own mood darkened as she pondered her first holiday season without Frankie (who loved her parties, even if he often showed up high) and without Leo (who made a point of wearing some tacky superhero costume for her Halloween fetes). Eleanor took a deep breath. The two men she loved most, lost in just one year. Anna was right, 2020 must be better. *Not so many terrible losses. Please, God.*

"Welcome back, Eleanor." The tea master greeted them.

His silver goatee, wire-rimmed gold glasses, paisley ascot, and copper suspenders said diehard steampunk. Shelves of teas in large bell jars were decorated with nineteenth century portraits of couples in tailored, long suitcoats, goggles perched atop brown fedoras, starched high collars, and neckties, and with gold watches slung from fancy fobs.

Studying the exotic tisanes, those earthy teas corked in test tubes and the extensive tea list, Anna murmured, "No wonder you like it here. It looks like a laboratory."

"Indeed," the tea master smiled widely. "I call it my laboratorium. Let me put on the kettle!" Beaming, he adjusted his glasses, which were fogged from the steam of the boiling kettle. "New shipment just in from China."

"What's brewing today?" Eleanor asked. She gestured for Anna to join her at the counter, where two tall glass beakers with tea leaves in the bottom were soon steaming.

"Russian Caravan for you, Eleanor," the tea master said as he poured her a porcelain cup of the bold black brew. "You'll like the heavy malt finish of Pekoe." He regarded Anna intently. "And for your friend, Earl Grey with just a touch of cream and a ginger snap!"

His ritualistic tea-making was more performance art than ceremony. They took their teapots back to the tiny table with its lace tablecloth. Eleanor noticed that Anna's lustrous hair was growing back after her shockingly bad cut. Were they close enough yet for her to suggest another hair stylist? Her own, perhaps.

"When do you start your new job at the global health NGO, Eleanor?"

Eleanor thought Anna must have a sixth sense for following up on suspects, especially when they were found innocent. "Next month," Eleanor answered. "It was hopeless at Fortura. At least in global health, I can put my biochemistry skills to work developing vaccines for all the epidemics that often strike Third World countries . . . and it's only a matter of time before we suffer a terrible pandemic here," Eleanor said thoughtfully. "I want to be on the front lines when it does."

Anna hunched her shoulders and shivered a moment, even though it was a sunny day. "God forbid," she said. "I heard Fortura filed for bankruptcy to escape paying out a $300-million settlement with the Justice Department. But the Cushman family has not been held personally accountable."

"I've sold my shares." Eleanor frowned.

Now she had enough to personally support the Obliterate Opioids movement and fund the Franklin Kiernan Foundation focusing on public health education and treatment of addiction. She had planned to offer a carefully managed monthly stipend to Toni Fleishman, but Leo had left his daughter the financial—if not the emotional—support she'd craved. Eleanor had heard Toni married a man she'd met in rehab and was trying to stay clean.

"Oh!" Eleanor stood up from the table abruptly. "I can't forget to get catnip."

"I thought you only had a dog." Anna joined her again at the tea racks.

"Thomas has moved in with his cat." Eleanor smiled, blushing slightly. She hadn't told hardly anyone that he and his burly Manx had moved in with her.

For just an instant, Anna seemed a little startled, perhaps even put off, by her announcement.

Does she judge me for sleeping with Thomas? Like some sort of bodyguard cliché? It's really none of her business. Eleanor resolved to keep her personal life more to herself.

Anna fiddled with a test tube of lapsang souchong. Then she asked softly, "Does your dog, Brodie, ever attack his cat?"

"No, Mortimer is the alpha." Eleanor smiled. "Of us all." The truth was she and Thomas had settled into a comfortable, quotidian intimacy. Quickly, Eleanor retreated to a subject that was not too personal. "Well, there was just one big and very loud hissy fight between Mortimer and my dog. And then, Brodie sensibly decided they would be best friends. Sometimes they even sleep together."

Anna moved away from Eleanor to study an opened burlap bag of bergamot. Eleanor followed and sifted through the tangy, orange tea leaves. *Does Anna have someone special waiting for her at home? Does she have a lover?* Eleanor realized she really knew nothing about Anna Crane's personal life, except that she wasn't married. It occurred to Eleanor if she ever wanted a deeper intimacy with another woman, it might be someone like Anna.

Is this the last time we'll meet?

The thought of never seeing Anna again saddened Eleanor. But their personal and professional worlds didn't orbit each other. Yet Eleanor felt somehow coupled with Anna after all they'd both been through together. They had trusted each other with their lives. Men experienced this with war buddies—the life-enhancing and sometimes life-long intimacy of surviving the trenches together.

What do I really want from this woman?

The two women stood silently contemplating more tea shelves. Eleanor noted Anna didn't go for the bath teas, as Thomas would have.

"Lavender gray is Thomas's favorite," Eleanor ventured, not wanting to confide too much more about Thomas because Anna didn't seem to like him. Perhaps because the only time Anna had met Thomas was when he was trying to take over her first murder case.

Anna's brow furrowed with indecision. Her sudden insecurity and tentativeness startled Eleanor.

"Let's sit down again. Our tea is getting cold," Anna said, and retreated to their table. For a while she gazed out the window, watching the parade of tattooed hipsters, a woeful homeless woman, and harried tourists.

Eleanor waited for Anna to continue. But Anna simply stared down at her empty cup and its cluster of tea leaves, as if trying to decipher her own future.

At last, Anna straightened in her rickety chair and said, "I wanted to talk to you about something I've been feeling . . . but my job doesn't allow it." She glanced at the door, as if she might suddenly run out of the teahouse.

"Of course, you can tell me," Eleanor said. She fought an instinct to reach out and offer a touch to Anna. Eleanor said hopefully, "We're becoming . . . I hope we might be becoming . . . well, friends."

Her words settled them both—an unspoken agreement.

Anna poured herself another cup of tea, taking her time. "Yes," she nodded firmly and held up her cup in a toast. "To . . . to *friendship*."

Eleanor lightly clicked her teacup to Anna's. She noticed the delicate porcelain was chipped; the next tea drinker might break it. She'd have to tell the tea master. "Your job allows friendship with a former suspect, doesn't it?"

"Getting close to a suspect, at any stage . . . well, it's not . . . encouraged." Anna was silent a few more moments.

"Well, *I'm* encouraging it," Eleanor nodded firmly. "After all we've been through, Anna, shouldn't we trust each other?"

Anna leaned back in her chair as if to regain her balance. "I don't usually tell people about this," Anna began in a measured tone. "The reason I blame myself for Rafe's injury—I had a clear premonition about the crash. And I didn't tell my partner." Anna hunched her shoulders, shaking her head. "People closest to me . . . even if I can't protect them, can't stop fate . . . shouldn't I always tell them what I *see*?"

Eleanor felt a rush of emotion she couldn't quite name. She leaned toward Anna and encouraged, "You had a premonition? Doesn't mean you could have changed what happened to your partner." What she wanted to immediately ask was—*Ever had a premonition about me? Did you know I was innocent?*

"Did you and your twin ever share a sixth sense?" Anna asked. "Often twins do."

Eleanor shook her head. "None whatsoever. I wish we had. Maybe then . . ." Waves of grief tightened Eleanor's throat and washed over her body like an undertow. Now, it was Eleanor who was herself losing her balance, the way sand slips underfoot in the surf. "Don't you think I would've saved Frankie's life if I'd known *that* was the day he would overdose?"

"We never really know," Anna murmured. "We just *think* we know."

"Did you know when your sister died? Did you have a premonition?"

"No," Anna sighed. "Not the night someone ran her over." Anna gathered resolve. "But I did know several other times. My premonitions helped her survive . . . for a while."

"Yes," Eleanor nodded sadly. "For a while." They sat in silence, each sipping their tea. At last, Eleanor said softly. "So, Anna, have you always had . . . premonitions? Have you always, well, just known things?"

Anna gazed down at her tea, swirling it in the fragile cup. "There was this teacher, Mr. Cooley, who taught me to be very careful who I told about my . . . clairsentience, he called it. It was knowing and sensing things without knowing how."

Eleanor was fascinated by what struck her as more a confession than a simple acknowledgment. Of course, there was some alternative science about intuition, but Eleanor had not paid much attention. It intrigued her now, drew her in. "What did you know about me?"

"I always see more clearly when I am not close to somebody," Anna explained.

Eleanor had read about the telltale colors shimmering around people that TV psychics described. Frankie had been a late-night addict of those kinds of metphysical shows. "So, you see . . . so-called auras?"

Anna's brows knitted with frustration as she explained. "Not always, I mostly see images or memories that don't belong to me. It's like seeing and hearing colors other people don't." Anna lips tightened as if she feared she had confided too much.

No one sees the colors I see.

Eleanor suddenly remembered a scrap of dialogue she'd noted in her journal. It was one of those evenings she'd visited her brother. He'd insisted they watch an old 1970s movie, *The War Widow*, on YouTube. The film was also set in a New

England tearoom, more old-fashioned and primmer than this steampunk teahouse but equally intimate.

During WWI, a lonely woman, well-bred and bored, languished in a culture that allowed her to be only a wife and mother. Drawn into an unlikely liaison with a Bohemian woman photographer, the two fell into an artistic and revitalizing Boston marriage, which evolved courageously into a love they both chose, even though their future would be clouded by prejudice and loss—not the diverse mating dances of today.

Eleanor sat back. *What more does Anna know about me? Does she pick up that I've even been thinking about a film with a love affair between women?*

The idea unsettled, yet intrigued Eleanor, and she fretted with her teacup.

"Don't make any big decisions," her neurologist had warned after the head injury. Venturing into any sensual relationship with a woman would certainly count as a big decision. Eleanor's skull ached with a rising alarm. She scooted her chair back from the small table and crossed her legs.

"Well, Anna," Eleanor said coolly, "knowing things about people . . . isn't this kind of an invasion of privacy?"

"Doesn't happen all the time." Anna leaned forward, as if to reassure her. "Sometimes when I was working cold cases and completely detached." She hesitated. "But most often when someone touches me . . . physically. Just images."

Eleanor couldn't help but ask, "Did it happen with me?"

"Only a few times," Anna admitted.

It unnerved Eleanor, but she had to ask, "What do you see . . . about us?"

"I see us . . . together," Anna said softly.

"Where? Here?" Eleanor thought, *What about Thomas?*

"Not here," Anna said lightly. "I see us . . . someplace else."

"Someplace else?" Eleanor was quiet a moment, and then an idea popped into Eleanor's mind. "Maybe we should try traveling together, Anna. My brother and I were veteran vagabonds—before I got caught up in Fortura work. Frankie always said it's the best way to know if you're a good fit . . . traveling together."

What am I offering? Eleanor's inner voice demanded.

"Travel is always . . . a good idea," Anna said with a slight smile. "Besides, I'm taking a brief sabbatical from my job while the captain considers Rafe's and my request to form a special task force on the fentanyl case."

Eleanor was relieved to change the subject. "You and Rafe certainly deserve it," she said heartily, "especially after you helped pin down Jackson's fentanyl lab ring. Surely, you've both proven yourselves. Say, Thomas is working on another big FBI drug case now. Maybe he could help you and Rafe out with the Northwest traffickers."

Anna nodding thoughtfully. "Sure, I could work with the FBI, now that we're not fighting each other."

"Over the case?"

Anna smiled. "Over *you*."

Eleanor laughed, surprised to feel herself blushing. "A truce, then." She reached over and poured Anna another cup of tea. "I can help, too, if you'll let me."

Anna's face clouded. "I've not yet solved the most important case of all . . . my sister, Lizzie's hit-and-run. The Georgia detective is stonewalling me."

"If you really want to pursue this, I can analyze blood, DNA, and other forensics." Eleanor realized she really could make good on the offer in her new lab where she'd been given complete independence—and more power for good than she'd ever had at Fortura. Besides, it would be wonderful sometimes to work with Anna, to be of service to her.

"Really?" Anna brightened.

"The perks of a nonprofit," she said. "And my own lab."

"And your billionaire boss." Anna grinned. "I've finally got some time now on leave to go to Atlanta, track down the detective on Lizzie's case—"

Eleanor reached out to touch Anna's sleeve but held back. "If you'd like, I'll come with you," she offered. "My new job doesn't start yet. Thomas can take care of Mortimer and Brodie, or they can take care of him."

Their eyes met.

"I'd love that," Anna said.

"Okay, then. We'll work it out." Eleanor stood. Careful not to touch Anna, Eleanor guided them back toward the counter where the tea master was brewing more exotic blends. "Besides, I bet you'll be a fabulous travel mate, even though you left behind the Deep South's humidity. It's just undeniable, like living in a sauna. You can't escape it."

"I like saunas," was all Anna said.

The tea master held high another steaming beaker of tea. "Now, let's sample a botanical and maybe an all-time classic. My favorite chai," he pronounced as he poured them each a cup. "Say, you two look like you work together."

"Crane and Kiernan," Eleanor nodded, with a wry and affectionate glance at Anna. "Our first case."

THE END

ACKNOWLEDGMENTS

Every book has allies who are the inspiration and guidance backstage, behind the story. I am so grateful for the many editors who have encouraged me, especially during the pandemic: the late Merloyd Lawrence, Christy Ottaviano, Maureen Michelson, Linda Gunnarson, Leslie Meredith, and Marlene Blessing. Tracey Conway, with her perceptions and line editing, read *Stiletto* many times, and it was always better for her red pen. Dana Kennedy Silberstein's intuitive gifts are an inspiration. Vanessa Adams, with her social media skills and research, is invaluable. Two of my favorite editors and mystery buffs are my sister, Paula Peterson Roth, and my brother, Dana Mark Peterson, whose "advise and consent" are vital to my writing. Other authors—all essential workers—whose own work gives me deep nourishment are Sy Montgomery, my life-long podmate, and poets Jane Hirshfield, Joy Harjo, Linda Hogan, and Pamela Uchuk.

Every week, my remarkable students support, delight, and engage me in the craft of writing. Publishing "Sherpa" Mary Bisbee-Beek, my literary agents Elizabeth Wales and Anne Depue, and film agent Mary Alice Kier are wonder-workers in the midwifery of books and stories. My friend and sister author Mary Anne Mercer joins me every Tuesday for our "tea and mystery" afternoons. Black Earth Institute, whose other writers also work for the Earth, is an enduring alliance for my mind and my work. Astute editors Brooke Warner and Lauren Wise and artist/designer Julie Metz were the first to see this new novel. I applaud their nimble, independent spirit and far-sighted publishing model, which respects and responds so collaboratively to authors. Artist and designer Alison Kan Grevstad is an eloquent guide to all things visual. My coauthors for our kid's book, master illustrators Wendell Minor and Ed Young, always remind me of why stories and heart-stirring art can change lives, no matter the age.

Every writer has physical and spiritual counselors who help us survive our demanding avocation. I'm grateful to be well and thriving because of the medical wisdom of acupuncturist and RN James Dowling, Dr. Raya Mawad, RN Brittany Lutnick, PA Joanna L. Fesler, and Mickey Portalatin.

My "twin brother," Krystian Jezka, is an enduring and generous partner, who gives me hope for the future. My good neighbors, Mindy Exum, Haleh Nekoorad Long, and Jon Long, who also happen to be culinary geniuses, have nurtured and advised. Anne and Geoff Barker lent me their pilot expertise. My friends John Keister and Dan Miller always encourage and entertain. Musical companions Dianochka Shvets, Mark Cooper, and our Seattle Metropolitan Singers keep my voice strong.

Daily feline playmates Loki and Tao, Rita and Tako and canine companions Ella, Brodie, Mattie, and Fiona offer life-saving walks and humor. My wise Jungian analyst Anne DeVore has given me years of creative counsel. Always grateful to my quick-witted and competent editorial assistant, H.R. Dowling, my daily muse of the Salish Sea—also a major character in this novel—bonds me to the enduring songs and the other animals of my watery homeland.

ABOUT THE AUTHOR

B renda Peterson is a novelist, memoirist, and nature writer, the author of over twenty books, including *I Want to Be Left Behind*, selected as a Top Ten Best Nonfiction book by the *Christian Science Monitor* and an Indie Next Great Read by Independent Booksellers. Her novel, *Duck and Cover*, was a *New York Times* Notable Book of the Year. Her most recent books are *Wolf Nation: The Life, Death, and Return of Wild American Wolves*, the children's books *Wild Orca* and *Catastrophe by the Sea*, and the illustrated book, *Crane Maiden*. Her work has appeared on NPR and in the *New York Times*, the *Christian Science Monitor*, *Tikkun*, the *Seattle Times*, *Orion*, and *Oprah* magazine. Sign up for news about the sequel to *Stiletto* at www.BrendaPetersonBooks.com.

Author photo © Yuri Makino

SELECTED TITLES FROM SHE WRITES PRESS

She Writes Press is an independent publishing
company founded to serve women writers everywhere.
Visit us at www.shewritespress.com.

Murder Under The Bridge: A Palestine Mystery by Kate
Raphael. $16.95, 978-1-63152-960-3. Rania, a Palestinian
police detective with a young son, meets cheeky Jewish
American feminist Chloe at an Israeli checkpoint—and soon
becomes embroiled in a murder case that implicates the highest
echelons of the Israeli military.

The Great Bravura by Jill Dearman. $16.95, 978-1-63152-
989-4. Who killed Susie—or did she actually disappear? The
Great Bravura, a dashing lesbian magician living in a fantastical
and noirish 1947 New York City, must solve this mystery—
before she goes to the electric chair.

On a Quiet Street: A Dr. Pepper Hunt Mystery by J. L.
Doucette. $16.95, 978- 163152-537-7. A funeral takes the
place of a wedding when a woman is strangled just days before
her wedding to a district attorney—and Pepper, whose former
patient happens to be the brother of the victim, is soon drawn
into the investigation.

A Child Lost: A Henrietta and Inspector Howard Novel by Michelle Cox. $16.95, 978-1-63152-836-1. Clive and Henrietta are confronted with two cases: a spiritualist woman operating on the edge of town who's been accused of robbing people, and an German immigrant woman who's been lost in the halls of Dunning, the infamous Chicago insane asylum. When a little girl is also mistakenly taken there, the Howards rush to find her, suspecting something darker may be happening . . .

A Girl Like You: A Henrietta and Inspector Howard Novel by Michelle Cox. $16.95, 978-1-63152-016-7. When the floor matron at the dance hall where Henrietta works as a taxi dancer turns up dead, aloof Inspector Clive Howard appears on the scene—and convinces Henrietta to go undercover for him, plunging her into Chicago's gritty underworld.

Last Seen by J. L. Doucette. $16.95, 978-1-63152-202-4. When a traumatized reporter goes missing in the Wyoming wilderness, the therapist who knows her secrets is drawn into the investigation—and she comes face-to-face with terrifying answers regarding her own difficult past.